Dead Air

Dead Air

Kerri Lee Miller

NORTH STAR PRESS OF ST. CLOUD, INC.

Cover design: Seal Dwyer
Back cover photo: Ann Marsden

ISBN: 0-87839-188-6

First Edition: August 2002

Printed in the United States of America
by Versa Press, East Peoria, Illinois

Published by
North Star Press of St. Cloud, Inc.
P.O. Box 451
St. Cloud, Minnesota 56302

Dedicated to

Greg, for always believing.

Prologue

TIJUANA, MEXICO

December 20

Dawn was still two hours away when the figure appeared, broken and battered, out of the desert. The rancher's dog saw her first, sending up a frightened howl that woke his master. The rancher cursed and rolled out of bed, vowing to box the mangy hound's ears.

Stumbling through his dark house, he reached the door and flipped on the powerful yard light, opening his mouth to call the dog. "*Madre de Dios*," he whispered, his heart galloping.

She stood at the edge of the circle of light, blood covering one side of her face and throat, her features swollen and misshapen. Long dark hair hung to her shoulders where shreds of what had been a white blouse, remained. Her legs were bare and blood-streaked.

"What do you w-want?" The rancher wished he'd brought his rifle to the door.

"*Por favore, senor*. I need—" She crumpled to the ground, and the dog let out a strange whimper. The rancher froze, torn between locking his door and stepping out into the yard. With a backward glance toward the bedroom where his wife still slept, he crossed the pebbly sand and gingerly approached the girl.

She was lying on her side, her hair flung across her face, her small hands curled into fists. The knuckles were scraped raw. With trembling fingers, he pushed her swathe of hair back and touched her throat. Her skin felt warm. Bending, he scooped her into his arms, surprised at the featherweight of her. She might be younger than he thought.

The rancher carried her into his house and laid her on the floor of his living room. Flipping on a small lamp, he hurried into the kitchen for warm water and clean towels. Crouching over her, he dabbed a damp towel on her face, wincing at the mass of cuts and bruises. She would carry permanent scars, he thought. If she lived.

When he'd removed the blood from her face, he started on her throat, catching his breath as he saw a dark circle of bruises emerge. Someone had tied something around her throat. Sighing, he sat back on his heels. What had this *nina* been through?

Getting to his feet, he padded down the short hallway and into the darkened bedroom. "Mama? You'd better come see what has come to our door."

ST. PAUL

March 1, 3:36 P.M.

THE BARRACUDA PEERED OUT INTO the hot sea of lights and swallowed against the cold fury in her throat. There was blood in the water and the sharks could taste it. Sweat broke out at her hairline, and she resisted the urge to wipe it away. Three weeks on the job. A baptism by fire.

"Liz, is the governor planning an apology for his comments about women soldiers? The local chapter of N.O.W. is calling for his resignation."

Liz Barracosta eyed the reporter, noting the avid gleam in her eyes. They had one hell of a story, and there was little she could do to quash it. "Governor Hamm has no plans at this time to elaborate any further on his interview with *Patriot Magazine*." Even if they had to put a muzzle on him, she thought grimly.

"Will Governor Hamm resign?"

She speared the reporter with a look that could cut glass. "Absolutely not."

"Does the governor believe that he's been quoted incorrectly, Liz?"

The press secretary swiveled, her narrowed gaze landing on the newspaper reporter. His contempt for Edward "Bunyan" Hamm was well known. "He hasn't said that, to my knowledge."

"Then the governor really did say that he cannot think of one woman who has ever distinguished herself in the military?" The radio reporter's eyes gleamed behind his glasses. "And he said that places like West Point and V.M.I. made a terrible mistake letting women in. He stands by that, Liz?"

"He has not said that he was misquoted, Evan."

"What does Mrs. Hamm think of her husband's comments?"

Her fingers tightened on the edge of the podium. "She has no comment." She held up her hands as the reporters shouted more questions. "Look, I think I've answered all of the questions about this that I can. Please note on your schedules that tomorrow's visit to a Saint Paul high school has been moved up an hour. Good day."

Cate McCoy slid the beta tape into the editor and chortled as an image of the Barracuda came up on the screen. Tangling with the press secretary always gave her a shot of adrenaline. "She'd like to take our heads off, Andy. Look at her face."

Andraya Costinopoulos grinned, eyeing the video she'd shot. "We don't call her the Barracuda for nothing, McCoy."

The tape sped backwards and Cate logged on to the computer, ready to select sound bites from the news conference. "I think we're in for a long night, Andy. They'll want this for the ten o'clock show too, I'm sure."

She watched the replay of the press secretary's performance, noting the way the woman's lips curled in with fury as the questioning went on. By the end of the news conference she was smearing her lipstick on her teeth. "You know, Andy, I'd guess the Barracuda considers herself a feminist. She probably wasn't very happy about defending her boss for this."

Andy pointed to a stack of tapes beside the editing deck. "That's the picketing stuff at the university." She ejected the first tape and slid another into the machine. They watched as images of the governor running a gauntlet of irate young women rolled across the screen. The protesters had been waiting for him as he arrived at the college to give a speech, and they'd swarmed toward him, fended off by the governor's bodyguards.

"Speaking of feminists," Andy said, "did you see the writer who did all those books about women's rights and stuff like that? I think I saw her at the college today."

Cate tapped on the keyboard, logging a soundbite. "Which writer?"

"She was on *Meet the Press* a while back, talking about women candidates for president."

Cate swiveled to face Andy. "Millicent Pine? She's here?"

Andy snapped her fingers. "Yeah, that's right. Millicent Pine. She was at the protest, kind of watching the whole thing." Andy leaned over and turned up the volume. "This is where he starts to talk." She chuckled. "You can almost see him getting ready to stick his foot in his mouth."

The shot zoomed in, and Cate spotted the long scar that creased the governor's face from his cheekbone to his jaw, disappearing into the dark beard that curved around his chin. Eddie Hamm claimed he'd cut himself with the first axe his father had ever given him, but some suggested it had come from a bar fight during his rowdy days as a 101st Airborne paratrooper.

His deep voice boomed from the editing system's speakers. "I just want to tell you people something."

"Here it comes," murmured Cate, shooting an amused glance at Andy.

"If you women want respect, you should be earning it out there on the battlefield, instead of whining about sexual harassment and discrimination all the time."

Cate's voice rang out on the tape. "Governor Hamm?"

He speared her with annoyed glare.

"How do you expect women to be trained as leaders on the battlefield if they're shut out of places like West Point, as you advocated to *Patriot Magazine*?"

Cheers and catcalls rose from the protesters, and the impromptu press conference ended abruptly as Liz Barracosta finally broke through the throng of reporters and grabbed the governor's arm, turning him toward the main door to the college. "You'll be late for your speech, Governor."

Cate smirked as the editing screen went dark. "I'd love to be fly on the wall when he gets home tonight. Deborah Hamm must be ready to kill him if the Barracuda doesn't get to him first."

Cate slipped through the heavy door and felt tropical air glide over her bare skin. Water glimmered in the dim light coming through the glass enclosure, and she breathed deep of the chlorine scent. Andy was still editing with one eye on the clock, but Cate had slipped away to her gym, a twenty-four-hour place in downtown Saint Paul, deciding that she needed exercise more than sleep.

Pulling a towel from around her waist, Cate tucked her chin length hair into a bathing cap, slid into the heated pool and pushed off from the edge, moving into a slow breaststroke. She was exhausted after her weekend trip to Boston to see her parents. They were divorcing after thirty-six years of marriage and selling the house. Cate and her younger sister had been summoned to select any family heirlooms they wanted before the division of property began.

She flipped onto her back and stroked the length of the pool, studying the silhouette of the indoor ferns and fig trees against the glass walls. It reminded her of her mother's backyard garden, and Cate felt a pang that someone else would soon be tending to it. Her parents had spent most of her adolescence bickering and had gone their separate ways when first she, then Cara had gone off to college, but somehow they'd never divorced.

She reached the wall and turned, plunging under the water's surface and pulling hard for the opposite end. Rising to take a breath, her heart pounding, she let out a gasp as she collided with another figure.

"Sorry. Didn't see you there."

The woman blinked water from her eyes, her skin pulled taut by the swimming cap she wore over her hair. She was openly annoyed. "I was in my lane when you suddenly veered out of yours."

Cate shook her head. "I'm pretty sure it was the other way around. I'm quite familiar . . ." Her words trailed off as the other woman pulled her bathing cap from her hair and Cate spotted the trademark silver streak that began at her widow's peak. "You're Millicent Pine."

The other woman nodded shortly.

"My photographer saw you at the protest today, at the college."

Pine's eyebrows rose. Tiny drops of water sparkled in them. "You were one of the television people those students were performing for?"

Cate flushed, resting her feet on the bottom of the pool. "I got the impression they were pretty upset with the governor."

"What do you think happened when the cameras went away?" Her eyes were strange, pale, almost colorless irises around dark pupils. "It was just a show for television. All style, no substance."

Cate stared at her, reaching for the ladder, her hands curving around the cool aluminum. She'd always admired this woman. "Sometimes television can do what no other medium can. Even books like yours."

"You're a fan, then?" Her mouth seemed to curve down at the prospect.

"No," Cate said, pulling herself onto the first step. "A friend of mine stocks your books in his store."

"A *man*," she said mockingly. "He must be quite enlightened."

Cate stepped up onto the rubber matting around the pool, yanking her own bathing cap off. Her hair fell in damp strands around her face. "I'll tell him you said that." She added, "You're here to write about Governor Hamm?"

The author regarded her from the center of the pool, her skin brown and shining. She had a dark mid-winter tan. "Let's just say I'm here to renew some old acquaintances." She snapped her cap back on and took a deep breath. "Pleasure making yours." She plunged under water, streaking like a heat-seeking missile for the far side of the pool.

Cate pushed through the glass door and shivered in the cool air of the locker room. What a jerk. The woman had ruined her workout and been an ass on top of it. Adam would be so disappointed. He even sold her early stuff in his store.

5

She drew her gym bag from a metal locker and rolled her suit off over her wet skin, still fuming. What goes around comes around, she thought, and Millicent Pine deserved everything she got. Cate draped a towel over her head and rubbed her hair, her hands stilling abruptly. Maybe that was it. Maybe Millicent Pine was the perfect person to go one on one with the governor, if she truly was here to do a story on him.

For the three months since he'd won the election, he'd been fawned over by the national press. The requests had poured in so rapidly from all over the world that his staff had taken to just pinning them up on a large bulletin board and throwing darts at them to decide who got a few precious moments with him.

Cate slid into her sweats, thinking about election night. All three network affiliates had declared the Republican candidate the winner early in the evening, but Edward Hamm had refused to concede, insisting that turnout in the rural, northern part of the state was going to break all records. It did.

At eight forty-five, Cate's station retracted their projection and declared the race too close to call. By ten twenty, numbers started coming in from the outer most regions of the state, including what they called the "paddle districts," where ballots were brought in by canoe through the Boundary Waters and counted by hand.

By midnight, the man who'd marketed himself as a modern-day Paul Bunyan was the new governor, and three months later, Eddie 'Bunyan' Hamm was still charming the public and press alike with his stories of painting his dad's dairy cow blue so he could have his own version of Babe, the blue ox.

2

SAINT PAUL, MINNESOTA

March 20, 5:59 P.M.

ICY SNOWFLAKES PROPELLED BY A MARCH wind flung themselves at Cate's face as she waited for her cue. Her teeth chattered loudly into the microphone, and she muttered, "Come on."

"Thirty seconds, Cate. Hang in there." The producer's voice purred into her ear through the earpiece Cate wore, and she pictured him snug in his booth back at the station, a wall of monitors in front of him, her shivering face filling one of the boxes. Sean would have his can of Fresca next to him and his headphones on upside down, so that the strap that connected the earpieces hung below his chin. He'd be warm and comfortable and in no damn hurry.

"Ten seconds, Cate. Last cue."

Cate nodded, trying to still the shuddering rippling through her body. The glamorous life of a TV reporter, she thought sourly, looking into the camera lens and smiling slightly as she was introduced.

"Dan, Governor Hamm's interview with *Patriot Magazine* has been the subject of protests, hundreds of angry calls to the capitol and furious demands for an apology. Today a group of community leaders, politicians, and even some retired military personnel came to the state capitol to demand a meeting, but so far they've been met with resistance from the governor's staff."

Cate listened as the taped story began, stamping her feet and shoving her gloved hands into her pockets. "Why is the Capitol always the coldest spot in the Twin Cities, Andy? We're going to have to start building bonfires before our live shots."

"Forty seconds to the tag, Cate."

Cate nodded into the camera's eye, watching Andy adjust the shot. The photographer wore a down parka and a ski mask that covered the lower part of her face. She looked like the suspects that showed up on bank robbery surveillance tapes.

Cate cleared her throat, waiting for the final words of her package. "Governor Hamm's office will not say whether they will agree to a meeting, and the governor is still insisting he has nothing to apologize for. But, Dan, if Governor Hamm is feeling the heat now, it's only going to get worse. Channel 3 has learned that Millicent Pine, a nationally known author and women's rights advocate is preparing a major profile about the governor for *Vanity Fair* magazine. Word is that she plans to turn the profile into a book." Cate nodded into the lens. "Dan, back to you."

Cate waited until they'd moved onto the next story before pulling her earpiece out and scurrying for the live truck. Her college roommate's position as a photographer's assistant at *Vanity Fair* had given her a nice little scoop. She huddled in front of the blasting vents, rubbing her chilled hands.

Andy put her head inside. "Coming to McChesney's tonight, Cate? Remember, it's Terry's going-away party."

"Another one? That's the third this month." Ever since Michaela Snow had been named News Director at Channel 3, there'd been a mass exodus to the competition and out of the market.

"I know." Andy nodded, pulling the ski mask up over her head and smoothing her hair. "I thought when we got rid of that dickhead Corning things would be better, but Snow is just as bad in her own way."

Mason Corning had spent eighteen months taking the perennially third-rated station to new lows, even airing a series on topless maids during a recent sweeps period. But the numbers that reflected how many viewers were watching had remained dismal, and Corning had finally been told to slink back to the small Iowa station he'd come from. The station owner had replaced him with a hotshot from Los Angeles who'd vowed to "whip the place into shape," but so far it hadn't happened.

"I think I'll skip the party tonight, Andy. I'm bushed." Cate slid behind the wheel of her Mustang, sporty and sharp in the summer, foolhardy in the Minnesota winter. "I think I've still got a bit of jet lag."

"Maybe it's that big birthday you've got coming up," Andy smirked. "You know, three and a half decades is quite a milestone, McCoy."

"You're not too far behind me, even if you act like you're twelve most of the time."

Andy laughed. "Speaking of which, I'll be robbin' the cradle again tonight."

"Sunny's back in town, huh?"

"Fresh off a big win at the Texas Rodeo. Rode that buckin' bronco 'til he couldn't buck no more." She winked. "That boy is great in the saddle."

Cate chuckled. "Well, have fun and watch those shots of tequila." She waved as she put the car in reverse. "See you Monday."

Liz Barracosta flipped off the small television set in her office and threw the remote onto her desk. "Bitch," she snarled, striding to the window and pulling the blinds aside. Forty yards away, she could see the mast on Channel 3's live truck being lowered as the technician prepared to wrap up the live shot.

"How did they find out about Millicent Pine?"

The press secretary whirled, biting back an angry reply. Eddie Hamm's niece stood in the doorway. "They have their sources, Jill."

"I'll bet my uncle will want a better answer than that."

She studied the girl, tempted to order her out of the office. Liz had taken the job when the governor's staff had come begging, overwhelmed by the onslaught of the media demands. She'd wrestled a big salary out of them and a corner office, but they'd had the last laugh, sticking her with Jill Hamm as her press assistant. Liz suspected she was there to spy for Lamar Bates, the governor's chief of staff.

"Look, I'll tell you what I told the governor. The less we talk about Millicent Pine the better." She moved away from the window and sat down in the soft leather chair behind her desk. They'd hidden the chair's two-thousand-dollar price tag in the governor's mansion redecoration budget. The press would've had a field day. "If we refuse to cooperate with her, she'll eventually have to pack up and go away." She looked at the girl. "You just keep writing press releases. I've got Millicent Pine well under control."

9

The lights of downtown Saint Paul glowed in the cold dusk as Cate headed toward the river, passing dark office buildings and the new hockey arena. Turning right, she drove along the riverbank, the modern arcs and pillars of the High Bridge rising in the distance. Her condo occupied a crescent of land at the river's edge, land that had once been so polluted the city had all but abandoned it. But it's proximity to the water and good economic times had brought clean-up crews and then a developer. The result was an elegant cluster of boutiques and condos, surrounded by a river-front garden.

Cate passed the guard shack and turned into the underground garage, grateful for its heat. She pulled her briefcase from the car and joined her next-door neighbor on the elevator. "Adam! Slow night at the book store?"

The elevator doors closed as they traveled upwards.

"Bad weather is keeping everyone home. I figured it was a good night to hunker down with Sherlock."

Cate nodded, catching the doors as they slid open and holding them so he could maneuver out of the small elevator cabin. Partially paralyzed during a skiing accident ten years before, he used a single metal crutch to get around. "Do you want me to take Sherlock for a quick run? I've got to go downstairs to get my mail anyway."

Adam Doyle paused in the small landing between their doors, the recessed lighting burnishing his face. He was one of the most striking men Cate knew, with looks that they used to call Black Irish. Thick dark hair and bluish gray eyes the color of a wintry lake. His social life was as dismal as hers.

"No plans tonight, Cate?"

She ducked from his penetrating gaze, digging into her briefcase for her keys. "Butt out, Adam."

He sighed, leaning on his crutch as he jiggled his key into the lock. "Is he still in Europe?"

She shrugged. "I try not to think about it."

A sharp yip greeted him as he opened the door. "At least you know Sherlock thinks you're hot stuff." He stepped back, leaning on his crutch, as a whirling dervish of black fur burst into the hallway and headed straight for Cate.

"Down, Sherlock." Cate knelt to pet the excited Labrador. "I see obedience school is really working. He knows not to leap on you but he makes a beeline for any woman in a five-mile radius. Must be quite a chick magnet."

Adam's mouth twisted. "That's why I'll be spending my Friday night with a dog and my socially-challenged neighbor." He limped into his condo, calling out, "Want some wine? Sherlock wants you to stay."

"I'll be over in a minute," Cate said, opening her own door. "I have to feed Walter and inspect the damage he's done today."

Adam's voice reached her through the half-open door. "Speaking of which, that animal turned my favorite rubber tree into shreds the last time you brought him over here. He's not invited."

Cate looked down at the large orange-and-white cat. "Another social faux pas, Walter. Pretty soon we'll be out of friends." She bent to pick him up, closing her eyes as he nuzzled her under the chin. He'd cost her room-mates, boyfriends, and a huge security deposit to the condo management but he'd survived all of them.

Cate carried him into her living room, her mind skittering over Adam's pointed observation. She'd been alone for nearly two years, unable to call it formally over with the man she now followed through his bylines. She'd last seen his name on an article datelined Madrid. It had been two months since she'd had a letter from him.

Cate poured out a bowl of cat food for Walter, kicked off her shoes and crossed the hall, tapping lightly and pushing the door open. Strains of Melissa Etheridge's first album greeted her, along with what smelled like Adam's hot artichoke dip.

"I love it when you take pity on me," she said, flopping down on his huge leather couch and taking in the view from his floor-to-ceiling windows. "I might've been reduced to eating Walter's Friskies if you'd left me to my own devices."

Adam brought a bottle of wine into the living room and handed her a corkscrew. "Do you think Walter Cronkite would be offended if he knew that you'd named your rapacious feline after him?"

Cate pulled the cork out of the bottle and splashed Zinfandel into two goblets. "Rapacious? He only weighs twenty-one pounds." She took a long sip and stretched out on the couch. "I don't know what I like best about your place, Adam, the view or your books."

Bookcases circled the entire living room, and Cate knew there were more in Adam's bedroom. He'd even mounted shelves in his bathroom. Studded with classic literature, the bulk of Adam's collection was devoted to mysteries, from Hemingway to Christie to Chandler to some of the newer writers. Cate thought he must have as many books in his home as he did at

11

his bookstore. An independent store owner, he'd been fighting off the large chains for several years. "How's business?"

He shrugged, limping into the room, his crutch in one hand, a large bowl of dip and chips in the other. Setting it on a low table, he sat down next to her, accepting a glass of wine. "Up and down. The months after Christmas and before summer are always the toughest."

"Still seeing that cute little thing from Doubleday?"

He eyed her over the rim of his glass, the lamplight hollowing his eyes and cheekbones. "Two dates is not quite what I'd call 'seeing,' Cate. It was over when she headed off to Costa Rica for a scuba-diving trip." He gestured toward his crutch, propped against arm of the couch. "Salt water rusts metal."

"Not aluminum," she said, sipping her wine. "Besides, you can always get a new one."

His mouth twisted. "Which is just what she did. A new guy who can do all the things she wants to do."

Cate scooped a dollop of creamy dip onto a chip and munched, gazing out into the blackness beyond his window. In the summer, Adam could watch the barges and towboats work the Mississippi, their cargos moving slowly past as they headed downstream. Tonight, though, the river was partially frozen and the only lights came from the houseboats that people lived on year round. "Have you ever seen the place where the Mississippi begins?"

He shook his head. "It's in the woods up north, isn't it?"

Cate nodded. "It bubbles out of the ground at this small spring in Itasca State Park. You can actually step across it." She swallowed some wine. "Hard to believe it flows all the way to the Gulf of Mexico from that one little trickle."

Adam looked at her. "Is this where I'm *not* supposed to mention that a certain city called New Orleans sits on the Gulf of Mexico? One-time home of a certain newspaper reporter?"

Cate hooked a swathe of hair behind her ear and spotted the concern in his eyes. "I haven't gotten a letter from him in eight weeks." She reached for another chip to escape his steady gaze. "It's . . . I'm here and he's . . ." she gestured with the tortilla chip, "somewhere out there. End of story."

She touched the rim of her glass against Adam's. "End of story," she said again.

He nodded, his gaze on the blackness beyond the window. "Time to write a new one," he murmured. "Chapter one. There's this lonely reporter . . ."

3

SAINT PAUL

March 22, 10:17 A.M.

CATE PULLED THE COLLAR OF HER WOOL COAT tighter and shielded her eyes from the sun's glare. The reflection off the snow-covered capitol lawn was blinding. "Whose crazy idea was it to have a demonstration on the capitol steps, *outside*, in March?"

Andy shifted her camera to her shoulder, focusing on the growing crowd as people streamed toward the broad stairs that led up to Minnesota's state capitol. Cold air fogged up her lens, and she pulled a hanky from her parka pocket to wipe it off. "I have a feeling they were denied permission to be inside in the rotunda. Probably too many people."

Cate nodded. "Looks like they've got at least three hundred now, and more are coming." She waved to another photographer from a competing station. "Think the governor will show up?"

Andy smiled. "Sure hope so. No telling what he'll say."

They moved deeper into the gathering demonstrators, getting shots of signs that read "I'm proud of my sex!" and "Women are Combat-Ready!" One demonstrator shouted into Cate's microphone, "Eddie Bunyan Hamm spent too much time in the woods if he thinks we're going to put up with this."

Cate and Andy moved off to the side as someone grabbed a bullhorn and began to shout at the crowd. "Thank you all for coming on this cold morning."

Cheers and whistles filled the air. "We thought it was important to show Governor Hamm that we are not going to simply shut up and go away, although he seems to expect that." More cheers. "We have asked repeatedly for a meeting with the governor, but he has refused to talk to us. So we are here today to let him know that his comments in *Patriot Magazine* will not stand!"

Someone blew an air horn, and the raucous sound bounced off the white walls of the capitol dome. Several legislators had joined the demonstration, and the bullhorn was passed to the minority leader of the Senate, a woman with a tight gray perm and the stern visage of her Norwegian ancestors.

"Folks, I'm glad to see you here today. Governor Hamm owes you an apology and until he gives you one, I think you should keep the pressure on."

The demonstrators screamed and whistled. The lawmaker held out her hands to quiet them. "Governor Hamm likes to talk about his upbringing up there in northern Minnesota, how he grew up on his family's land and worked at his grandfather's lumber mill." The legislator chuckled. "Hell, if he says he's the king of the lumberjacks, who's gonna' argue?"

The crowd laughed.

The minority leader breathed into her hands and rubbed them together, her face red with cold. "I think we can all appreciate the governor's . . . *personality* . . . but when he starts talking about what women can and can't do," she thundered, "that's where we draw the line!" A deafening roar rose from the demonstrators, and they surged forward, some of them grabbing the legislator's hands. "Keep up the good work! I'm with you all the way!"

"Edd-y Hamm has got to know. Apol-o-gize or we won't go!" The man with the bullhorn picked up the chant. "Edd-y Hamm has got to know. Apol-o-gize or we won't go! Edd-y Hamm . . ."

The Barracuda tapped on the polished oak door and slipped inside before the governor's secretary could stop her. Hamm was standing at his window, the chants of the demonstrators coming in through the glass, even though he couldn't see the crowd from his vantage point. "That bitch can forget about the light rail line she had her heart set on."

Liz Barracosta smiled. It hadn't taken the rookie politician long to catch onto the art of political payback. But they had bigger fish to fry right now. "Governor?"

He turned, winter daylight tinting the scar that ran the length of his right cheek a bluish color. He stroked his fingers over his thick beard. "What?"

"We've got to decide what we're going to tell the press."

His eyes narrowed. "Screw the press. What've they ever done for me?"

Barracosta nodded, tamping down her impatience. While he held a pity party for himself, news photographers were out there taping stuff they'd use for *years*. "Yes, that's true, Governor, they haven't been very nice to you, but we can't let what's happening out there go . . ." she paused, searching for the right word, "unanswered. I think we should draw up a statement. I'll take it out there and read it. Something to the effect of . . ."

"Uncle Edward?"

Liz whirled. Jill Hamm stood in the doorway, her cheeks flushed, her eyes wide. She was wearing a black suit with a scarlet scarf tied at her throat, an outfit identical to one Liz had worn last Thursday.

"Jill!" Liz's voice was curt. "The governor and I were discussing something important. Could you please come back later?"

The girl's eyes darted past her boss's face to her uncle. "Uncle Eddie," she murmured, "I can't stand to hear those things they're saying about you! Why aren't you out there defending yourself?"

"No!" Liz softened her voice as the governor's eyebrows shot up. "Governor, that would be a mistake. It's just what the demonstrators and the news crews want." She gestured toward the window. "A confrontation between you and that screaming rabble."

The governor flushed, blood rushing into his face. "Why shouldn't I go out there? I have nothing to be sorry about."

She could see his temperature gauge rising.

"Since when do I have to hide in my office?" He glanced around, calling out toward his secretary's desk. "Alice, get security and tell them we're on the move."

Liz raised her voice. "Governor, if you do this it's against my advice and judgment, and it is a serious mistake."

That stopped him. Liz ignored Jill's sigh. "You can't win this confrontation. Pick a better place. Agree to a meeting. Write a letter maybe— anything but go out there."

He stared at her for a moment, his bodyguards rustling into the doorway, eyes eager. Edward Hamm had made the security detail fun again. "Ready, Governor?"

The governor reached for his favorite coat, a red-and-black plaid wool that dated back to his lumberjacking days. "Let's go." He glared at Liz, the love of the fight flaring his nostrils and reddening his cheeks. "Barracosta. They told me you had balls."

The chanting was so loud Cate had to shout to be heard over the din. "Andy! The governor is coming down the stairs!" Andy swiveled quickly, focusing her camera lens with one hand, using the other to steady the camera on her shoulder. She was wearing gloves with the fingertips cut off so she could work the lens. "I've got him."

They moved through the crowd, Cate opening a path for her photographer while Andy rolled tape, keeping the governor framed up as he descended the shallow granite stairs. Cate and Andy stopped on a wide plaza that separated two levels of stairs as Hamm approached the podium, waving off the bullhorn.

"I've never run away from a fight in my life!"

The crowd surged forward, now nearly five hundred people standing on the steps, their chants accompanied by puffs of silvery steam as humid breath met the cold wintery air. "Edd-y Hamm has got to know! Apol-o-gize or we won't go!" The governor's security detail eyed the demonstrators, warning them with stern looks not to get too close.

"I've got nothing to apologize for." His plaid coat swung open as he pointed at the crowd. "Any soldier worth his salt is gonna' tell you he doesn't want a woman in the foxhole with him when the sh—when the crap hits the fan."

The demonstrators roared with anger and Andy spun away from the governor to record their reaction. A young black woman broke out of the crowd and strode toward the podium. The governor's bodyguards shifted uneasily. "Governor Hamm, we're here to let you know how offended," the word rang out, ricocheting among the protesters, "we are by what you said in that interview."

The governor shrugged, his eyes narrowed against the reflection of sunshine on snow. "I served my country and kicked some ass, and that's more than most of you can say."

Cate's mouth dropped open, and she shot a glance at Andy's camera to make sure the tape was still rolling. She whispered to Andy, "Get a shot of the Barracuda over there." Andy turned, focusing in on Liz Barracosta's face, her silver hair easy to spot in the crowd.

Hamm waited for the crowd to quiet. "You elected me because you wanted me to speak my mind. Well, that's just what I'm doing. Take it or leave it." He spun around in a plaid blur, ascending the stairs two at a time and disappearing back inside the capitol.

Millicent Pine slipped her notebook into her purse and permitted herself a brief smile. This was going to make a terrific lead for her profile of the lumberjack-turned-politician. Her editor at *Vanity Fair* would eat it up. They'd probably move her deadline forward, and that was fine. She was eager to finish this assignment and get back to her other story.

She slipped through the dispersing crowd and headed for her car in a distant parking lot. She'd taken pains today to be unobtrusive, but she suspected that the governor's press secretary had spotted her during the melee. Liz Barracosta is one to be wary of, she thought. As she fumbled with her keys, Millicent remembered Liz Barracosta when she'd been working for Senator Pound in Washington. The woman's confrontations with reporters were legendary. Rumor had it that she'd once snatched the tape out of a reporter's cassette recorder and ground it beneath her heel when an interview had gone badly.

Millicent Pine headed for downtown Saint Paul, eager to make her phone calls to New York. Turning the corner, she spotted the Saint Paul Hotel's historic façade. She made it a point to avoid chain hotels when she traveled, and this one had an excellent restaurant perfect for her expense account. She handed over her keys to the valet and crossed the elegant lobby. She would draw a hot bath to thaw out her fingers and toes, and then call New York from the tub. She smiled to herself. This story couldn't have had a better beginning, and there were more fireworks to come.

4

Saint Paul

4:52 P.M.

"Happy fortieth, Cate!"

Cate ground her teeth, curving her lips into what Andy called her iceberg smile, ice cold on top, deadly underneath.

"I'm turning thirty-five today, Allison, but thank you."

The blonde anchor tilted her head, blue eyes widening, one eyebrow arched. Cate had seen the pose before. It was meant to convey serious interest whether the topic was last night's plane crash or tomorrow's wind chills. "Thirty-five. Forty." Her eyes hardened. "It's still a lot of candles on the cake, isn't it?"

Heat burned in Cate's stomach, flushing over her chest and into her cheeks. She'd disliked this Barbie doll from the day that idiot Mason Corning had pronounced her the station's great white hope. White being the operative word, Cate thought grimly. In a news market that trailed many others for on-camera diversity, Scandinavian blondes were in great demand. The blonder the better.

The news directors didn't talk about it, but somehow all of the black anchors ended up on weekend or morning shows, where the stakes weren't as high. The ice princesses sat front and center, no matter how young or inexperienced. Allison Anderson was twenty-seven.

"Allison?" The station's makeup artist rounded the corner. "Let's get going on your face. I have a new blush I want to try on you with that pink suit."

The anchor nodded, sending Cate a veiled look. "I was just wishing Cate a happy birthday, Mary Ann." She winked, bending to stage whisper in the cosmetician's ear as they walked down the corridor. "Maybe she's so crabby 'cause there's no man to celebrate with."

Cate shot daggers into the anchor's back and strode into the newsroom, surprised to see a group of reporters and photographers clustered near the assignments desk. She glanced at her watch. Six minutes to news time. "What's going on?"

Heads turned and Cate caught the sheepish grin on Gino Benedict's face. Competitive and driven, he was the station's most award-winning photographer, but there were whispers that he staged shots, telling his subjects to do and say certain things to make the story better.

Cate scanned the faces, the tinny sound of a siren bleating out of the dispatch center's scanner in the background. "Come on, Gino. Give it up."

In the center of the newsroom, a producer slammed down a phone, gathered up a sheaf of papers and sprinted for the control booth. The six o'clock newscast was three minutes away.

Benedict leaned toward her. "I'll deny it if you tell anyone it came from me. Deal?"

Cate nodded, disliking the malicious gleam in his eye, but intrigued despite herself. Hey, reporters lived for this stuff. "Deal."

"The Snow Queen is a little hotter than we thought." His dark eyes flared, primed for her reaction.

Cate's groaned. "Not another hockey player."

Benedict smirked. "She's *branching* out." He leered, and the others burst out laughing.

Cate's eyebrows rose. "What are you talking about?"

A reporter settled into the newsroom camera chair in the middle of the newsroom, and bright lights came on above him. He put on a lapel mike and waited for the newscast to begin. Cate noticed it was Barry Fallon. She turned back to Benedict. "Come on, I have a live shot on the set in three minutes."

The music from the newscast's open began, and Cate glanced up at the bank of television monitors above the assignments desk. Looked like the competition was leading with a story about a snowmobile through the ice.

Gino Benedict's hand fell on her shoulder, and he leaned in close. Cate could smell the scent of damp wool on him. "A certain news director was

spotted in the bathroom of a downtown Minneapolis bar last weekend performing a certain service for a certain quarterback. It'll be in the paper
tomorrow."

Cate reared back. "In the paper?"

Benedict's hand tightened on her shoulder. "In the gossip column."

Cate shook her head as if to clear her vision and headed for the news set,
her mind spinning. "Holy shit," she muttered to herself. "Holy shit."

Millicent Pine eyed her adversary over her martini glass. They'd been fenc-
ing for the last hour, their feints and thrusts unnoticed by any of the other
patrons of the Saint Paul Grill. She took a mouthful of booze and set the glass
down, fitting it into the circle her first two drinks had engraved on the paper
napkin.

The Barracuda smiled. "We've known each other for a long time,
Millicent. Why don't we just put our cards on the table?"

The journalist tilted her head. "You make it sound like we're old friends,
Liz, but we both know that isn't true. You sent me hate mail for six months
after my story on the good senator."

Liz forced a smile. "Your hatchet job on Ron Pound in the *Post* was a
long time ago. I've moved on."

Pine sipped her drink, watching the Barracuda close her lips over a tiny
plastic spear and pull two cocktail onions into her mouth. "Have you, Liz?"

The other woman's eyes narrowed, gleaming obsidian in the low light.

"You told Ron Pound to lie to me," Millicent said, her voice low. "He as
much as admitted it during the interview." She paused. "Right after he admitted to an affair with his chief of staff's seventeen-year-old daughter."

Barracosta toyed with the empty spear. "If this is supposed to persuade
me to grant you an interview with the governor, Millicent, it's not working."
She tilted her wrist and peered at her watch. "I've got an early meeting with
a reporter from *Time* who also wants a sit-down, and he's probably going to
get it." She swallowed the rest of her drink, the sheen of gin on her lips. "You
know why?"

Millicent saw a man at the bar spot Liz and lean over to point her out to
his companion. Even Governor Hamm's press secretary was a celebrity these
days. "Because he can fell a tree with a single blow?"

"Funny." The Barracuda's lips tightened, the shine gone. "I wish that
agenda you bring to every story was so amusing." She leaned forward, press-

ing against the lip of the small table. "Millicent, face it. You see yourself as some kind of *crusader*, taking up the cause of women's rights far and wide." She tilted her head, condescension in her eyes. "That's so seventies. Feminism is a dirty word for the Gen X-ers, in case you hadn't noticed. "

"Liz, I'm writing the profile whether he cooperates or not."

"Sounds like it'll be the printed version of what TV reporters call dead air." She glanced at her watch again, and gathered her purse and coat from the extra chair.

Millicent played her ace. "You know better than that, Liz, and that's why you're here." She slid a finger down the side of her glass, moisture dampening her fingertips. "You never intended to let me interview Hamm. You just wanted to see what I've got."

Barracosta acknowledged that, putting her purse and coat back on the chair, sensing there was more.

"Well, here it is."

Muted alarm spread over the other woman's face, and her gaze dropped to the photograph Pine slid onto the table between them.

"Eddie Hamm wasn't bad to look at when he was a young army recruit, was he?"

Barracosta stared at the picture.

Pine gestured toward the photo. "He had the kind of face you'd remember. Even thirty years later."

A second photograph covered the first. It was black and white and featured a young woman with upswept hair, large eyes, and a wide smile. The girl wasn't more than twenty-one.

"Carolee Baldwin." Pine's tone was as tough as Teflon. "Pretty enough to be a pool girl at one of those swanky hotels in West Palm Beach."

"Florida," Liz said flatly.

Pine tapped the photo with a finger, the nail short and unvarnished. "But they don't pay the girls much, so Carolee had to moonlight." Her gaze trapped Barracosta's. "Guess what she did to make ends meet?"

"I have a pretty good idea."

Pine nodded, her eyes somber. "She turned tricks on the side. Met her customers at a motel that was just a few blocks away." She separated the two photos and laid them side-by-side on the table.

"The governor has never pretended to be a saint, Millicent."

Pine ignored her. "Edward Hamm had just come through some long weeks of paratrooper training with the 82nd Airborne, and he had a week's leave before he would be shipped out. Chances were high he'd be going to Vietnam."

The Barracuda shifted restlessly, signaling the waiter for another round. "And as we all know, Millicent, he did end up in Vietnam, where he earned a bronze star. That's certainly not classified information."

"But in the fall of 1973, Eddie Hamm was a soldier on a different mission. Pack in seven days of R&R before reporting for duty." Millicent looked at her. "He and two buddies, Pete Escobar and John Grace, decided to head south." Her eyes were hard. "They didn't have much money so they pooled their cash on low-rent motels and gas for the car." She paused as the waiter arrived with the drinks. Barracosta shoved a fistful of money at him, and he disappeared.

"By the time they got to West Palm and paid for their hotel room, they were broke, but Eddie had already spotted Carolee."

Barracosta dunked her cocktail onions in her gin and pried them off the stick, chewing delicately.

"Boys will be boys."

"He spent two evenings with her and asked for a third." Pine squeezed the lime in her fresh drink and looked at the photograph of Carolee Baldwin. "But when Carolee asked to be paid, Hamm didn't have the money. All he had was a pocket watch his father had given to him as a boy. Josef Hamm had received it from his father when he was a young man. On the inside of the case, it had an engraving of an evergreen tree." She looked at Liz. "You've probably seen the governor pull it out from time to time."

Liz returned her stare, giving nothing away. "Is this going somewhere?"

"Carolee Baldwin wanted the watch in exchange for her services." Millicent traced the outline of Hamm's cocky smile in the photograph. "Hamm refused and pulled a knife. He was probably only going to threaten her with it, but Carolee had a temper. Still does."

Pine paused, moving the pictures around again. "She tried to hit him, and he grabbed her. The knife slid across her right breast. Carolee saw the blood and screamed bloody murder. The motel manager rushed to the room and saw Hamm running away before the cops showed up." Pine's lips pursed. "That was the last time Carolee saw Edward Hamm, Liz, until he won the election and made national news. But she still remembers him."

Barracosta's fingers curled around the stem of her glass, and she twisted it back and forth. "A compelling story, Millicent. Could even be damaging. If it's true." She smiled. "But where's the proof? You can't seriously expect me to take the word of some burned-out hooker who must be in her, let's see, early fifties by now." She sat back in her chair.

A police report joined the photographs. "Officer Diaz is retired now. He eventually made assistant chief. He prides himself on his memory." She smiled slightly. "We spent the afternoon on the golf course."

Barracosta looked at the report but didn't touch it.

Pine smiled slightly. "There is also a photograph of the three friends on the beach. The hotel where they stayed and met Carolee is in the background. John Grace's mother found it in his things after he was killed in Vietnam." She looked at the press secretary. "And just so you know. Carolee Baldwin is far from a 'burned-out hooker' these days. She owns a chain of upscale Mexican restaurants. She's living in Boulder City, Nevada."

Barracosta ran her fingers through her pewter hair, her eyes on the collage of photographs and other papers. She rubbed her hands together, an engraved silver ring catching the light. "Well, it appears we've got some trouble." She rose. "I'll be back in a minute." Pine saw her reaching for her cell phone as she pushed through the bar's glass doors.

She was gone for fifteen minutes. "The governor's chief of staff is willing to see us in about an hour. He lives out in Marine on St. Croix, and it's hard to find. Maybe I should drive."

Pine eyed the press secretary's empty glass. "I think we should take a cab, Liz."

The Barracuda stood up, her gaze on the photographs. "You don't have to worry, Millicent. I find that I'm suddenly stone-cold sober."

5

Saint Paul

March 23, 4:32 P.M.

Nᴇᴡѕ ᴏꜰ Mɪʟʟɪᴄᴇɴᴛ Pɪɴᴇ's ᴅɪѕᴀᴘᴘᴇᴀʀᴀɴᴄᴇ hit the Associated Press wire thirty minutes before the five o'clock newscast. Cate was at the state capitol, putting the finishing touches on a story about the power struggle between pro-choice and pro-life factions within the House Democratic caucus when her phone rang. "What do you mean, 'missing'?"

The executive producer snapped, "Missing, Cate. As in not there. Not anywhere!"

"Who discovered it?"

"The A.P. says her editor reported her missing when she didn't answer calls to her cell phone and hotel room. Says her car is still in the hotel parking ramp, and her room appears to have been empty since the maid turned down the bedcovers two nights ago."

Cate thought for a second. "Could she have taken off for another assignment?"

"Without her car?" Noah Hamilton pounded some computer keys. "We're gonna' lead with this at five. I need you to put together about a minute thirty on her." More pounding. "I think we've got some file vid of her when she won the Book Critics Award a few years back."

"Okay. We might also have some video of her from two days ago. She was there when Hamm confronted those protesters on the capitol steps."

"Good. Get the script in the newscast lineup, and I'll warn the show producer what's going on. I'll have someone on the desk call the police."

Thirty minutes later, Cate stood outside on the capitol steps, a weak sun warming her face as she waited for her cue from the producer. They'd found a couple of shots of Millicent Pine from the day of the protest, and they'd blended that with file video the station had dropped in. Now, Cate hoped she could remember what she'd written without glancing down at her notes too much. Eye contact with the camera always had a bigger impact.

"We're coming to you in fifteen, Cate."

Cate nodded into the camera lens, aware that the producer was watching her in a wall monitor back at the station. She heard Allison Anderson read the intro, stumbling over Millicent Pine's name.

"Allison, police confirm that Millicent Pine has been missing for nearly forty-eight hours. You'll remember that we first reported four days ago that she was coming to the Twin Cities to profile Governor Hamm for *Vanity Fair*."

Cate glanced down at the small television monitor propped below Andy's tripod and saw that video of Millicent Pine was rolling. "Governor Hamm's press secretary, Liz Barracosta, said that the governor would not cooperate with the profile, but that apparently did not deter Ms. Pine."

Cate glanced again at the monitor and saw video of Pine accepting an award. "Millicent Pine is perhaps best known for her award winning book on the oppression of women under the rule of Afghanistan's Taliban. She worked closely with Gloria Steinem during a period in the early eighties and won the Pulitzer Prize for her newspaper column in the *Washington Post* during the Reagan Administration."

The video ended and Cate looked into the camera lens. "Millicent Pine was last seen in the bar of the Saint Paul Grill with Liz Barracosta. The governor's press secretary had no comment late today. Back to you."

Liz Barracosta stood up behind her desk, shook the police officer's hand and watched him settle uncomfortably into the chrome-and-leather chair. Tall and thin with small eyes and a curved, expressionless forehead that had earned him the adolescent nickname of "serpenthead," the Clipper was given his new handle in the police academy. Unable, at first, to hit even the paper targets at the shooting range, Sid Dahl practiced diligently with his pistol until he could pass the marksmanship section of his training. But since then, he'd been known as the Clipper, a marksman who struggled to do more than just clip his target.

In spite of that, the Clipper had risen through the ranks of the Saint Paul Police Department to homicide detective. He had an impressive clear rate and was known to despise the press. Liz had heard about his legendary revenge on a cop reporter he hated.

The television journalist had been doing a live report in front of a house in which officers were serving a search warrant. As the reporter broadcast from the lawn, viewers could see police officers in the background carrying boxes out the front door. Just as the reporter launched into the details of the raid, then-officer Sid Dahl had come out of the door with a box, eyes straight ahead, face stern. Protruding from the carton was an over-sized sex aid, which could clearly be seen behind the unwitting reporter's head as Dahl marched by.

"Cute trick with the dildo." Liz said, sitting down.

He looked at her, his small eyes empty. "What time did you and Miss Pine finish your drinks Tuesday night?" He flipped open a crumpled notepad, drawing a Bic pen from his breast pocket.

Liz smiled. "I see. I'm persona non grata too because I work with the press." She straightened the green scarf at her throat. "Fine, Detective, we'll play it straight. "

"Do you know what time it was, Miss Barracosta?"

"Around ten fifteen, I think."

His gaze flicked up at her.

"I know because we had an appointment to meet Governor Hamm's chief of staff at his home at eleven and I was worried about being late. The roads were icy."

He scribbled for several seconds. "Why were you going to Mr. Bates' house at that hour?"

Barracosta's fingertips tingled, and she picked up a heavy paperweight, holding the cool granite in her palm. "I was trying to help Millicent with her story about the governor. She thought if she could make her case to Mr. Bates, the chief of staff, personally, he might talk Governor Hamm into an interview."

"Even though it was likely that Miss Pine's story wouldn't be flattering to the governor?"

Liz studied the speckles in the green stone, rubbing her thumb along its jagged edge. "That's an old trick with journalists, Detective Dahl. They believe that if they threaten a negative story, their subjects will feel they have to defend themselves." She replaced the paperweight. "I knew what Millicent was trying to do, but I felt the governor could hold his own with her." She looked him in the eye. "He can be very charming when he makes the effort."

"Don't flatter me too much, Liz. I like my press secretaries on the mean side."

Liz stood, startled by the governor's sudden appearance in her doorway. "Governor, this is Detective Dahl. We were just going over some details about Millicent Pine's disappearance."

Edward Hamm stroked his beard, his blue eyes inquisitive. "That pit bull? Glad she's gone." He folded his large frame into the only other available chair.

Dahl looked at him. "Did you know that Miss Barracosta wanted you to grant Miss Pine an interview?"

Hamm frowned and pointed at Liz. "You called her an 'unethical bitch.'" He tapped his temple, eyes on the detective. "I've got a mind like a steel trap, Officer. Comes from memorizing all those coordinates from my paratrooper days."

Dahl jotted something on his pad. "It's Detective, Governor. Did Millicent Pine threaten you in any way?"

"Threaten me?" Hamm kicked booted feet up onto the edge of Liz's desk. "No, not in any physical sense, if that's what you mean. But I don't worry too much about threats, Officer. That's what my permit is for."

Liz winced. One of the governor's greatest press debacles had erupted when a reporter had discovered he'd applied for a gun permit. In Minnesota, the issuance of permits was up to the discretion of the sheriff and police chief, and Hamm had been turned down twice before. He'd finally gotten one after being elected governor. The media furor had prompted Bates' first phone call to her. "Governor, I . . . ."

Hamm barked out a throaty laugh, rising to his feet. "They call her Barracuda, Officer, and for good reason." He winked at the detective. "Don't let her sting you. Good night."

The governor's leather boots creaked down the hall as Detective Dahl studied her. "It appears Governor Hamm didn't know you were 'helping' Miss Pine."

Liz flushed. "This is a very delicate business, Detective. You walk a fine line between the boss and the press."

He blinked. "Did you call Miss Pine an 'unethical bitch?'"

Perspiration tickled her scalp. "Yes. I wanted Governor Hamm to be very wary of Miss Pine if an interview arrangement was ever reached."

He jotted something, flipping a wrinkled page to squint at his writing. "You told my partner earlier today that you suggested that you and Miss Pine drive together to Mr. Bates' home. Is that right?"

Liz nodded. "I told Millicent it was in a small town on the Saint Croix River and might be hard to find at night."

"And she agreed?"

Liz shifted in her chair, the soft leather sticking to her nylon-covered thighs. "She was a bit concerned about the amount of alcohol I'd had to drink, but I assured her that I was fine to drive."

"And what did she say to that?"

"We agreed that I would order some food to take out with us while she went up to her room to change into warmer clothes."

His gaze dropped to her hands and Liz laced her fingers together. "What happened then?"

"As I told your partner, she left and never came back. I waited another half hour and tried calling her room but there was no answer. I finally left."

"Did you ever go upstairs to her room or send anyone from the hotel up there?"

"No. I figured she'd gotten a call from her editor or something had delayed her and we would reschedule the next day."

Their eyes met. "Were you surprised when she never called to set up another appointment?"

Liz shrugged. "She's a big girl, Detective. She slipped into Afghanistan illegally once. She can take care of herself."

8:13 P.M.

Cate emptied the bottle of Zinfandel into their wine glasses and carried hers to the large window that looked out on the river. She could hear Adam in the kitchen cleaning up the plates from their meal. The lights from the houseboat moored against the opposite bank glowed yellow in the drizzly night and Cate imagined ragged chunks of river ice bumping against the bow as they broke off and flowed downstream. Spring was finally coming but winter surrendered very reluctantly in Minnesota.

"I forgot to tell you," Adam called over the sound of the dishwasher. "I brought you a couple of Millicent Pine's books from the shop."

Cate turned as he emerged from the kitchen, his black sweater pushed up over his forearms. His hair was uncombed, and she noticed he was letting it grow a little longer. "After the way she treated me at the pool that night, I'm not sure I want to read anything she's written."

He propped his crutch against the armrest of the couch and lowered himself onto it, gesturing toward the glass coffee table. "I brought you the book on the Taliban. This one," he said handing her a thick volume, I found in my own collection."

Cate read the title, *The Future of Feminism,* and smiled. "Adam, the women out there just don't know what they're missing. A great cook and a closet feminist." She sighed, opening the book's cover. "Somebody's going to snap you up and then where will I be?"

Adam regarded her, his blue eyes serious. "Tending the flame for he who shall remain nameless."

There was an uneasy silence. Cate said finally, "I saw his byline yesterday. He's in Northern Ireland."

She read the dedication page. It said, "To my sister. Doing the work of the angels." "That's interesting," she said, showing Adam the inscription.

Adam read it. "I think her Islamic friends put a death sentence on her head after this book came out a couple of years ago. Cancel that summer vacation in Kabul."

"She's had a fascinating career." Cate flipped through the book, pausing to scan paragraphs in various chapters.

Adam sipped his wine. "Any chance she got a hot tip on another story and left to investigate it?"

Cate shook her head. "Sounds kind of unlikely. She didn't even tell her editors where she was going. They're pretty worried." Cate's cell phone chirped, and she reached for her purse. "Hello?"

"McCoy? Andy."

"Hey. What's up?"

"Plenty. You'd better get over here."

Cate pulled a reporter's pad out of her purse. "Where are you?" Andy reeled off an address. "The Tamarack Nature Center? That's in White Bear Lake, isn't it?"

"Yeah. The place is closed, and the cops have brought in huge floodlights. My buddy in dispatch says a witness saw Millicent Pine here with a woman Tuesday night."

29

"In the nature center?" Adrenaline surged through Cate's veins, and she gathered up her purse. "I'll be there as quick as I can. Roll on everything."

At one minute to ten, Cate stood shivering at the edge of the nature center, waiting for her cue. The police officers, angry that reporters had been tipped off, had moved Cate and Andy back to the street so that it was difficult to see what they were doing. But they had the story, and in thirty seconds they were going to break it.

"News open in twenty, Cate, and then we're coming to you." The producer's voice was tense.

Cate adjusted her earpiece, which allowed her to hear the producer and the on-air programming. She listened to the music that signified the beginning of the newscast while Andy checked the shot through her viewfinder. The rain had diminished to a light mist, but it had soaked both of them.

"Stand by, Cate."

Cate heard Dan Gilbert recap the story about Millicent Pine's disappearance and toss it to Allison. Allison said, "But there are new developments tonight in the case. We go live now to political reporter Cate McCoy in White Bear Lake. Cate?"

Cate took her cue. "Dan and Allison, investigators have been here in the Tamarack Nature Center since early evening. They're combing the woods and marshes for evidence that might support a witness' claim that he saw Millicent Pine in the company of another woman here Tuesday night."

Cate glanced down at the monitor and saw videotape of the police at work. "The police received that information after television broadcasts of Ms. Pine's disappearance earlier tonight. Police aren't saying much, but the witness apparently told them that he was in the nature center around eleven o'clock Tuesday night when he saw two women near the parking lot."

The video ended and a sound bite of Detective Sid Dahl came up. "The witness contacted us this evening, and we're simply following up on some of the information he told us."

Cate was back on live. "This is the first solid lead police have had since Ms. Pine disappeared two days ago. We'll be following this story and have more for you as it develops."

6

LAS VEGAS, NEVADA

9:20 P.M.

D ELLA DEFRANCISCO FOUGHT THE URGE to clap her hands over her ears and scream. A headache pounded at her temples, and the cacophony of the casino was painful. She glanced at her watch. Two hours until she could call it a day. Or a night. You never knew which it was inside the Athena. Built to resemble ancient Greece, the casino's soaring pillars and marbled ruins were bathed in a warm Mediterranean light around the clock. The owners even mixed the pure oxygen they pumped into the gambling rooms with the scents of citrus and the ocean. Della suspected the gamblers hardly noticed.

Dodging a couple who wore wedges of cheese on their heads and T-shirts that said 'Wisconsin Dairy Association,' Della crossed the busy room, catching the eye of a dealer and murmuring a hello. The night's take would be high, judging from the number of people on the floor this early. Her boss would be pleased.

She paused to observe a round of blackjack, her gaze on an obese man who had just watched his pile of chips switch positions on the table. He was bellowing for a waitress, and she shot a warning glance at the girl who arrived to serve him. The girl nodded and Della moved on. She glanced at her watch again. The evening was moving excruciatingly slowly.

"Miss DeFrancisco? There's a phone call for you."

31

Finally. Della spun to thank the young man who'd delivered the message and moved quickly to an in-house phone on the wall. "Della DeFrancisco here."

"Detective Sid Dahl. Saint Paul Police Department."

Della's heart raced. "Saint Paul? Minnesota?"

"Yes. We found your number in Miss Pine's things. We're investigating her disappearance."

Della's fingers clenched the receiver as her headache throbbed. The worry that she'd tried to quell for two days burst into full-fledged panic. "What . . . happened?" Her mouth felt like she'd eaten sand.

"Miss Pine has been missing since Tuesday night."

A woman screamed "Jackpot!" and Della closed her eyes.

The detective's voice was matter of fact. "We've spoken with her editors and a couple of other contacts we found in her organizer."

An image of Millicent swam into her mind. She'd been joking that she might need one of Della's old lariats from her cowhand days to bring the governor to his knees. Della had pressed a kiss on her mouth at the airport and reminded her to call when she had time.

"Miss DeFrancisco? I'm sorry to spring this on you over the phone, but I'd like to ask you a few questions."

Della swallowed hard. She longed for some water. "Of course. Go ahead."

"Have you heard from Miss Pine since she arrived in Minnesota?"

"No. I've been feeding her cats. She usually calls to see how they're doing."

"Did she mention any other trips she had planned?"

Della hesitated. "No, although I know she was going to fly to North Carolina at some point to research the governor's military background. But I think she was planning that for May."

"Can you think of any reason she would've left Minnesota so abruptly? An emergency call from a family member, perhaps?"

Della thought for a moment. "I don't think so, Detective. Her father died about ten years ago and her mother is remarried and living in Italy." She signaled a passing waitress and pointed at a glass on her tray. The girl handed her a flute of mineral water.

Della swallowed a mouthful of the water, listening as the detective typed something on what sounded like an old-fashioned typewriter.

"That's all for now. If you hear from Miss Pine, please let us know."

Della blurted out, "Wait!"

"Yes?" Impatience edged his voice.

"I need to know more. What kind of leads . . ."

"Miss DeFrancisco," he interrupted. "We know very little. Just that she had a late meeting with someone and never made it. We're still interviewing witnesses and gathering evidence."

Della went cold. "Evidence?"

"This is a homicide investigation. Please call if you think of anything."

The receiver slipped from Della's fingers and bumped against the wall. She stared numbly into the crowd. Homicide. Oh, God. Her gaze sought out the cashier's cage and the huge wall vault she knew was behind it. Should she have told the detective about the packet Millicent had given her?

It was hidden on one of the vault shelves, behind a tall stack of bound one hundred dollar bills. Millicent had pressed the envelope into her hand at the airport. "Hide this as if it were your deepest darkest secret, Del." She'd smiled. "Not that you have any from me." Her fingers had curled over Della's, the envelope bulky in Della's palm. "I'll need it when I get back."

Edward Hamm grinned around the thick stogie clamped between his teeth and pushed away from the table, patting his belly. "Used to be a washboard, Simon, back in the old lumberjackin' days, but politics has made me soft."

The director cupped a hand over his own rounded stomach and waved away a puff of smoke drifting toward him. "Politics, Hollywood. It's all the same, Governor." He had a strong British accent. "That's why I'm eager to get back into the field and live like a real man for a change."

The third man at the table shook his head mutely, and the director squinted at him. The governor winked, gesturing with his cigar. "My buddy Pete here thinks 'the field' is hiking into the desert about thirty miles and frying up a little rattlesnake meat for your supper." Hamm chuckled. "Escobar's picture is in the dictionary next to the word 'hard core.'"

The director fanned smoke from his face. "I believe that's two words, Governor." He studied the other man. "How did you two make your acquaintance?"

Escobar's eyes were cool. "Paratrooper training."

Hamm broke in. "Pete taught me about double and triple checking my gear. He . . . well, that's for another night. Might even make a great movie." He plucked the cigar from his mouth, blowing smoke from his pursed lips. "I owe Pete a lot."

"Eddie!" A tall woman in khaki shorts, a denim blouse and knee socks strode into the room. "You know you're not allowed to smoke in here." She leaned over the governor's shoulder and plucked the cigar out of his hand, looking at it with distaste. Her brown hair was scraped into a ponytail and her rimless glasses slid down her nose. "The governor's mansion is like a museum, Edward."

"How was the meeting, sweetheart?" Hamm rolled his eyes at Escobar and turned toward the director. "Deborah's leading a bird watching tour up north next weekend, Simon. You ought to go along."

Deborah Hamm stubbed out her husband's cigar and broke it in half. "Mr. Divine has better things to do than follow me around in the woods." Her glasses glinted in the light from the chandelier. "Although we are on the lookout for a . . ."

Simon Divine smiled politely. "I will be busy scouting locations for my movie, but thank you, Mrs. Hamm, for the kind invitation."

"Well if you change your mind, we'd love to have you."

"Deborah?"

Divine started, twisting toward the door, where a woman leaned against the frame.

She smiled at him, a jeweled pin in her hair shimmering in the chandelier's light. She wore tight dark riding pants and a violet blouse. Her hair was pulled back into a glossy roll at the nape of her neck.

Eddie Hamm grinned at the director's reaction. "Simon, this is Ana, Pete's wife."

Divine reached for his wine glass. "Perhaps I'll find time in my schedule after all. A walk in the woods might be just the thing."

March 26, 12:18 P.M.

"Now there's a beautiful sight, McCoy. Check that out."

Cate looked up from her sandwich and followed Andy's line of sight. Sunny Cortina was crossing Rice Park, his lazy saddle-sprung lope attracting plenty of attention. His large silver buckle caught the pale afternoon sun.

"Hi, Sunny." He sat down on the wide lip of the fountain where she and Andy were having a picnic lunch, bundled up against the brisk wind off the river. "Want some chips?"

He shook his head. "Gotta' stay in fighting shape. Next rodeo is coming up Saturday in Abilene."

Andy kissed the corner of his mouth, running a lascivious hand up his jean-clad thigh. "I think you're in great shape, darlin'." She nibbled his ear.

Cate rolled her eyes. "Born and bred in Duluth, and she sounds like a cowpoke every time you come to town. Next she'll be wearing a Stetson to work."

Andy jabbed Cate in the ribs and stood up. "We'd better put this story together, McCoy, or we're not going to make deadline." She bent to kiss Sunny again. "My place at six thirty?"

"Wild horses couldn't keep me away." He pinched her rear end as she bent over to pick up her camera. "And I know a wild little pony when I see one."

The newsroom was in chaos when Cate and Andy walked in thirty minutes later, and an assignments editor shouted their names when he spotted them. The two exchanged puzzled glances as they approached the raised desk from which the assignments desk staff kept track of the everyday mayhem.

"I've been paging the hell out of you, Andy. Where have you been?"

Andy pulled out her pager and groaned when she saw the low battery sign. "Sorry, Tim. What's going on?"

A phone rang, and he snatched it up. "Channel Three News. Please hold." He shouted at one of his minions to attend to it. "We think we may know who the Tamarack witness is. We got a tip call from the guy's sister." He broke off, shouting into the dispatch center, "I just heard four engines being sent to New Brighton! Keep an eye on it."

"Why would the guy's sister call us?" Cate pulled her notebook from her purse.

"Loves Channel Three. Watches us every night."

Andy smirked at Cate. "So she's the one."

He opened a file. "Here's the number, Cate."

"What about our six o'clock story?"

He punched a button on his phone and picked it up. "Channel Three. Can you hold?" He frowned. "What was your question?"

"Thanks, Tim. I'll talk to the producer."

Cate went over to the producer's desk, waiting while she finished a phone conversation with another reporter. "I don't care if you think the story's stupid, Laura. I've got a minute thirty hole in my newscast to fill and you're it." She replaced the phone and grimaced. "Save me from anchor wannabes. I think they're worse than the real thing." She turned back to her computer, pounding hard on the keyboard. "What's up, McCoy?"

"I've got a good lead on the witness the cops are talking to about Millicent Pine. How about if we blow off the live shot on my story today and it runs as a straight package? That way, I can get going on this other thing for the ten o'clock show."

The producer ran a distracted hand through her hair and nodded. "Fine. Straight pack. You owe me."

Ninety minutes later, Cate and Andy were on their way to stake out Ellis Emerson's house. "So much for my date, McCoy."

"Sunny will keep the sheets warm for you, Andy."

Emerson's sister had given them his address. Cate wasn't sure what kind of a reception they would get. "I think we turn at the next light."

The news van swung into a quiet cul de sac where porch lights on large farmhouse-style homes glowed in the chilly dusk. Cate spotted a car in the driveway of Emerson's house and warned Andy to park some distance away. "I think he's home. Why don't you get the camera out and roll as I go up to his door."

Andy nodded. "You can wear the wireless mike. That way we'll get sound even if he slams the door in your face." She turned off the car. "Which he probably will."

Cate slid the small transmitter into her pocket and clipped the microphone to her coat's lapel. Andy stood on the driver's side of the van with camera propped against the hood, trying to be unobtrusive.

Cate approached the house, butterflies in her stomach. You never knew what a person would do when a reporter showed up, uninvited, on his front doorstep. Cate had had the families of victims scream obscenities at her and threaten to call the police. She'd had others invite her in and give her long interviews about the deceased. The mother of a young man who'd been killed by a drunken fifteen-year-old driver had been so convincing, it had sparked new legislation at the state capitol. She had a feeling there would be no such interviews tonight.

The doorbell was an annoying electronic buzzer, out of keeping with the retro-prairie construction of the house. Cate waited, pulling cold air into her lungs. Small crescents of grainy snow still bracketed Emerson's garden, but the night had a wet marshy scent to it, as if the mid-winter thaw had stirred the plants and creatures in the nearby wetlands.

The door opened abruptly and Cate stepped back, startled.

"Yes?"

"Mr. Emerson," Cate said, moving to the right so Andy would have a clear shot of him in the lighted doorway.

"Who are you?"

"I spoke with your sister today, and she said you might be willing to . . ."

He was peering out into the darkness, and Cate prayed he wouldn't spot the camera before she could explain. "If you're trying to sell me something, miss . . ."

Cate smiled, drawing his gaze back to her face. "I'm not in sales, Mr. Emerson. I'm a reporter for Channel Three."

His eyes widened, and he peered out into his yard again. "Is that your van down the street there?"

Cate looked over her shoulder, relieved to see that Andy was only a dark outline. "Yes it is." She turned back to him. "We're aware that you talked to the police, Mr. Emerson, about Millicent Pine's disappearance." His gaze shifted back to her, eyes narrowed. "I'm sure you know that there's a lot of interest in this case. I was hoping you might tell me what you saw at the nature center that night."

He frowned, glancing over his shoulder into the recesses of his house. Stepping outside, he pulled the door halfway closed. "My wife is very upset that I'm even involved in this. She says if I had been where I was supposed to be, none of this would've happened."

Cate drew her notebook from her purse. "Would you mind if I took a few notes, Mr. Emerson?"

He ignored her, running a hand through thinning blond hair. "But that's my quiet time, the only time I can get away and think without all of . . . this." He gestured toward the house, lowering his voice. "We have a new baby in the house and a toddler. You can see why things get kind of hectic sometimes."

Cate nodded. "So you go to the nature center for a little solitude." She smiled sympathetically. "What were you doing the night you saw the women in the parking lot?"

He shot another look over her shoulder. "You're not recording this are you? My wife would be very upset if I was on television."

Cate made her pitch. "I'd like to do an interview with you, Mr. Emerson. You've got an important piece of the puzzle in this case and our viewers are very concerned about what happened to Miss Pine. Would you mind just doing a quick . . . ?"

He was shaking his head. "No TV interviews. I'll tell you what I saw, but no cameras."

"That's fine." Cate knew Andy was listening through the mike she wore and would turn off the camera. "I'll just take some notes, then."

He shoved his hands in his pockets, hunching his shoulders against the damp chill. "I'd gone over to Tamarack around nine o'clock that night, after the kids and my wife were in bed. I like to jog, and it was a perfect night for it. The moon was full, and it wasn't too cold." He shrugged. "I guess I just lost track of the time."

"When did you first see the women?" Cate was scribbling furiously to get it all down.

"I heard them before I saw them." He exhaled, and frosty air puffed out of his mouth. "One of them was laughing."

She looked up at him, pen poised over paper. "Laughing?"

He nodded. "Yeah, I thought it was weird too, because I thought I'd heard them arguing before that." He looked over her shoulder into the quiet street. "I was just coming out of the woods, kind of to the left of the center's clubhouse there, when I spotted them standing near the picnic table."

"Where is the table?"

"To the right of the parking lot on this little grassy area. I figured they must've walked over like I did."

"What did you see?"

He rubbed the back of his neck. "I was sort of far away. There's a path that leads from the building around the left side of the parking lot, so I was about a hundred feet away from them."

"But the moon was full," Cate prompted.

He looked at her. "I heard the laughing, and I kind of looked over my shoulder, and I saw them standing there. The woman who was laughing hugged the other woman, like they were good friends or something. They stood there like that for about ten seconds, maybe more."

Cate said, "That's a long hug," wondering how he kept such precise track of the time.

"I'm a boys track coach at the high school," he replied. "I have a stop-watch around my neck half the day."

"What happened next?"

He shrugged. "I turned around and just kept walking. I felt like I was . . . interrupting something, I guess."

Cate studied her notes, looking up as she heard a voice call, "Ell?" from the interior of the house.

"I've got to go," he said, shifting nervously. "My wife is looking for me."

38

"One more thing, Mr. Emerson," Cate said, scanning her brain for any loose ends. Once the cops found out she'd talked to him they'd read him the riot act. This was her first and last chance. "What made you think one of the women was Millicent Pine?"

He glanced over his shoulder, eager to go back inside. "I noticed her hair. It was black and frizzy. It kind of stuck out all over the place." He swirled his hands over his head and Cate nodded. Millicent Pine's untamed wiry curls were hard to miss. "Then I saw her picture on television, and I knew it was her."

"How about the other woman?"

He shook his head. "I didn't see much of her. She had her back to me. I just heard her laugh." He turned away from Cate to go inside. "Kind of gives me the creeps now."

7

Saint Paul, Minnesota

March 24, 8:45 P.M.

Cate was pouring the last of the Friskies into Walter's bowl when Adam knocked on her door and let himself in, Sherlock bounding in behind him. "Found something you might be interested in."

"I hope you and your pooch aren't hungry. I haven't been grocery shopping in a month." Cate bent to caress the Labrador's silky head, smiling at the dog's adoring gaze.

"Thanks anyway," Adam said dryly, his crutch swiping a plant stand as he maneuvered into her living room. "It's starting to look like a jungle in here."

"I might've gone a little crazy at the last plant sale." Cate joined him on the couch. "It's my way of coping with winter."

"Must take you an hour to water all of them," he grumbled, looking around for his dog. "Sherlock. Sit." The Labrador spun away from his surveillance of the cat's dinner and scrambled to his haunches in front of Adam. "Good boy. Now relax." The dog flopped down on his paws, burying his black nose between them.

"I have a bottle of tequila Andy's boyfriend brought me from Texas. Want a margarita?"

Adam shook his head. "I'm not staying long. I just wanted to tell you something I found out yesterday while you were snooping around that poor guy's house. Emerson, was it?"

Cate nodded. "Yeah. Too bad the 'poor guy' wouldn't do an interview." She shrugged. "We got the story on the air, anyway." Cate curled her legs underneath her and leaned toward him, catching the scent of his aftershave.

"Did you know that Millicent Pine once put a restraining order on Liz Barracosta when they were both working in Washington?"

Cate stared at him. "You're kidding. How do you know that?"

"One of my friends works at Harbor House now." Seeing Cate's frown he added, "The New York publishing house that handles all of Pine's books. He says the editors there were worried when they knew that Millicent would be dealing with Liz Barracosta again."

"So the Barracuda's reputation goes way back."

Adam nodded. "My friend says Barracosta sent Millicent Pine some pretty ugly hate mail after she did a profile on Ron Pound."

Cate said, "I've heard something about that, but I didn't live here then."

"It was back in the late eighties." He rubbed his leg, and Cate wondered if he was in pain. He wouldn't welcome any questions about it. "Apparently the senator admitted to an affair with his chief of staff's daughter. Pine's article ran on the front page of the *Washington Post,* and Pound announced two days later he wouldn't run again."

Cate thought for a moment. "Did Liz threaten her?"

"That's what my buddy says. He says Pine's editor even saw some of the letters."

"I wonder if I could double check that. It was a long time . . ." She grinned as he pulled a slip of paper from his jeans pocket. It was a phone number with a Washington, D.C., area code. "I'm going to have to put you on the payroll."

He levered himself off the couch, wincing as he dragged his crutch under one arm. "They're sure about the protective, but I knew you'd want to do your own checking." The plant stand teetered again as he moved out of the living room, Sherlock at his heels.

Cate followed, putting a hand on his arm, feeling the rigid muscles beneath his shirt. He rarely missed a workout, aware that his upper body had to compensate for his partial paralysis. "Adam, thank you. I'll let you know what happens."

He looked at her, his eyes more blue than gray. "Good night, Cate. Come on, Sherlock."

41

March 26, 7:23 A.M.

Liz Barracosta sat down in her plush leather chair and pulled her wool coat tight around her shivering body. The day had dawned bright and sunny, but she felt as cold as a northern lake. She wondered if she was coming down with something.

"Liz?"

She looked up. Jill Hamm stood in the doorway. "Yes."

"The police are here again."

Nausea bubbled up in her empty stomach, and she swallowed hard to quell the rising bile. "Give me a minute and then show them in, Jill. Thank you."

Liz shed her coat and swiped some lipstick on her mouth, tucking the makeup away as Detective Dahl was led in. "Good morning, Detective." Liz's handshake was firm.

"Good morning."

Liz asked Jill to bring two coffees and sat back down in her chair. "What can I do for you?"

He looked past her to the blue and gold day outside the window. "Kind of makes the winters all worth it, doesn't it?"

Tension tightened her jaw. "Sometimes it seems like spring will never come. But you aren't here to talk about the weather," her voice hardened, "and I'm quite busy, Detective."

The Clipper's brown eyes shifted back to her. They were as opaque as mud. "I don't think you told us everything you and Miss Pine discussed the night she disappeared, Miss Barracosta."

The door swung open, and Jill carried in two dark blue mugs emblazoned with the state seal. She lingered by the door until Liz gave her a stern look. She took a sip of coffee, searing the roof of her mouth. "What do you mean?"

"Why didn't you mention Miss Pine's plans to reveal the incident with Carolee Baldwin?" He blew on his coffee, his eyes unreadable over the rim.

Clammy fear wormed out of her upset stomach and spread over her chest. Her heart skipped, and she laced her fingers together to keep them from trembling.

He set his mug on the edge of her desk and sat forward, daylight washing over his face. "You're playing with fire, Miss Barracosta." His authori-

42

tarian tone startled her. "You were the last person seen with her. You're the person with something to gain if she never shows up." His eyes dipped to her entwined fingers. "And you lied."

"A lie of omission, then, Detective." She unclenched her jaw, meeting his gaze. "I think you can understand why I would've guarded that information very closely. I don't even know if it's true."

"You weren't trying to get her in to see the governor. You were trying to talk her out of it." He shoved his coffee cup aside and folded his arms. She noticed his hands had black hair on the tops of them.

"I knew that information could be very damaging to Governor Hamm. I thought Millicent should talk it over with Lamar Bates before we notified the governor."

He stood up, drawing a piece of paper from his breast pocket and dropping it on her desk. "That's a search warrant for your car. We're impounding it."

Liz shot out of her seat, her face flushed. "Impounding it! On what grounds?"

He seemed surprised by her reaction and stepped back, his gaze assessing. "I think Millicent Pine got in your car that night but you took her somewhere else. I'm going to find out where that was."

He pulled the door open, brushing by Jill Hamm where she crouched on the carpet. But Liz didn't see her. She was at the window, watching officers swarm over her car where it sat in its reserved parking space.

Cate glanced at her watch for the third time in as many minutes and grimaced. If Hamm didn't come out soon, she was either going to miss her deadline or be forced to write the story without his soundbites. Neither of which would work. Indigestion rumbled in her stomach, and a silent clock ticked in her head. How had Hamm managed to dodge them?

Just then the door swung open, and the governor's security detail stepped out. Reporters swarmed around them, and Edward Hamm shot them angry glares, muttering, "Vultures," under his breath.

"Governor, have you spoken to Liz Barracosta since her car was seized by the police?"

"Has Liz told you what she and Millicent Pine were talking about that night?"

"Governor, did you tell your press secretary to get rid of Millicent Pine?"

The last question stopped him, and the governor froze in the midst of ducking into the back seat of his turbo-charged BMW. The state patrol had leased it after Hamm had refused to be chauffeured around in his predecessor's Lincoln Town Car, arguing that his drivers would need the BMW's extra horsepower to elude the media. "Did I order Liz Barracosta to get rid of that reporter? Was that the question?" He flushed a dangerous purple.

The reporter who'd asked the question smirked. "Not literally, Governor. But did you tell Liz to . . ."

Hamm interrupted, "That's just the kind of stupid question I'd expect from the press." His voice dripped with contempt. "But since I have to spell it out for you people, I will. No, I did not tell my press secretary to 'get rid of' that woman. I had no plans to do an interview with her, and as far as I'm concerned that's the end of it." He looked around, staring furiously into the black lenses of the cameras. "Everybody got that?" He whirled around, throwing himself into the back of the car and slamming the door.

Cate grinned at Andy. "Just in time. Let's go . . ." Her words faded as she spotted Jill Hamm. "Jill?"

The girl stepped down into the glare of the lights, eyes wide, as microphones were thrust in her face. "I don't really know what I can say."

A reporter asked, "Were you there when the police came to impound Liz Barracosta's car?"

The girl nodded. "Yes, I was. I showed the detective into Liz's office. She had asked me for a few minutes to compose herself."

"Did she seem nervous?"

"Was she scared?"

"Did she try to leave?"

Cate noticed that the barrage of questions didn't seem to frighten the young press assistant. "She did seem . . . concerned, but, no, she didn't try to leave."

"Has Liz told you what she and Millicent Pine were talking about that night?"

Jill shook her head. "Miss Barracosta doesn't confide in me." Her smile was pained.

Cate pushed her microphone closer to the girl. "Do you know why Millicent Pine requested a meeting with Liz? Hadn't she already been denied an interview with the governor?"

The girl's blue eyes shone like sapphires in the bright television lights. "All I know is that on the day Channel 3 reported that Miss Pine was coming here to do a profile on my uncle, Liz told me, 'I've got Millicent Pine well under control.'" She smiled, dipping her head and looking up at them from under her lashes. "Those were her exact words."

Cate's story that night at ten featured the bombshell about the protection order Millicent Pine had once filed against the Barracuda in Washington, D.C. She had also included the impoundment of the Barracuda's car, the governor's angry response, and the sound bite from Jill Hamm about Liz's ability to 'control' Pine.

When she'd finished the live shot, the producer said, "Great job" in her ear, and Cate passed the compliment on to Andy, who was breaking down her equipment. The photographer smiled, lifting her camera into her van. "What's up for tomorrow?"

Cate thought for a second. "I think we ought to get Barry to work the cop angle. He's got better contacts down there than I do. I want to know what the cops have that prompted that search warrant today."

"They've probably sealed the warrant, huh?"

Cate nodded. Police officers frequently put warrants under seal when they didn't want the news media to know what they had. "But Barry should be able to get something out of them, even the notorious Detective Dahl."

Andy snorted. "Isn't he the one who—-?"

Cate laughed, remembering the infamous live shot. "The one and only. See you tomorrow."

8

THE GOVERNOR'S MANSION

March 27, 9:00 P.M.

DINNER WAS OVER, AND THE SMALL GROUP had moved into the living room,
arranging themselves on the uncomfortable couch and overstuffed chairs.
The drapes had been drawn over the large windows that looked out on
Summit Avenue, the city's version of Newport, Rhode Island's, Bellevue
Avenue. Historic mansions built by lumber barons and railroad kings lined
the street, many of them now divided into spacious apartments or purchased
by corporations because they were too expensive to heat.

The Governor's Mansion sat back off the street, protected by a black
wrought iron fence. Inside it was filled with dark woodwork and antiques
and more than one governor had chosen to use the mansion for state dinners
and entertaining, sleeping most nights at their private homes. The Hamms
divided their time between the mansion and their tree farm in northern
Minnesota.

"Anybody want another drink before I tell the staff they can call it quits
for the night?" The governor gestured around the group with his cigar, handing his beer glass to the maid. Rumor had it that the mansion staff had been
thrilled to see Eddie Hamm's predecessor move out. The Capertons had had
a nasty habit of summoning the servers with a bell.

Hamm sat back in his chair, puffing smoke rings into the air and looked
at his chief of staff. "You called the meeting, Bates. The floor's all yours."

The chief of staff looked around the small circle, his expression grim. "We have to address the Barracosta situation. Quickly. Any ideas?"

The administration's legislative liaison spoke up. "She's toast." The woman pointed to a newspaper lying on the coffee table. "From the moment the press found out she'd been served with that warrant, it was over. She has no credibility."

The governor's legal counsel agreed. "She's in some serious trouble, Governor. She's clearly a chief suspect in Millicent Pine's disappearance."

Deborah Hamm cleared her throat, and Hamm turned to his wife. "Something to say, honey?" Deborah Hamm wore baggy jeans and a mis-shapen sweater. A pair of ultra light binoculars was looped around her neck from her day of bird watching. "She's trouble, Edward. I'd cut her loose."

The governor thought about it, finally shaking his head. "No, I'm not one of those political weasels who cuts and runs when the flak starts flying." He put out his cigar, puffing a last smoke ring out of rounded lips. "Six weeks ago we were up to our asses in alligators, and you all said she was the answer. Now you're ready to throw her overboard." He caught sight of Pete Escobar standing in the doorway. "Pete, what would you do?"

The governor's advisors exchanged annoyed glances as the large ex-paratrooper shrugged, rubbing muddy hands together. "Ed, all I know is when we were under fire back in the old days, we didn't leave one of our guys behind if things went wrong. But that was war. I don't know a damn thing about politics." He pulled a handkerchief from his back pocket and cleaned his hands with it. "Do you have a minute? I want to show you some-thing out back."

The governor stood. "You heard the man, Bates. The 82nd doesn't run away from a fight. Barracosta stays. For now." He crossed the room, clearly eager to escape. "See you in the morning."

Deborah Hamm shrugged. "He never would listen to common sense," she said, her voice resonant with years of frustration. She rose. "'Bout the only way to wise him up is tighten up those purse strings." She followed her husband out of the room and the legislative liaison gave a low whistle.

"Whoa. So it's true."

Bates eyebrows arched. "What's true?"

"That their daddies set up this match made in heaven, and old Eddie and Debbie hate each others' guts."

Lamar Bates glared at the young woman and turned to the governor's lawyer. "Do you have any idea as to what Escobar is doing out there?"

The attorney frowned. "No one seems to know. Rumor has it he's building some kind of war memorial or something."

The legislative liaison gasped. "In the back yard? Does the Historical Society know?"

Bates grimaced, swallowing the last of his coffee. "Who wants to tell the governor he needs permission to build anything on the mansion grounds?" They looked at one another. "Me neither. We'll let it ride for a while."

Cate slipped into the hot bubble bath, wincing as the water flowed up over her chest and shoulders. She'd gone to the gym after work and spent a rigorous hour of weightlifting. She knew she'd be sore tomorrow, but the heavy workout had helped relieve a lot of stress. For a week, she'd worked double shifts covering the Pine disappearance.

She started as the bathroom door squeaked open and Walter sidled in, curling up on the bath mat to watch her. Her cat had been alone for much of the last month too, but he was, unfortunately, used to that. She'd rescued him as a kitten from a shelter when she was working as a reporter in Tallahassee, Florida. That had been two television jobs ago and her schedule hadn't eased much. Only the pay had gotten better.

She smoothed a bar of soap down her arm and thought about the moves she'd made since graduating with a journalism degree. Each time she'd said goodbye to friends and, in many cases, a blossoming relationship to make the next jump up the news market ladder. She'd ended up in the Twin Cities four years ago and had latched onto the political beat when the reporter who'd had it got out of the business. Now, with Eddie "Bunyan" Hamm's election, she was covering the best political story in the country, and the ambition that had driven her from market to market had cooled a bit.

Cate slid underwater, letting the scented warmth envelope her. The knots in her shoulders were loosening, and she felt pleasantly sleepy. She would read for half an hour and then get a good night's sleep. She stood up, reaching for a towel as a loud beep echoed through her apartment, followed by the voice of the nighttime assignments desk editor. "Cate? Aaron here. Snow wants you and Andy to fly out to Las Vegas tomorrow. Barry got a tip from the cops that some bimbo out there says the governor hit her back in the seventies when she was a hooker in Florida. Call me when you get home and we'll set everything up. Thanks."

March 28, 6:10 A.M.

"How many drinks have those idiots behind us had already?" Andy sat up, smoothing her dark hair and shooting an annoyed glare behind her. They were on the redeye to Las Vegas along with a planeload of rollicking low rollers, and the photographer's plan to sleep most of the way had been foiled by the rowdy group. Bloody Marys were flowing, and several of the passengers were practicing card counting on their tray tables.

Andy glanced at the papers Cate was reading and sighed. "You might as well tell me what Barry came up with."

Cate said admiringly, "Barry is the poster boy for persistence paying off." She sipped from her cup of tea. "He never gives up." She outlined for Andy how the cop reporter had spent several days working his sources in the Saint Paul Police Department, and one of them had finally come through. He'd told Barry that Millicent Pine had been about to blow the lid off a story about the governor and a young hooker he'd met in West Palm Beach. The woman had called the police but no charges had ever been filed. Cate's mission was to track down the woman and get an interview. She also planned to make a trip out to Boulder City, where Pine lived.

"How many days do you think we'll be here?"

Cate shrugged. "Enough time to soak up some desert sun and hit the casinos." She reached into her coat pocket and drew out a silver dollar. "I've got to pop this into a slot machine while we're there."

"Big spender," Andy grumbled, drawing a wad of twenties from her jeans. "I'm going to double this on the blackjack tables. Then, Sunny and I are going to take a long riding trip into the Canadian Rockies this summer."

"Won't that be fun," Cate said. "Saddle sores and sunburn. So romantic."

A flight attendant passed through the cabin, collecting glasses and warning them to fasten their seatbelts. The plane dipped through the clouds and emerged into a warm sunny day. In thirty minutes, they'd collected their baggage and equipment, picked up a rental car and were heading toward the strip.

"Let's drop off our stuff at the hotel and then see if we can find Carolee Baldwin's restaurant."

Andy steered them through the stop-and-go traffic on the main strip, finally pulling into the circular drive at the Athena Hotel and Casino. "Sounds like a plan."

Baldwin's business sat several blocks off the strip, a low adobe building with dramatic landscaping and a small tasteful sign that said "Bella Luna's." "Doesn't look like a brothel, does it," Andy said, parking at the end of a lot situated beyond the restaurant.

"I think Miss Baldwin's days on the wrong side of the tracks were over a long time ago, but I'll bet that's how she ended up out here." Cate got out of the car and inhaled the dry air. "Looks like she invested some of those ill-gotten gains pretty well, though."

They circled the restaurant, following a curving sidewalk around to the front. Cate tried the door, tugging on it when it wouldn't open. "Locked, damn it." Cupping her hands at her temples, she peered in through a large bay window. "I can't tell if there's anyone in there."

"I think I saw a car at the other end of the parking lot. Maybe one of the kitchen staff is here."

"Good idea. Let's go knock on the service door."

They retraced their steps to the back, and Cate rapped on a metal door that said "Employees Only." When nothing happened, she knocked again. The door was yanked open by a young man in a white apron. "We're closed."

"We're not here to eat," Cate said, noting the large knife he held in his hand. "We're looking for Ms. Baldwin. The owner."

The man's eyes traveled between them, his expression decidedly unhelpful. "She's not here."

Cate ground her teeth. "Do you know where we can find her? It's kind of urgent."

"She's in Brazil." He stepped back, trying to close the door but Andy put her foot in the opening.

"Just hold on," Cate said. "Are you sure Ms. Baldwin is out of town?"

He nodded. "Her daughter lives there. She goes every year." He pulled on the door, managing to dislodge Andy's foot. "Come back when we're open," he said, slamming it shut.

Cate kicked the door. "What a jerk!"

They crossed the parking lot, getting into the rental car. "Now what?"

Cate unfolded the map the rental agency had given them and pointed to a dot on it. "Boulder City. Maybe we can cut our losses and dig up something at her house."

Liz Barracosta stared at her telephone, cursing its silence, yet relieved that it hadn't rung. She knew Lamar Bates had lost his bid to oust her last night but there were other ways to skin a cat. This morning she'd walked in on a staff meeting. The participants had had the grace to look embarrassed, and the meeting had broken up, but she knew they'd simply rescheduled it for later.

Bates was freezing her out, and word had spread quickly through the capitol. Calls weren't being returned, and even Jill Hamm was averting her eyes when they met in the corridor. She'd like to smack the girl. She'd made her sound like some kind of power-hungry maniac to those reporters last night.

Liz pushed away from her desk and went to the window, her gaze caught by the news crew that had set up on the sidewalk. The noon newscast's top story was, undoubtedly, her implication in Millicent Pine's disappearance and the impoundment of her car. A few more days of this and her reputation would be dog meat. Unsalvageable. Like those ships that lay at the bottom of the ocean so deep even divers in tiny submarines couldn't retrieve their treasures. Maybe she'd quit her job, and take off for a desert island. Take up scuba diving herself.

The jangle of the phone startled her, and Liz spun to stare at it. Had the governor had second thoughts about keeping her on? Was he even now summoning her to his office to fire her? She moved to her desk and snatched it up, barking a firm, "Barracosta here," into the receiver.

"Liz? Chandler Coates."

Relief rushed through her, and she leaned against the desk. "Yes, Chandler. Have you talked to the police yet?"

Her attorney paused, and Liz pictured him running an uncomfortable hand through his hair. She'd retained him yesterday after the visit from Detective Dahl. "We have to meet, Liz. As soon as possible."

She swallowed hard. "How about lunch? I can meet you somewhere in about forty minutes."

"Yes, let's do that. Good."

They agreed on the restaurant and time, and Liz started to hang up the phone but paused. "Chandler, I need my car back. This rental car is going to get expensive."

"Then you'd better think of a good explanation." The lawyer's tone was clipped.

Liz frowned, her fingers clenched around the phone. "For what?"

"For what they found in the trunk of your car."

51

9

LAS VEGAS, NEVADA

2:18 P.M.

CATE SQUINTED IN THE LATE AFTERNOON SUN, pointing toward the sign. It hung on the painted fence that encircled Millicent Pine's backyard. "Beware of killer felines, huh?" She grinned. "Cute. I didn't have Pine down for a cat lover."

Andy slid her camera onto the tripod and peered through the viewfinder, focusing on the exterior of the house. "Never can tell, McCoy." She zoomed in and then pulled out gradually. "Who'd suspect you harbor one of the nastiest, man-eating cats this side of the Mississippi in your apartment?" She shifted the tripod and camera, shooting the house from another angle.

She hoisted the camera onto her shoulder and looked at Cate. "Okay, I think we have enough exteriors. What next?"

Cate eyed the front door. "We knock and then we prowl." She glanced back at the driveway. "I'm assuming that car is Pine's, and she got a ride to the airport."

They approached the double doors, and Cate lifted the brass knocker. The door was suddenly flung open.

The tall woman in the doorway spat out, "Who the hell are you?"

Cate hoped Andy was rolling. "Cate McCoy. I'm a report—"

She pointed at Andy. "If you don't turn that thing off, I'm calling the police. You're on private property."

Cate glanced over her shoulder at Andy and nodded. Turning back to the woman, she said, "We're a news crew out of the Twin Cities, and we're investigating Millicent Pine's disappearance."

The woman sneered, tossing long dark hair over her shoulder. Her dark eyes were dismissive. "Don't waste my time." She tried to close the door but Cate stopped her.

"Are you Ms. Pine's roommate?"

The woman leaned into Cate's face, and she caught the scent of sandalwood. Her eyes were bloodshot.

"It's none of your business who I am. The only thing you need to know is that I have permission to be here and you don't. So get out." She stepped back and slammed the door.

Cate and Andy trudged back to the car, stowing the gear into the trunk and driving quickly away. When they were headed back to Las Vegas, Cate said dispiritedly, "Two strikes. Carolee Baldwin is in Brazil, and we've been chased off of Pine's property by some banshee woman." She shook her head. "Snow isn't going to be happy."

Andy pushed a pair of wraparounds onto her nose and looked at Cate. "Screw her. This was a fishing expedition, and she knew it. So we came up dry. It happens."

Cate looked out the window, noting clusters of new homes springing out of the desert landscape. "A lot of new construction out here." She thought for a moment. "Wonder why Millicent Pine chose to live here."

"Good climate, lots of sunshine. Beats the Siberian tundra we live in half the year."

Cate smiled, resuming her gaze out the window. Finally, she said, "We need a night on the town, Andy. A little drinking, a little gambling, and a good dinner. How about it?"

"Lead on, McCoy. I can feel our luck turning already."

Liz Barracosta tilted her head back and drew hot moist air into her lungs. She'd been in the sauna for fifteen minutes, back pressed to the warm wood, a soft towel wrapped around her waist. The panic had begun to recede. They weren't going to arrest her today. If the police had been coming for her, they would've caught her in her office.

Her closed eyelids flickered as she envisioned the scene. Handcuffed wrists in front of her, Detective Dahl leading her through the warren of

53

offices in the governor's suite. Shocked faces would appear over dividers and around office doors to witness her procession. Jill Hamm's triumph quickly masked as concern. Lamar Bates' relief that she could no longer taint the governor with her presence.

Liz opened her eyes and ran her fingers through her silver hair. It felt dry and lifeless. The pressure was also showing on her face. Just this morning, she'd glimpsed a new crease between her eyebrows, a wrinkle even the thickest concealer would soon be unable to hide. She ran a hand down her throat, feeling the tautness that she'd labored many miles in the pool to maintain. They didn't have pools in prison.

She stretched out on the upper bench, resting her head on a folded towel. The sauna rocks hissed, and Liz closed her eyes again, letting her mind drift, but the same pounding questions rushed in to fill the vacuum. How had it gotten there? Someone must have put it there. Someone with access to her car. But who?

Images of her meeting with Chandler Coates the day before filled her mind. He'd been solicitous when she'd arrived at the restaurant, a small place on Cathedral Hill where they weren't likely to be seen. He'd poured her some wine and asked how she was holding up, but Liz saw the questions in his eyes, the same questions the detectives must be asking themselves as they worked the case.

How *could* she explain it? How had Millicent Pine's reporter's pad ended up in the trunk of her car? With a smear of blood on it? Liz remembered Pine making notes in the small notebook the night they'd met at the Saint Paul Grill, but Pine had taken it with her when she'd left.

Chandler had leaned across the table, his dark suit somber in the midst of the restaurant's fresh flowers and yellow walls. "Did she give you the notebook, Liz? Perhaps you wrote the address of Bates' house on it for her."

Liz had thought hard, sifting through her memory of the night, aware that it was hazy from the amount of alcohol she'd consumed. No. She'd ended the phone call with Lamar Bates and told Millicent the name of the town he lived in, but not the exact address. That's when she'd suggested that she drive them both to his house.

Coates had sat back in his chair, his gray eyes serious. "What did you do that night after Millicent Pine didn't return to the restaurant?"

"I tried to call her room on my cell phone, and then I left. I thought she might've gotten a call from her editor."

Coates picked up a spoon, eyeing his reflection in the shiny hollow. "At ten o'clock at night, Liz?"

Liz had looked away from him. "I don't know, Chandler. I'd had a lot to drink. I told you that! I wasn't thinking clearly." She twisted the stem of her wine glass. "I was happy to get a reprieve from her. I thought it would give us another day to come up with some kind of response to the Baldwin thing."

He nodded, pausing while the waiter delivered their food. "I can understand that. But it looks bad." He picked up his fork and speared a cherry tomato. "What did you do after that?"

She watched him eat, nausea roiling her stomach. "I drove home."

"Did anyone see you?"

She pictured the darkened street, the dim streetlights. "No, probably not. Most of my neighbors are young professionals or people with families. They go to bed pretty early."

He took a sip of wine, mulling it over, as he dabbed his mouth with a starched napkin. "Did you walk to your mailbox for the mail? Pick up your newspaper on the front lawn? Do anything that someone looking out their window might've seen that night and noted the time?"

Liz shook her head slowly. "I don't think so, Chandler. But I was there, just the same."

He looked at her. "We'd better start figuring out how to prove it."

Cate crossed her fingers and yanked hard on the slot machine handle, watching in dismay as cherries, followed by a joker and then a palm tree popped up in the horizontal window. That was her last quarter of the twenty bucks she'd begun playing with just an hour ago, and she had nothing to show for it. Andy, on the other hand, was riding high.

Cate wended her way through the slots, past the video poker and out into the center of the casino, where the blackjack tables stood. Catching sight of her photographer among a small circle of players at one of the tables, she headed that way, stopping to accept a glass of champagne from a waitress. As she sipped the wine, Cate's gaze traveled around the room, skipping over brightly clad tourists and young couples, senior citizens with plastic cups of quarters in their hands, and an elegantly gowned woman who stood behind a tuxedoed man, his arm outstretched to place a bet at the craps table.

She spotted Andy again, noting the pile of chips in front of her. She probably had enough for two vacations by now. Cate caught her eye and toasted her with her champagne glass, her gaze snagged by a flash of white behind Andy. Wasn't that the woman . . . ? Cate moved a little closer, straining to see her amid the crowds of people. Yes.

Setting the champagne down on the edge of a table, she walked quickly toward the blackjack tables, nearly certain that the woman had not yet caught sight of her. Her dark hair had been caught up in a twist at the back of her head, and she'd exchanged her denim for a dark blue business suit and a crisp white blouse, but Cate had recognized her immediately.

Slipping up next to Andy, Cate waited while the dealer dealt the cards and then whispered, "Don't look now, but the banshee has tracked us down here."

Andy frowned, her eyes still on her cards. "What are you talking about, McCoy?" She plucked a chip from her stack and handed it to Cate. "Here's a twenty to keep you busy for another hour."

"Andy," Cate said more urgently. "The woman who was at Millicent Pine's house today is here. She's standing right behind you."

Andy said, "Hit me," to the dealer and glanced quickly over her shoulder. "I don't see anyone back there."

Cate twisted around, searching the milling crowd. The woman had disappeared. "She was there." Pocketing the chip Andy had given her, Cate muttered, "Fine. I'll get lost, but she *was* there. Let me know when you've broken the bank."

Cate wandered away from the tables toward a small lounge that looked dark and quiet. A sign outside the door advertised a jazz trio. The woman stood just inside talking to an older man with a deep suntan and a mint green sports coat. Cate approached them, meeting her surprised gaze. "Hi."

The woman murmured something to the man, and he left, shooting a hard glance at Cate as he passed. "What are you doing here?" She took a long pull on a cigarette and dropped it in the glass she was holding, the hot ash making a sizzling sound.

"Haven't we already been over that? Or is this your private property too?" Cate saw the heavy ring of keys that encircled her left wrist.

"Why have you followed me here?"

Cate gestured behind her. "We're staying here."

The woman hesitated, her eyes sweeping over Cate. She swirled the cigarette butt in the glass. "I see. My apologies." She put the glass down and stepped out of the dusky lounge light. "That's no way for me to treat a guest of the hotel."

"You work here?"

She nodded. "I'm the floor manager. I thought after—Millicent's . . ."

Cate looked past the woman into the lounge. "Do you think we could talk for a minute?"

The woman studied her. "Why?"

Cate said, "I can tell you things about the investigation you probably don't know."

She guided Cate to a small table with a flickering candle in the center. She drew a cigarette from her pocket and held it to the flame. The jazz trio announced they were taking a short break. "You're a journalist."

"Yes." Cate quelled the urge to wave smoke out of her face. Why did nicotine and gambling seem to go together? "I work for a television station in the Twin Cities."

"It's cold there, isn't it?" The woman stared at the glowing tip of the cigarette, the candlelight washing red and brown into her hair. "What's your name?"

"Cate McCoy."

"Della DeFrancisco. Millicent and I—" She broke off, stress showing in her drawn brows and tight mouth. "I was worried when she didn't call."

Cate leaned forward. "Did Millicent ever talk about a Liz Barracosta to you?" She noted the other woman's frown. "A woman she knew when she was covering politics in Washington."

Della shook her head. "No, the name doesn't sound familiar. Why?"

"That's who Millicent was seen with shortly before she disappeared. Didn't the police tell you any of this?"

"All the police would say was that she was missing." She looked past Cate's shoulder to the busy casino. The lounge was an oasis of quiet.

Cate pushed the ashtray and smoldering cigarette away. "Did Millicent tell you about what she planned to do while she was in Minnesota? About anyone she'd arranged to meet with?"

The woman hesitated and adrenaline surged through Cate. She knew something. "Just that she planned to push hard for an interview with the governor." She swept a nervous hand over her hair and looked out into the casino again. "I have to get back to work, Miss McCoy." She rose. "I'm sorry I couldn't help you."

Disappointed, Cate dug into her purse for a card and pressed it into the woman's hand. "We're leaving tomorrow. If you think of anything, call me at that number." Cate shook her hand. "Thank you for talking to me."

Della nodded distantly. "Enjoy your stay at the hotel."

Two hours later, Cate was about to slip into her pajamas when someone knocked on the door. Cate threw Andy a surprised look. "That must be room service already."

Andy yawned from the center of the bed, money scattered around her. She'd finally left the tables at quarter past midnight, hungry and tired and considerably richer. She pulled a fifty out of the pile and tossed it at Cate. "Here. Give him this."

"Miss Gottrocks," Cate muttered, crossing the spacious room and pulling the door open. But instead of a waiter, Della DeFrancisco stood on the threshold. "I hoped you might still be up."

Cate stepped back. "Come in. Andy, this is Della DeFrancisco. You may remember her from earlier today."

Andy swept her money into a pile and thrust a hand at the woman. "Nice to meet you. Cate tells me you run the casino."

Della smiled. "I see we've been very good to you tonight."

Andy winked. "I just know when to call it a night." She whisked a pair of jeans and a couple of shirts from a chair and said, "Please sit down."

Cate said, "Did you think of something else you wanted to tell us?"

The woman laid an oversized envelope in her lap and placed a protective hand on it. She looked at Cate. "I don't know what Millicent would want me to do."

Cate and Andy sat down in chairs opposite her. "About what," Cate asked softly.

Della took a deep breath and froze when there was a sharp knock at the door. Andy said, "That will be room service. I'll take care of it."

Cate noticed the woman's hand trembling where it lay over the envelope. "What did you want to tell me, Miss DeFrancisco?"

She spoke haltingly. "I drove Millicent to the airport the day she flew to Minnesota. Before she left, she gave me this." She uncovered the envelope and looked at it in her lap. "She warned me to guard it." Her shoulders rose as she took a steadying breath. "She even joked that I should treat it as if 'it was my deepest darkest secret.' So I put it in the casino vault."

"Do you know what's in there?"

Andy carried the room service tray in, placing it on the bureau and joining them again. "Sorry for the interruption."

"I haven't opened it. She asked me not to." Her fingers shook as she smoothed a lock of hair into the twist at the nape of her neck. "It may be connected to the story she's working on."

Cate's eyes widened. "About Governor Hamm?"

Della nodded, looking between them. "I don't think she wanted to travel with it, and she was concerned about leaving it at her house for several weeks."

The woman's fingers curled over the envelope, and Cate warned herself to calm down. She wanted to snatch it and tear it open, but when Della handed it to her, she took it slowly, glancing over her shoulder to ensure that the hotel room door was closed and locked. Sliding a fingernail under the sealed edge, she pulled the flap open.

Peering inside, she drew the contents out and laid them on the table. The three women stared. Cate looked up at Della. "Does this make any sense to you?"

10

STILLWATER, MINNESOTA

April 7, 1:51 P.M.

LIZ BARRACOSTA COVERED HER EYES AS THE GOVERNOR tore off his windbreaker and began stripping to the waist.

"Can't bear to see Eddie Hamm half naked?"

Peering over her fingers, Liz mustered a weak smile for the newspaper reporter who stood next to her. "Hi, Glenda." Three days ago her paper had run a series of letters to the editor demanding that Liz be arrested.

Glenda Diamond gestured with a half-chewed pencil toward the spectacle unfolding before them. "If I wasn't seeing this I wouldn't believe it."

The governor and a second man stood in a clearing, a huge crowd encircling them. Short thick logs lay at their feet, and the sharpened axes they held glinted in the unseasonably warm sun. The blue river sparkled behind them. The summerlike weather was the talk of all of the meteorologists.

Glenda's photographer, a short stocky woman with a crew cut, joined them. She sniffed the air. "Smell that?" Liz frowned and the photographer grinned.

"Testosterone." She peered through the lens of one of the cameras hanging around her neck and clicked off several shots.

Liz muffled a groan and watched the governor. She knew his bared chest and bulging belly were sure to make the front pages of newspapers across the country. He'd been scheduled to make a brief speech and then work the crowd at the annual Lumberjack Days festival. But when a young man had shouted out a sneering challenge, Hamm had spun around, spotted the kid in the crowd and picked up the gauntlet.

The newspaper photographer crouched to get a low angle shot as Hamm rolled his arms and twisted right and left to limber up for the contest, smiling widely for the media. His competitor, a burly guy half his age, wore a thin t-shirt that emphasized his powerful biceps.

A short man clad in jeans and a flannel shirt entered the makeshift ring. Shouting into a tinny microphone, he said, "Ladies and gentlemen. Welcome to a history-making event here on the shores of the scenic Saint Croix River." The crowd cheered. "Lumberjack Days may never be the same." The audience chuckled.

The emcee sketched a bow in Hamm's direction. "On that side, the governor of the great state of Minnesota and a lumberjack legend in his day. Edward "Bunyan" Hamm." The crowd cheered, chanting, "Bunyan. Bunyan." Hamm waved as Liz cringed.

"You couldn't talk him out of it, huh?" The reporter was scribbling furiously.

Liz looked at her. "I'm not exactly wielding a lot of influence these days, Glenda. No thanks to your newspaper."

The reporter blushed, looking away as the emcee continued. "On the other side, one of the best lumberjacks this side of the Mississippi, Jac Champenau." Cheers and catcalls filled the air as the younger man hefted his six-pound axe over his head, his body hard and muscled.

"He's never going to live this down," Liz murmured, standing her ground as the excited crowd jostled for a better view. She saw Glenda jot it down.

"Now, folks, here's how this is going to work." The emcee pointed at the two-foot wooden blocks. "We call this the underhand chop. Both men will step up on their blocks and when I say go, they'll begin chopping." He looked into the excited faces of the audience. "The lumberjack must chop halfway through one side of the block, turn around and chop through the back side. The key, my friends, is accuracy and speed."

"And a few missing marbles," Liz said, glancing around to see if there were any ambulance crews in the vicinity. One false move and Hamm might serve out the rest of his term with a missing limb.

"All right. Are we ready?"

The crowd burst into applause as the governor and his challenger stepped up onto their blocks, positioning their feet on the opposite ends. Hefting their axes, they paused. The emcee looked at each man, assessing his readiness. Satisfied that all was in order, he raised one hand. Liz held her breath. The emcee said, "Go!"

Shouts of encouragement filled the air as the two men brought their axes down in sweeping arcs, burying them in the span of wood between their spread legs. Liz watched as the governor chopped again and again, his bare chest covered in sweat, his face a deep plum color. Champenau was breathing hard too, as the audience pressed forward for a better view.

A large hand fell on her shoulder and Liz spun, expecting to see the dour expression of Lamar Bates. She knew the chief of staff would be furious about this. Instead, it was the Clipper, his normally pale face flushed in the heat.

"Miss Barracosta?"

The azure sky wheeled above her, and Liz felt suddenly off balance. She needed to sit down. "What are you doing here, Detective?"

"We need a formal statement from you at headquarters. Can you please come with me?"

People near them turned, and their curious stares scorched her skin.

"Am I under arrest?" A loud cheer went up in the crowd, and Liz thought for one disorienting moment that it was approval for the police presence.

"No, Miss Barracosta, you're not," the detective said, his muddy eyes on her face. The unspoken "yet" hung between them. "But we need to take you in for questioning. You may call your lawyer when we get there." He nodded to two officers standing at the edge of the crowd, and they moved in, circling her as she was led to the waiting patrol car.

Cate opened her eyes with a jolt, unsure what had awakened her. She was stretched out on her couch, the spy novel she'd been reading folded in her lap. Walter snoozed next to her. She sat up as the phone rang. Must be the station, she thought, reaching for it. An unanswered phone only prompted more calls until the employee finally gave in and picked it up. "Cate McCoy here."

"Cate? Nathan on the assignments desk."

Cate sighed. "Yeah, Nathan."

"They just took Liz Barracosta in for questioning in the Pine case."

Cate sat up. "Holy shit!" Springing up, she looked around for her briefcase. "Hold on." She pulled a reporters pad out and flipped it open. "Okay. Please tell me we had a camera there."

"We got it all."

Cate's heart slowed a little, and she took a deep breath. This was the first time in over a week there was news in the Pine case. "Thank God. Now where did it happen?"

"In Stillwater at Lumberjack Days. The governor was chopping wood and the . . ."

"Hold on. Did you say 'chopping wood'?"

The assignments editor chuckled. "The photographer says Governor Hamm was chopping wood in some contest, and the Barracuda was watching, and the cops came up and told her she had to go downtown with them."

Cate muttered, "Unreal. Do we have a photog at the police department?"

"Bases covered, but you might want to get down there pretty quick."

"I'm on my way."

The chief of police was a tall, powerfully built African-American who had political ambitions beyond running a medium-sized police department. Which is why, Cate knew, he was in on a Saturday. John Yancy wanted to be mayor, and he was surveying the assembled press with the stern demeanor of a man who would watch his performance on his VCR later in the privacy of his own home.

Cate said, "Chief Yancy, is Liz Barracosta under arrest?"

The chief adjusted his tie, looking into the television cameras. "She is not under arrest at this time."

Cate followed up, raising her voice to be heard above the shouts of other reporters. "Is she your primary suspect?"

Yancy paused. "We have asked Miss Barracosta to give us a formal statement. That's all I can tell you."

A newspaper reporter bellowed, "Do you think Liz Barracosta can tell you where Millicent Pine is?"

The chief looked at the man, his eyes hard. "We hope someone can, Mr. Snyder."

Snyder followed up. "Do you think Millicent Pine is still alive, chief?"

"We hope to know more about that by the end of the day. Thank you." He pushed past them and went into police headquarters as reporters scrambled to file their stories.

Three hours later, Cate stood in front of the Governor's mansion waiting as her package rolled on the six o'clock weekend news. Her story began with the videotape of Governor Hamm, wood chips flying as he whipped his competition. It continued with the Barracuda's shocked face as she was led away by the Clipper and his pals. The piece ended with a terse statement from the governor. "I have complete faith in the police department and the district attorney," he'd said, his face still flushed from the exercise, tiny splinters stuck in his hair and beard. "I'm confident they'll get to the truth of the matter."

Cate came back on camera. "If that sounds like less than full support for his press secretary, Jay, sources close to the administration tell us that's just how Governor Hamm wanted it to sound."

She looked into the camera lens, her gaze steady. "It is no secret that Chief of Staff Lamar Bates has advised the governor to distance himself from this case. Back to you."

Cate unhooked her earpiece and patted the photographer on the shoulder. "Good job on that crash-and-burn edit, Al. Things were tight there for a while."

The photographer grinned. "Never a dull moment with you, McCoy. Now I know why Andy was complaining about finding gray hair."

Cate chuckled as her cell phone rang. Digging it out of her briefcase, she flipped it open. "Cate McCoy."

"Cate? Adam here."

"Hi! How about if I bring some Chinese home and we have dinner at my place?"

"You may want to hold off on the food when I tell you what I've come up with." Something rustled in the background, and Cate's heart skipped. He'd translated the papers in the envelope Della DeFrancisco had given her. "But I don't want to do that over a cellular line."

Cate headed for her car, sliding behind the wheel. "I'll be there in fifteen minutes."

When he opened his door, the aroma of hot dough and melting cheese curled out into the hallway.

"You ordered pizza," Cate exclaimed, slipping past him into his apartment and greeting his dog. "You're too good to me."

Sherlock's tail thumped the carpet as he caught sight of her, excited growls escaping his throat. Cate knelt to press a kiss on his black nose, catching Adam's expression as she straightened. "What? You never kiss Sherlock?" Cate stroked the Labrador's silky head. "No wonder he comes to me for a little tender loving care."

Adam was leaning heavily on his cane as he maneuvered around the kitchen. His face was pale against the navy shirt he wore, and Cate hesitated. "Leg hurting tonight," she finally asked, her tone casual.

Their eyes met, his impenetrable. "Pepperoni or Canadian bacon?"

Cate reached for the pizza box, cheeks burning from the rebuff. She carried it into the living room, returning for plates and napkins. When they were settled on the couch, plates of pizza on their laps, she said quietly, "You're my best friend, Adam. You and Andy."

He bit into a slice of pizza, thick lashes shielding his reaction. Cate watched him out of the corner of her eye, pretending to taste her food. He still hadn't gotten to the barber, and a dark sweep of hair brushed his left temple. "I'll just say this, then. You can trust me. The way I trust you."

They finished their food in silence, flipping pepperoni to his dog. After they'd cleared the debris, he carried a sheaf of papers to the coffee table, turning on a second lamp. "I don't know what you're going to make of this, Cate, but here's what I've found."

Cate leaned forward, glad their attention was back on work. "First tell me what's on the tape."

He picked up the micro-cassette, turning it over in his hand. "It appears to be an interview of some kind with a young girl." He gave her the tape. "My Spanish is pretty good, but there were colloquialisms that I couldn't translate. I tried every Spanish dictionary we had at the store."

Cate looked at the small square of plastic. "Is the interviewer Millicent Pine?"

Adam nodded. "It sounds like her. She's also speaking Spanish, and there's a third woman in the room, but you can't hear her because she's off-mike."

"What does the girl say?"

Adam took a paper from the table and handed it to her. "That's a rough translation, but you'll notice that there are parts missing. I think the tape was turned off several times."

Cate scanned the written conversation, frowning as she read. "So the girl is saying that she was in a car somewhere, and she was taken out into the desert?"

Adam nodded grimly. "That's the first place the tape stops, probably because the girl was upset. Read on."

Cate's eyes flew across the paper, the words making her hands tremble. "The driver attacked her, raping her and beating her." She looked at him. "How old do you think she is?"

He thought for a moment. "No more than fifteen. Probably younger."

Cate went back to the translated dialogue. The girl had described sleeping on the ground, probably knocked unconscious, Cate thought, and awakening to find the man gone. "I'll bet the bastard left her for dead, poor thing." Cate shuddered. "But she was able to find help?"

"She tells Pine that she saw *el arbol de Navidad.* A Christmas tree, probably in somebody's window. Sounds like she wandered out of the desert onto someone's doorstep."

"So Millicent did this interview around Christmas, then?"

Adam nodded. "We don't know how long it was after the rape and beating that Pine interviewed her, but she sounds weak on the tape. I would guess that it was within the week." He glanced at his watch. "Today's April seventh so that could make it almost exactly four months ago."

Cate read down to the bottom of the page. "She says she doesn't know who the man was. How do you think Millicent found out about it?"

Adam shrugged. "Who knows? Maybe a tip, maybe she was approached by someone when she was in Mexico recently. Nevada isn't all that far from the border."

Cate's gaze was snagged by a paragraph at the bottom of the page. "What's that?"

Adam leaned over her, and Cate caught the scent of something sharp and clean. "Oh. Yeah, I thought that was weird too." He scraped his fingers through his hair. "The tape had been turned off and then was turned back on, almost as if the girl said something that Millicent wanted to catch."

Cate read aloud from the paper, "'Gerte is dead. She saw them.'"

Adam scratched Sherlock's ears, cradling the dog's large head in his lap. "Then the girl is sobbing so hard I can't make out what she says next."

"How about the other paper?" Cate picked up a page with dense Spanish writing on it that had also been folded into the envelope.

"Well, this is where it gets even weirder." Adam gestured to the paper she held. "That's part of an autopsy report."

Cate stared at him. "Do you think the girl died? The one Millicent was interviewing?"

66

Adam shook his head. "I don't think it's the same girl." He took the paper, scanning it, puzzlement evident on his face. "This appears to be a girl of seventeen or eighteen years of age. The coroner doesn't know. But she died of several knife wounds to her throat and stomach."

"Oh, Adam!" Cate looked at the paper in his hand, pushing her hair behind her ears. "Why was that in the envelope with the tape if they're not the same girl?" She paused, thinking. "I wonder what Millicent was planning to do with this?"

"Here's one more question as long as we're asking. Why did the dead girl have gold paint on her fingers?"

11

GOVERNOR'S MANSION

April 9, 7:38 P.M.

LAMAR BATES WATCHED HIS BOSS KNEAD his shoulder, permitting himself a secret smile over the governor's pain. He flushed when he saw Peter Escobar studying him. Had Escobar taken up permanent residence at the mansion? What would the press make of that when it got out?

"Governor," he said, "I don't think we can hold the national media off much longer on this Barracosta thing." He gestured toward the windows. "They've all got crews camped out there beyond the gates, and we're under a lot of pressure to say something."

"Nosey bastards," Hamm muttered, fingers probing his right biceps. He'd refused to see a doctor for what appeared to be strained muscles after Saturday's competition and had spent Sunday in seclusion, tending to his aches and pains.

"Ed, why don't we kill two birds with one stone?" Escobar's voice was rusty, as if he didn't use it often enough, and Bates puzzled over what Hamm saw in the man. He seemed to be nothing more than a burned-out veteran who'd found a juicy meal ticket. Escobar, Bates was tempted to point out, had advised the governor to keep Barracosta on his staff, even as the police were moving in.

"What did you have in mind, Pete?" Hamm reached for his bottle of Pig's Eye beer and took a long swallow.

The ex-paratrooper rose and strode to the windows, pulling back the curtain to peer out on the media horde just beyond the wrought-iron gate. "Give them what they want but get something in return."

Bates rolled his eyes, anger flooding through him when he saw the governor's interested expression. Now the idiot was plotting press strategy. "What are you talking about, Mr. Escobar?" His voice was carefully modulated.

The former soldier ignored Bates. "We need money for our memorial, right?"

Hamm nodded, one hand curled around the neck of the beer bottle. "I like where this is goin', Pete."

"Let's invite the vultures back there and show them what we've got so far. We'll tell everyone we need some cash to keep it going, and then you can answer their questions afterwards." Escobar's dark eyes gleamed.

Lamar Bates shook his head. "Governor, I'm not sure that's such a good idea."

Hamm's eyebrows rose. "Why not? You treat those monkeys out there too well, Bates." He polished off his beer and reached for another, snatching his hand back as Deborah Hamm walked in the room. Her hair was windblown, and she had a flush of sunburn across the bridge of her nose.

"I saw that, Eddie," she said, eyeing the silver bucket filled with crushed ice and bottles of Pig's Eye. "You obviously didn't get a good enough look at yourself on TV the other day."

The governor flushed, sinking into the cushions of the couch as his wife glared at him. "Pete and I have a long run planned tonight, honey, as soon as we can sneak by the press out there."

"Beer is only going to slow you down, then." She bent to pick up the bucket, cradling it in her arms. "Remember that we've got Congressman Albertson and his wife coming to dinner tonight. Seven sharp."

"Yes, dear." The governor watched his wife's retreating form and drew a bottle from underneath the cushions. Twisting the top off, he grinned at the other two men as he took a long swallow. Smacking his lips, he said, "Call a press conference for nine tomorrow morning, Bates. Pete will show you what to do."

Liz Barracosta saw the truth in her attorney's eyes as she opened the door of her house and pulled him inside, the questions and catcalls of the press following him like a swarm of killer bees. Leading him into the kitchen, she slid into a chair at one end of a large oak table, running a hand through her limp hair. Her eyes were red-rimmed, and her twelve-hour interrogation had left its mark. "Thanks for coming, Chandler."

Coates nodded, his manner cool. "We could call the cops, Liz. Get that rabble outside moved out of here."

She waved a hand distractedly. "They'll go away eventually. What's the latest?"

He drew a file from his briefcase, and Liz spotted her name written on the tab. E. Barracosta. She would soon be a defendant in a kidnapping case, and the state would bring all of its resources, all of its force against her to see that she went to prison.

"Liz?" Coates was staring at her.

"Go ahead. I'm listening." She forced her eyes away from his file, focusing instead on the yellow legal pad he'd placed on the table between them.

"Let's go over what we know they have, Liz, and then we can discuss what we think they're not telling us." He made a note on the paper. "You were the last person seen with Millicent Pine March twenty-seventh. You say you arranged to drive out to Lamar Bates' house to discuss some information Ms. Pine had about the governor, but you never saw her after she went to her hotel room." He glanced up at her, and she nodded.

"That's right. I found out that she'd disappeared on the news the next afternoon."

Coates loosened his tie. "Here's what the police think." His hazel eyes held hers. "You two met, had several drinks, and she told you what she had on Governor Hamm. She warned you that she was preparing a story about it, and she wanted to interview the governor for his reaction."

"So far so good." Liz watched as he jotted another note.

"Here's where the accounts diverge. The police say you lured Ms. Pine into your car, telling her that you'd drive her to Mr. Bates' house to discuss the interview. Once she was in the car, you thought better of that and decided to take her out to a secluded park, where you would try to frighten her into burying the story."

Liz snorted. "Has anyone noticed that Millicent Pine is about four inches taller and probably fifty pounds heavier than I am. How could I force her to go anywhere with me if she didn't want to?"

The attorney's jaw tightened. "They believe you used a weapon, Liz."

She stared at him, blood rising under her skin, her eyes narrowed angrily. The sound of a large truck rumbled outside, and Liz knew it was the arrival of another satellite truck. That made five. She whispered, "Those bastards found the gun registration in Texas, didn't they?"

Coates nodded, a pulse jumping at the corner of his mouth.

So, that's why he'd been so distant. "Chandler, I can explain that."

He jotted something on his legal pad and looked at her. "I hope it's as convincing to me as it will be to a jury."

She swallowed, fingernails picking at the frayed end of a place mat. "I bought a gun seven years ago while I was working on a congressional campaign in Texas. It was registered and legal and everything was in order."

"Why did you think you needed a gun?"

Liz looked down at her hands, the knuckles reddened and lined in the muted daylight leaking in around blinds pulled tight to keep the prying eyes of the press out. "I was . . . attacked one night by a guy who worked for the campaign." She looked at the yellow pad, unwilling to meet his eyes. "He locked the front door from the inside and caught me back near the copier. I was making copies of a press release that was going out the next day."

Coates said quietly, "Did he rape you?"

She shook her head. "He forced me to my knees and tried to make me . . . do things to him, but I fought him off. He punched me in the face a couple of times and probably would've done some serious damage if the cleaning crew hadn't pounded on the door. They heard me screaming." Her gaze rose to meet his. "I bought a gun the next day and learned how to use it."

"What did you do with it when you left Texas?"

She plunged her fingers into her hair and cradled her forehead, eyes closed. "I brought it with me."

Coates groaned. "You had to know it was illegal to have an unregistered firearm in Minnesota, Liz. What were you thinking?"

"I was thinking good riddance, Chandler. I'd been here about eight months when my apartment was broken into. They stole the gun, and I couldn't report it because I'd never registered it. I was glad it was gone."

He looked at her, his eyes bleak. "You know what this means." His voice was flat, cold.

She nodded. "There's a paper trail that says I owned a gun and no paper trail that says I ever got rid of it." She rubbed her eyes, staring at the beige walls that surrounded them. "In other words, I'm screwed."

April 10, 8:55 A.M.

"We're screwed," Cate said with disgust, watching as the live truck operator lowered the microwave mast, signaling that they weren't going to be able to carry the governor's news conference live. She'd spent two hours biting her nails as the tech tried to troubleshoot it while the other stations were running their cable and setting up their shots for the nine o'clock event. They couldn't even use their satellite truck as a backup because it was in the shop for repairs. "Damn it all!"

Andy shrugged. "The beauty of live TV, McCoy, but we'll still get the story."

Cate watched another photographer adjusting his lights, the shadows in the backyard of the mansion playing havoc with the camera's color balance.

"When is Snow going to spend some money on equipment, Andy? That live truck has been on its last legs for six months now."

"Speaking of money, I heard the miserly Michaela bitching about how much our trip to Nevada cost her. I think she said something about throwing good money after bad."

An administration staffer hung the state seal on the front of the podium the governor would speak from, and Cate smirked as it skewed sideways after the minion walked away. "I knew she'd say that." Cate looked at Andy. "The witch."

"Everyone? Can I have your attention, please?" Jill Hamm was wearing a black suit with a hammered gold pin at her lapel. She seemed to be coping quite well with the Barracuda's absence, Cate thought.

"Governor Hamm and Lieutenant Colonel Escobar will be out here shortly. They will have a statement about the project they're working on and then there will be time for some questions." The girl smiled prettily and disappeared back into the mansion.

"She's loving this," Cate murmured to Andy, wondering what the "project" was that Hamm would be talking about.

"Think the Barracuda did it?" Andy eyed the podium through her viewfinder.

"Could be" Cate said. "Think about it. She threatened Millicent Pine a long time ago in Washington, and, even though we haven't been able to confirm it, Pine apparently came here with some pretty damaging information she wanted to spring on the governor."

"But to kidnap her, McCoy? That's kind of extreme, isn't it?"

Cate shrugged. "The Barracuda has "extreme" written all over her. Two words, Andy. Restraining order." Cate pushed her sunglasses up on her nose. "I think she's a control freak who let the situation get out of hand. She probably just intended to scare Pine but ended up hurting her or something."

Andy lifted her head and stared at Cate. "You think the Barracuda actually killed Millicent Pine?"

"No." Cate swept her hair behind one ear and thought for a moment. "But it wouldn't surprise me if she injured her somehow and then left her out in the middle of nowhere. Millicent Pine could've died of exposure, Andy. Who knows?"

Andy swiveled the camera as Governor Hamm emerged from the mansion, accompanied by a tall man with a military style brush cut. He was wearing camouflage pants and a khaki shirt, his eyes concealed behind dark sunglasses.

The governor stepped up to the podium, the bright sun burnishing his bushy dark hair. He held his shoulder stiffly and looked out at them with a dissatisfied air. Hamm drew his reading glasses out of his breast pocket and put them on, the frames too small for his face. He studied the paper on the podium for a moment, scanning what was obviously a prepared script, and then looked up at the assembled cameras, a smile on his lips. "My chief of staff likes it when I read what he writes, but this is one time when I want to speak from the heart."

Lamar Bates stood apart from the ceremony, and Cate couldn't read his expression behind his sunglasses.

The governor cleared his throat and put his glasses back into his pocket. "Lieutenant Colonel Escobar and I have been in our share of sticky situations." The two men exchanged a stern glance, and Escobar squared his shoulders, as if preparing to have a medal pinned to his chest. His jaw muscles worked as he chewed gum. "Most of what we've done we'll take to our graves. You just don't talk about that stuff."

"And if we told you we'd have to kill you," Cate drawled in Andy's ear.

"But that doesn't mean you ever forget what you did for your country and what your fellow soldiers did for you." He nodded at Escobar, and the ex-paratrooper lifted the cover from an easel, revealing a colorful architect's sketch. The cameras zoomed in. "That is the design we've chosen to honor the paratroopers that have served their country through many wars, and we're going to put it right there."

Hamm gestured to a wide oval that had been dug out of the grass of the mansion's backyard. Dirt had been turned over in anticipation of the first structure or planting of the memorial.

The sketch featured a stylized arch with four legs, reminiscent of the poles of a tent without the canvas or the shape of a parachute. Underneath it, the architect had drawn in green plants and bright flowers.

"But we need some help." The sun was directly overhead, and the governor's face was flushed. He hadn't dressed for the unseasonable warmth. "I'm asking all those veterans out there and any other Minnesotans who love their country to contribute to this cause." Perspiration dotted his face. "We've set up a special memorial fund and we're accepting donations." He looked into the camera lenses. "It's the least you can do to say thank you."

"Oh, God," Cate groaned under her breath. "Governor? Could you please comment on the police questioning of your press secretary Saturday?"

There was a subdued rustling as photographers tightened their shots and pens were poised expectantly over notepads.

Hamm's mouth turned down with disgust. "I might've known the press could care less about something important like this. You just want headlines for your tabloids. You all belong at the *National Enquirer*." He looked around as if measuring the distance he'd have to cover to escape.

A network reporter called out, "Are you saying you have no comment, Governor, about Ms. Barracosta?"

Hamm held his hands up. "All right," he shouted, taking a deep breath. "Here's my comment." He glared at them, glancing to his right where Escobar stood, the soldier's fists clenched. "It wouldn't surprise me if that reporter staged this whole thing just to get a story— "

The network reporter interrupted, his voice incredulous. "Are you saying you think Millicent Pine set this up herself?"

Other reporters jumped in. "Governor, is it your claim—"

"What about the evidence?"

"Governor, why would Millicent Pine do that?"

Lamar Bates slid out from under the crab apple tree and stepped up next to the governor, bending toward the cluster of microphones. "Governor Hamm has made his comment. He has other appointments." He gestured toward the mansion, and the governor strode away, flanked by Escobar's rigid form. "Please feel free to photograph the sketch and the memorial site. Thank you for coming."

Cate nodded at Andy, dialing her cell phone as the photographer moved to the edge of the dirt oval to get some tape of it. Noah Hamilton picked up the phone. "Noah? Cate here."

"I saw it," the executive producer said gleefully. "The competition ran the whole thing live. What a head case!"

"We're just getting some other shots, and then we'll be back."

Hamilton chuckled. "He's a gift from the gods, Cate." She could hear him pounding a keyboard. "Get here as soon as you can. Your story is going to lead every show."

12

SAINT PAUL

April 11, 11:14 A.M.

"LET'S DECIDE THE RULES OF THE ROAD." Cate looked across the table at the other woman, her brisk manner concealing her shock at the Barracuda's appearance. Liz Barracosta's silver hair hung lank and lifeless, framing a face that was pale and drained. Still, the air of authority that had always surrounded her like a cloud of pungent perfume was firmly in place. The haughty woman who'd terrorized reporters wasn't beaten, prime suspect or not.

"Fair enough," Barracosta said, dark eyes focused on the bland wall of her attorney's conference room. It had taken a decoy car and the cover of night to escape the media camped at her house.

Cate glanced down at her notes. She'd been shocked when Chandler Coates had called to say his client was interested in sitting down for an interview. "We're on the record from here on in."

Barracosta's chin lifted, and she pointed at Cate. "I want a list of the questions before we do anything."

"No deal. Liz, you know we would never agree to that."

Barracosta stared at her. "How do I know you won't edit the hell out of this and make me look like some crazy killer?"

Cate stared back. "You don't." She leaned forward, her hands flat on the table between them. "But, as you're well aware, this is your chance to tell your side and put a little reasonable doubt into the minds of the jury pool out there."

Barracosta bent her head, and Cate noticed the jagged part in her hair. The stress of being under virtual house arrest was showing.

"When do you want to do the interview?"

Triumph surged through Cate. Until now, she hadn't been certain she was really going to pull this off. Even after Barracosta's lawyer had called to say his client wanted to talk to her, Cate had suspected Coates would talk her out of it. "For some reason, she thinks you'll listen to her," he'd told her on the phone. "She thinks it's bad strategy to let the cops do all of the talking for her. She's a press secretary, after all." He'd sighed with frustration. "Just don't jerk her around, McCoy."

Cate looked at Liz. "I think we should do the interview tomorrow." Better strike when the iron is hot. "Can you get away from your house again without alerting everybody else?"

Barracosta tilted her head, her mouth drawn tight. "I'm becoming quite an expert at diversionary tactics."

When the telephone rang at two fifteen a.m., Cate knew it was Coates calling to tell her that the interview was off. Her scoop was down the drain. Pushing hair out of her eyes, she reached for the bedside lamp, flipping it on as she grabbed for the receiver. "Hello?" She cleared her throat, squinting at the clock. "Cate McCoy here."

"Cate? I need your help."

Cate sat up straight, Adam's voice clearing the cobwebs. "Adam! What's going on?"

"Sherlock is sick and I—" he took a deep breath, "and I can't carry him to the car, Cate—w-with this damn crutch and all."

Cate sprang out of bed, reaching for a pair of sweat pants and an old Saint Paul Saints t-shirt draped across a chair. "I'll be right there." She hung up, jamming her feet into a pair of slippers and stumbling over Walter as she raced for the kitchen. Scooping up her purse, she pushed the cat back when he would have followed her out the door. "Be back in a bit, pal."

Adam looked exhausted when he opened his door, and Cate guessed he'd had little sleep.

"Where is he?"

He led her to the kitchen where Sherlock lay on the tile, his eyes open, his tongue lolling out. A bowl of water next to him was full, and Cate knelt to feel his nose. It was hot and dry. She stood, looking around.

77

"Has he been vomiting?"

Adam bent stiffly, running his fingers lightly over the dog's head. "It started about two hours ago. He threw up his dinner and then kept retching until he finally ended up like this." The hand gripping the crutch was white with tension. "I called the animal hospital, and they told me to bring him in, that he might be poisoned, but I couldn't—"

Cate stroked the dog's dark head. "I'm glad you called. Go get the car, and I'll carry him downstairs and meet you at the front entrance." He hesitated, and Cate smiled at him. "Go ahead. He'll be all right, Adam."

The sun was sending spears of rosy light across the Mississippi when they finally got home, Sherlock still at the animal hospital for observation. The vet told them he suspected that the dog had gotten into some chocolate, toxic to canines even in small amounts. Adam had surmised that the teenager he paid to walk Sherlock every day at the bookstore had fed him a candy bar, unaware of its danger to dogs.

He unlocked his door and turned to her. "Let me make you breakfast, Cate. It's too late to go back to bed."

Cate glanced at his kitchen clock. "Sounds great, but I've got to shower first. Can you give me forty-five minutes to put on my TV face?" She ran her fingers through her hair. "I think I kind of frightened that young veterinarian."

Adam muttered something, and Cate paused on the way out of his door. "Better make that coffee strong. I could've sworn you just said something about 'autumn leaves.'"

He turned toward her, a large white egg cupped in his hand, his wintry eyes serious. "I said," he whispered, his jaw tightening, "you make me think of autumn, all gold and red and green—"

Cate's eyes widened as heat rushed into her face.

"And if he doesn't think that's beautiful, he's been looking at dog snouts for too long."

The air pulsed between them as her heart thudded. "Oh." She slipped out of the door.

"He really said that?" Andy pulled her camera out of the back of the van and set it on the ground, reaching in for the long canvas bag of lights. "God, if Sunny ever said anything half that romantic to me, I'd ride off into the sunset with him in a New York minute."

"Yeah, well, it was all I could do to sit there and choke down his eggs Benedict after that."

Andy handed Cate the tripod and slammed the hatchback door. "The man can cook, too? Girl, what the hell are you still doing hanging on for Mr. Foreign Correspondent?"

Cate shrugged, a headache beginning to throb at her temples. Three hours of sleep would do that. "I hope you're bringing plenty of tapes. I have a feeling the Barracuda will have a lot of say."

Andy patted the fanny pack that encircled her waist. "One in the camera and four more in here. I've also got lots of battery power."

They carried the gear across the street to Chandler Coates' town house. Built between two mansions on Summit Avenue, it stuck out like a modern sore thumb. He met them at the door and led them into a smallish sitting room.

"Mr. Coates. This is Andy Costinopoulos. She'll be shooting the interview today."

Coates nodded at Andy and sat down. "I'll tell you again, Miss McCoy. I think this is a serious mistake." The attorney drew an expensive pen from his breast pocket and turned it over between his fingers. "But, that said, I've told Liz that I will only intervene if I think she's saying something incriminating to the case."

Cate's stomach burned, and she felt weariness press like a leaden weight on her forehead. She wished she'd gotten a good night's sleep. "I hope you won't feel compelled to stop our interview. That always ruins the flow of the conversation." She forced an insincere smile.

He looked at her. "Ms. Barracosta will tell you what happened that night. Her version. And you're free to ask her questions about that. But she is not going to speculate about any evidence the police might have or go into great detail about what she told the police on Saturday." He took his glasses off and set them on the table. "This case may end up going to trial, Miss McCoy, and that's my top priority. Not your story."

Liz Barracosta appeared in the doorway, and Cate saw that she looked better than she had the day before, a light dusting of powder smoothing out her skin and a touch of red lipstick brightening her mouth. She shook hands with Cate and sat down as Andy attached a wireless microphone to her blouse.

The two women eyed each other. The Barracuda said, "Fire away."

April 12, 6:01 P.M.

Cate looked into the square box of the studio camera lens and listened as the last thirty seconds of her interview with Liz Barracosta played in her ear. She was sitting on the set next to Allison, who was peering into a small compact mirror, fixing her hair while she was off camera. The studio was cold, kept at polar temperatures so the anchors didn't perspire on the air. Cate doubted Allison sweated even in the most searing heat. Snakes were cold blooded, weren't they?

The floor director called out, "Fifteen seconds!" and Cate waited for the red light to go on atop camera two. "Liz Barracosta says she hasn't heard from Governor Hamm or any of his closest advisors since she was questioned. She has been suspended with pay." She swiveled away from the camera, addressing Allison. "Allison?"

Allison smiled and ignored the scripted question rolling by on the TelePrompTer, going on to the next story. Cate clenched her fists. Air hog, she thought, waiting for a commercial break before unclipping her mike and slipping out of the studio.

"Cate?" The assignments editor was holding a phone over his head. "Call from a viewer about your story."

Probably Detective Dahl, she thought, hurrying to her desk. Barracosta's protests of innocence and claims of police mistakes would not go over well. "Cate McCoy."

"That woman may be a lot of things but she's tellin' the truth about this one." The voice sounded hoarse and grumpy.

"I beg your pardon?"

There was a loud sigh on the other end. "That one you just did an article about on the news. She's my neighbor."

Cate exhaled wearily. The day felt like it had been thirty-six hours long. "And that's interesting because?"

He cackled in her ear. "Cause I got something you need to see, girl."

Cate winced as a loud crash was followed by an obnoxious dial tone.

Andy swerved to avoid a shorts-clad mother pushing a side-by-side baby carriage as they cruised into the Barracuda's neighborhood, spotting the crush of media at the far end of the street. They were obviously unaware that Liz had retreated to a friend's condo. "Warm weather brings out the soccer moms."

Cate smiled as spring-scented air rushed in the open window, brushing across her face, lifting her hair. "I love it," she said, closing her eyes and breathing deeply, feeling the headache she'd been fighting all day disappear. "It almost makes up for how much we suffer all winter."

Long shards of yellow light lay across greening lawns as they passed large suburban homes that all looked alike. Andy slowed as Cate leaned out of the window, reading house numbers on curbs and above doors.

"He didn't tell you which house was his, right?"

Cate shook her head. "All he said was that he was Liz Barracosta's neighbor, and he had something we'd want to see."

"I think this is it." Andy pulled into the brick driveway of a large house, it's forest green door sheltered by a graceful arch. A bay window refracted the waning sunlight. Andy turned off the engine. "Did the Barracuda's lawyer wonder why you wanted her address?"

Cate got out of the news van, looking around the tranquil neighborhood for a clue as to who her caller had been. "He started to ask and then his secretary buzzed him so he gave it to me and hung up."

Andy eyed the sprawling house in front of them. "Being a press secretary must pay pretty well, McCoy. Maybe we ought to think about a career change."

"She's not home." Cate spun in the direction of the voice to see a middle-aged woman with a gray pageboy and a small white dog on a leash. She was standing in the yard next door, her terrier frantically digging at a bedraggled flower bed.

"Thank you," Cate called, eliminating her as the caller. He'd definitely been male. "She asked us to make sure her lawn was getting enough water while she's gone," Cate lied.

The woman stared, her pageboy ruffling in the evening breeze. "Gone," she snorted. "Ought to be in jail where she belongs."

"Nice neighbors," Cate murmured, turning away from the woman's prying eyes to peer down the street.

"Over there," Andy said, nudging Cate.

Across the street, a short round man was standing in his doorway, waving them in as if guiding a jumbo jetliner to the gate.

"Must be our caller. Come on." They crossed the street, dogged by the woman's suspicious glare.

"You the news lady?" He studied Cate through thick glasses. "You look better on TV."

"Thank you," Cate said dryly, ignoring Andy's smirk. "Did you call me at the station about an hour ago?"

"Better come in," he said, gesturing them inside. "That nosey witch across the street is always snooping into my business." He shot a malevolent glare in the woman's direction. "But I'll fix her. And her little dog, too."

They followed him into a house so dark it might have been midnight. Heavy drapes covered every window and blinds blocked light that would've come in from his back door. Uneasiness tickled the back of Cate's neck.

"Can't stand the sun," he said, flipping on a dim lamp. "Pardon the mess."

'The mess' was a room full of furniture that had been shredded by something so sharp the stuffing was showing. Clouds of white polyester had popped out of his couch like bolls bursting with cotton at harvest time. A pillow lying on a chair had long scratches in it, and the material covering his recliner had jagged tears in it, the wooden frame of the chair showing through.

Cate wondered what kind of wild animals he was keeping when she spotted the eyes. At least a dozen pair glowed luminously from the shadows of the room, their dark pupils wide with dislike.

"You're a cat lover, Mr. . . . ?"

"Valentine. Douglas Valentine." He clicked his tongue, and three cats sped to his side, purring and pawing at his legs.

"I have a cat, too. A big orange one." Cate's voice trailed off as Valentine ignored her, whispering to his cats, his pudgy fingers stroking their heads.

She cleared her throat. "Mr. Valentine, what did you have to show me?"

He stopped stroking, peering up at her through his glasses. "I don't like her. Never did, you know."

"The Barracu—er, Ms. Barracosta?"

He nodded. "My wife thought she was nice. She even brought Kitty her medicine a couple of times."

Cate stifled the urge to tell him to get to the point. Patience was a virtue. Especially when she might get a story out of it.

"Did Ms. Barracosta give you something, Mr. Valentine?"

He shook his head, snapping, "Don't do that."

Cate turned to see Andy straightening quickly.

Valentine crossed the room, gathering a Siamese cat into his arms. "They don't like strangers."

Cate and Andy exchanged looks. "Mr. Valentine. I have a story to write for the ten o'clock newscast. Can you please tell me why you called?"

His double chins waggled as he released the cat, pulling a videotape from a stack on the top of his television. "Can't tell you. Gotta show you." He inserted the tape into his VCR. The screen buzzed with static and then cleared to reveal two Siamese kittens at play with a ball of yarn.

"Mr. Valentine," Cate said, ready to let him have it, when the picture changed to a shot of the neighborhood. It had obviously been recorded from Valentine's house and it encompassed his front lawn, the street and two houses. Street lamps and the glow from lamp-lit windows provided the illumination. A time and date were stamped on the bottom.

"Why were you taping Liz Barracosta's house?"

The round little man gave her a secretive smile and turned back to the screen, suddenly shouting, "There!"

Cate edged closer to see a small dog dart across the street and race into Valentine's front yard. The animal's white hair made him visible on the dark lawn, and they watched as he crept into a large circular flower bed. The dog looked around, almost as if he feared he was being watched and then abruptly turned into a whirling dervish of pale hair and paws. Dirt and flower petals flew in every direction.

"That wretched beast," Valentine cried, his voice rich with anguish. "My Kitty would've been heartbroken if she'd seen what that little bastard is doing to her rose garden."

Cate glanced at Andy and grit her teeth against a renewed throbbing at her temples. The headache was back. "Mr. Valentine, I really don't think this is anything we'd put on the air. Maybe you could call your town board about it."

She glanced at her watch, eager to escape the dark house, when a movement on the screen caught her eye. A car had pulled into Liz Barracosta's driveway and as the garage door rose, Barracosta emerged from the car and walked the short distance to her mailbox. It was too dark to see her face well, but Cate recognized her trademark silver hair.

The three of them watched as the press secretary pulled a bundle of mail from the box and paused to thumb through it. In a few moments she was back in her Jaguar and the garage door was gliding down.

Cate studied the recorded scene, her mind working. "Wait a minute!" She spun to see Valentine's smug grin.

"Took you long enough, girl."

13

CUAUHTEMOC, MEXICO

7:44 P.M.

THE TEACHER FINISHED HER SIMPLE MEAL OF TORTILLAS and fruit and smiled at the young girl who'd come to take the dishes away. "We are glad you're home, Marguerite," the girl said shyly, dipping her head, her hair covered by a small lace cap.

"It's good to be home, *niña*." She patted her lips with a rough cloth and stood, smiling when she saw her friend standing in the doorway. "Rachel!" The two women embraced.

"You were gone a long time, Marguerite," the older woman whispered. "Did your work go well?"

Marguerite drew her friend to a small wooden bench, holding her hand as they sat down. "I am feeling . . . dispirited, Rachel." Her hand tightened around the other woman's fingers, the knuckles reddened from rigorous farm work. "The villages are full of children who are sick and hungry, and their parents don't know what to do." She shook her head. "The floods did more damage than we even guessed. All of that water and yet many of the places I visited have no clean water to drink. It's terrible."

The other woman bowed her head briefly, praying for guidance. It pained her to have to add to her friend's worries. She looked into the younger woman's shadowed eyes. "We received a telegram for you, Marguerite, while you were gone."

Marguerite's brows drew together. "For me?"

Rachel drew the paper from the pocket of her habit. "Abraham decided that we should read it and try to get a message to you, but . . ."

Marguerite opened the yellow paper and scanned the words quickly. "Millicent missing. Stop. Need advice. Stop. Please contact immediately. Stop. Della." The paper shook in her hands. "When did this come?"

"Two weeks ago." She rose, drawing the trembling woman up from the couch. "What will you do?"

9:58 P.M.

Cate raced for the set, jabbing her earpiece into her right ear as she collapsed into the chair normally reserved for the sports anchor. Dan Gilbert gave her a preoccupied smile, tipping his chin up so the makeup artist could pat foundation powder down to the collar of his shirt. Cate smoothed her hair, wishing she'd touched up her lipstick. Gilbert's painted-on glow would make her look pale and washed out next to him.

"Two minutes!" The floor director was standing between two of the huge studio cameras. "Cate, you will be looking at camera two for your intro. The tag will be a two shot on camera one. Got that?"

Cate nodded tensely, looking down at the script in front of her. She would read it from the TelePrompTer, but it was always smart to have a backup. She'd seen too many anchors, faces frozen like deer in headlights, when the PrompTer went down because they couldn't shift gears to their written pages.

The newscast music filled the studio, and Cate watched the monitor as Dan Gilbert introduced himself. "Good evening. We begin tonight with new evidence that former press secretary Liz Barracosta was not with Millicent Pine when police say the journalist was kidnapped. Pine disappeared last month after meeting with Barracosta at a Saint Paul restaurant. Political reporter Cate McCoy joins us with this exclusive story. Cate?"

Cate nodded at Dan and turned smoothly to camera two. "Dan, police consider Liz Barracosta a prime suspect in the kidnapping of Millicent Pine. Part of their case involves the fact that the journalist was last seen with Barracosta, having drinks in the bar of the Saint Paul Grill. But Channel Three has uncovered timed and dated evidence that challenges the police timeline for the crime."

Cate's taped package began to roll, and she noted that even Gilbert was watching it. He usually spent his time off camera glancing at his scripts. Cate looked up at the monitor. Her interview with Douglas Valentine was playing. A calico swished his tail on Valentine's shoulder as he said, "I thought I was solving the mystery of my damaged flower beds. I never dreamed I was giving my neighbor an alibi."

Cate's recorded voice followed as shots of Liz Barracosta filled the screen. "And it does, indeed, appear to be a strong alibi for Barracosta. Here's why. Investigators allege that the former press secretary left the restaurant with Millicent Pine at 10:30 p.m., after which she apparently disappeared. Barracosta claims that Pine went to her room and never returned."

An interview done hastily ninety minutes ago with Liz Barracosta came on screen. "I thought she'd taken a call from her editor or something, so I waited about fifteen minutes, tried to call her room and finally left. I got home around 11:20 p.m."

Cate's voice track continued. "Barracosta's claim is backed up by this videotape." Grainy images of Liz Barracosta pulling into her driveway and walking down to the curb for her mail rolled on screen. The date and time stamp in the corner were unmistakable, and Cate's recorded voice track went on, "Notice the date and time on the videotape. It is 11:17 p.m. on the night of March 27th."

Another soundbite from Barracosta. "The police have wasted valuable time investigating the wrong person while the real kidnapper is still at large. Ms. Pine could be injured or in serious danger somewhere, and this department's bungling has allowed the true criminal in this case plenty of time to conceal himself. I expect to be completely exonerated by this department, and they owe me a sincere apology." The camera had zoomed in. "I'm not ruling out a civil lawsuit for harassment."

The taped story ended, and Cate read her tag on camera two. "A police department spokesman would only say that they are reviewing the videotape. Mr. Valentine says he came forward with the tape when he saw our interview with Liz Barracosta earlier. Ms. Barracosta's attorney says he'll be meeting with homicide investigators tomorrow. Dan?"

Eddie Hamm palmed the remote and flipped back to the program he'd been watching until Bates had called to alert him to the news story. Women in midriff-baring shirts and tiny shorts were bouncing on a trampoline. Eyes on the screen, he said, "Now she'll want her job back."

Pete Escobar nodded, opening two bottles of Pig's Eye and handing one of them to the governor. "Could be just what you thought, Ed. That reporter set it all up herself." He took a deep draught of beer. "Can't trust those weasels any further than you can throw 'em."

Hamm tilted the bottle to his lips. "How much money has come in for the project out there, Pete?"

Escobar's eyes narrowed. "Not as much as I'd hoped, but some. I think we've got pledges of about ten thousand dollars so far."

Hamm snorted in disgust, looking up to see Ana Escobar in the family room doorway. She wore tight black jeans that outlined her long legs and a black, fitted jacket. She had a riding crop in her hand. "Peter, may I speak to you for a moment?" Her voice was soft, her speech accented.

"Come in and have a brew, Annie," Hamm boomed. "Straddlin' a horse is thirsty work, if you know what I mean." He winked, polishing off his beer.

The woman's nostrils flared, and her smile was frosty. "Thank you, Governor, but I'm planning on an early night. I just need a few words with my husband."

Escobar rose, calling over his shoulder, "I'll tell the maid to bring a couple more Pig's Eyes, Ed. Be back in a minute."

The telephone rang at midnight, and Della DeFrancisco reached for it, wide awake, her heart slamming in her chest. Millicent knew that Thursdays were her night off. Maybe she had some crazy story about where she'd been, an interview that had suddenly come through in Belize or an assignment to the Middle East so secret she'd been warned to tell no one. Maybe . . . "Hello?"

"Della? It's Marguerite."

The adrenaline surge died, leaving her hands trembling in its wake and she bowed her head, the receiver cold and heavy. "Marguerite. It's good to hear from you." Her voice was drained.

"I'm sorry it's been so long. I've been traveling in the interior. I received your telegram and came into Chihuahua to a telephone as quickly as I could." There was a brief silence. "What has happened to Millicent?"

Della reached for her brandy and took a healthy slug. "She's missing, Marguerite. She disappeared while she was on a story in Minnesota."

"Minnesota?" It might as well have been Katmandu. "When did she . . . what was she doing there?"

The brandy curled warm in her stomach. "She went to try to interview the governor. Hamm, I think his name is. Her magazine editor assigned her the story." Della sensed the other woman's confusion. "He's a big celebrity, Marguerite. Kind of a larger-than-life sort of character. Millicent told me she thought she had a good story."

"What are the police saying?"

Della sighed. "Not much. I've been debating whether to go up there but it's just so confusing. All the police will say is that she disappeared from her hotel on March 27th. No one has seen her since." She swirled the brandy, inhaling the spicy fumes. "I've been talking to a television reporter. She says they're focusing on the governor's press secretary as a suspect."

"Suspect in what?"

Della closed her eyes. "Kidnapping, Marguerite."

"Dear Lord," Marguerite gasped, the sound swallowed in a burst of static.

Della wondered how long the connection from Mexico would last. "The reporter says they found Millicent's notebook in the trunk of this woman's car, and she was the person last seen with her." She wouldn't tell Marguerite about the blood. She could hardly think about it herself.

Long static-filled seconds ticked by. "I'm surprised Millicent took the assignment," the nun finally said. "She was working on something else."

Della's fingers tingled. "What do you mean? Another story?"

Marguerite's voice faded, swallowed in static as Della strained to hear her. "Yes." The static rose and all Della heard was, ". . . I gave her."

Cate stroked Sherlock's long nose, sharing a smile with Adam as the dog closed his eyes with a muffled groan. He was stretched out, his head on her thighs. "How long is he going to have to take the medicine the vet gave you?"

Adam handed her a plate with a gyro on it. They were sitting on his couch sharing a midnight snack. "A couple more days. We were lucky we got him to the vet as quickly as we did, Cate. Thanks to you."

"Your eggs Benedict was thanks enough, Adam." The memory of what he'd said that morning returned, and she blushed, taking a bite of the tender meat. "What did you think of the story tonight?"

"Intriguing."

She looked at him. "Do I hear a 'but' coming?"

His expression warmed, and his eyes flashed silver in the lamplight. He'd been waiting for her to ask. "Only that it doesn't answer all of the other questions."

Cate sighed, her mouth twisting wryly. "I should've known you'd be out here shredding my scoop as soon as I could get it on the air."

He set his plate on the coffee table and leaned forward, his hands clasped between his knees. Cate remembered how he'd cradled his dog's head, his fingers shaking, as the animal lay sick and frightened at the vet hospital. "You've got to be wondering about this too, Cate." His voice was low and even, not challenging. "How did Millicent Pine's notebook get into the trunk of Liz Barracosta's car if she wasn't involved?"

Cate set her own plate on the table and stood up, crossing the room to the windows. The full moon had opened a bright swathe in the velvet of the river and pewter-tipped waves curled to the surface. "It's strange" she said softly, her gaze on a cabin cruiser, it's running lights tiny colored stars in the blackness. "If the Barracuda didn't do it because she was trying to stop Millicent Pine from writing some hack-job story on the governor, then there's a whole other subplot out there that I haven't clued into."

She turned away from the view, scooping a handful of hair behind one ear. "Think about it, Adam. Someone with a motive strong enough to want Millicent Pine out of the way swooped in here and snatched her and took her somewhere, all without being seen. Weird."

He shook his head. "We don't know that the abductor wasn't seen, Cate. And that so-called 'subplot' may make sense when we know where to look."

"I'm open to suggestions."

He rose, gripping his cane and limped to his desk. It was a beautiful cherry wood he'd inherited from his father. Reaching into the top drawer, he drew out the cassette tape and the autopsy sheet. "This is where you begin."

14

CHANNEL THREE NEWSROOM

April 13, 6:56 P.M.

"S HE'S GOING TO KILL ME."

"Just put her in a headlock before you tell her, Noah. Then she can't hurt you too bad."

The executive producer grimaced, his uncertain gaze resting on Cate's face. "She's already pissed off that you guys went to Vegas and didn't turn up very much."

Andy snorted. "Typical tight-assed news director. You'd think it was her money."

Cate leaned across his desk, her eyes serious now. "Noah, you were left in charge while Michaela went home to take care of her mother."

"Didn't know she had a mother," Andy muttered. "Figured she hatched or something."

"It's your decision to send us down there if you think it's worthwhile." Cate gestured to the envelope that contained the tape and autopsy report. "Look, that's what Millicent Pine was working on when she accepted the Hamm story from her editor. We need to check it out."

He shifted in his chair, taking off his glasses and rubbing his eyes. "And you think a cassette tape of an interview and some autopsy that was done in Mexico more than a year ago is going to lead you to her kidnapper?" Hamilton shook his head. "Michaela's never going to buy that."

Cate grinned. "But we'll already be gone, Noah, by the time she finds out. That's the beauty of this plan."

He sighed. "Tell Beth to put you on the next flight to San Diego. You can cross the border there." He pointed at Cate with a nail-bitten finger. "But you'd better come up with something this time, or there'll be hell to pay."

The newsroom was quiet when Cate returned to her desk, most of the dayside reporters gone for the night, and the evening crew out covering stories. The digital clock over the assignments desk said 7:03:24, and Cate ran through a to-do list before their flight tomorrow morning. Dry-cleaning, packing, set up cat-sitting with Adam . . .

She rounded the corner and halted when she saw Chad Joosveldt sitting in her chair. He was hunched over a sheet of paper writing something. "Hey, Chad. What's up?"

The photographer swiveled in her chair, a half-written note in his hand. He was wearing jeans and a denim shirt with the station's logo on the breast pocket. Straight dark hair brushed his shoulders. "Hi, Cate. Hear you're headed to Mexico tomorrow." He smiled at her surprised look. "Andy asked to borrow credit card-cam."

The tiny camera was so small it could be hidden in a credit card-sized piece of plastic, which made it ideal for surveillance. Chad and Barry used it frequently for their cop shop investigative stories.

"What did you want to tell me?" Cate gestured to the paper he held in his hand and perched on the corner of a nearby desk.

"One of the homicide guys mentioned something about the Pine case today. I thought you'd want to hear it before you left."

"Definitely."

He twisted a small gold hoop in his ear, and Cate noticed the scratches on his hands. Rumor had it he was an accomplished mountain climber and was saving for a trip to Everest. "He said they're not giving up on Liz Barracosta as a suspect and that your story ignored something pretty important." Chad held up his hands. "That's what they're saying, Cate, not me."

She tilted her head, mind racing. What could she have missed? "Is there more evidence?"

He shifted in her chair, crumpling the half-finished note. "They think she had an accomplice."

Cate stared at him. It had never occurred to her but it wasn't completely implausible. Liz Barracosta could have had someone either near or even inside the hotel that night, waiting for her signal. Perhaps that person was her backup in case Millicent Pine refused to give up on the story she was writing. "Did they give you any hint about who they think it was?"

Chad shrugged. "No, but it does explain how she showed up on that guy's videotape at exactly the same time Pine was disappearing off the face of the earth." He rose. "Good luck, Cate. I'll let you know if I hear anything else."

Cate nodded, her memory clicking over anyone she'd recently seen with Liz Barracosta. Could Lamar Bates have been her accomplice? He'd been the one who had brought her on board when Hamm's poll numbers were so dismal. But she'd also heard he'd been eager to dump Barracosta when she'd become a suspect. If he'd helped, wasn't Bates afraid she'd implicate him to save herself?

Cate shouldered her briefcase and pushed through the back door to the parking lot. Her Mustang was parked at the far end, and as she crossed the blacktop, she could see it was in desperate need of a wash. It would have to wait until she came back, she thought, sliding into the buff-colored leather seat.

Steering out of the lot and onto the highway, Cate wondered if Adam was still at the bookstore. She exited at the next off-ramp, and headed for Grand Avenue, speeding down the long Saint Paul boulevard lined with trendy eateries and old Victorian houses. Adam's store, the Sleuthsayer, sat between a stylish tea shop and a place that sold every piece of gadgetry made for fly fishing, right down to hundreds of intricate flies and lures displayed in sliding drawers. Cate had interviewed the owner once for a story on taxes.

A group of people were coming out of the Sleuthsayer as Cate walked up the sidewalk. She spotted Adam standing in the doorway, shaking hands with a tall burly man, who smiled at her as she stood aside to let him pass on the stairs.

"Business picking up?"

Adam ushered her into the shop and closed the glass door.

"That was our monthly book club," he said, watching as an employee rearranged the chairs that had been set up in a semi-circle. Adam was wearing a white t-shirt under a loose gray sweater, the sleeves pushed up over forearms made powerful by the physical therapy he did for his leg. He looked at her. "Did you recognize the guy who passed you on the stairs?"

Cate pictured the man's face. Should she know him?

Adam smiled, handing her a glass of wine from the small table that had been set out for the discussion group. "Terrence Hardin."

"The journalist," Cate exclaimed, snapping her fingers. "I loved that book he wrote about the grave robbers in Egypt. What a terrific whodunit."

Adam spotted Sherlock nosing the cheese plate and whistled for the dog, pulling a biscuit from his jeans pocket and feeding it to him. "Hardin is working on his next book right now. Says he's researching the Mayan civilization."

"Cool." Cate sipped her wine, making a face as she swallowed. "This tastes like someone's home brew, Adam." She set the glass on the table. "Yuck."

He laughed. "It is. One of our club members presses his own grapes and bottles it every year. We all just take very small sips." He gripped his cane, leading her through the bookcases toward a trio of oversized chairs, brass lamps casting circles of light on their well-worn cushions.

Cate collapsed with a sigh, kicking her shoes off and wriggling her toes. Adam levered himself into the chair opposite her. "How did you persuade Terrance Hardin to show up for the book club?"

Adam shrugged. "Well, he lives just over the border in Wisconsin, and we've been stocking his books even when he was being published by an independent press." He rubbed Sherlock's ears, making the dog growl with pleasure. "I mentioned the tape of the interview and the autopsy report to him."

Cate's eyes widened. "Why?"

"He promised to keep it all confidential, Cate. He's a journalist. He understands that stuff." He leaned forward in the chair, lamplight shimmering around his head and shoulders, his eyes in smoky shadow. "He's just gotten back from nearly a year in Mexico. I thought he could give us a clue about Millicent's interview with the girl."

"What did he say?" Cate curled her feet underneath her, relaxing in the soft cushions.

"He said he didn't know anything about the story the girl told on the tape, but he did remember hearing about the gold fingertips on the dead girl. Apparently it was in the papers in Mexico City. He remembers the coroner concluding that she was a sniffer."

Cate combed her fingers through her hair, wishing absently that she'd had time for a cut and color before her trip. The auburn highlights her stylist blended in covered up an annoying gray patch right at her temple quite effectively. Her mind snapped back to the conversation. "What's a 'sniffer'?"

Adam winced. "It's not pretty, Cate. Mexico has a serious problem with kids who sniff glue and paint to get high. American kids do it too."

"So the police think the dead girl was sniffing gold paint?"

Adam nodded. "That's what Hardin remembers. He says the Mexico City newspaper ran a series on the problem."

"I guess I can find out for myself. Andy and I are leaving for San Diego in the morning. We're going to cross the border into Tijuana from there."

"How long will you be gone?" His expression was unreadable.

She smiled wryly. "At least until Michaela Snow orders us back. She's out of town and doesn't know we're going."

Adam ruffled his dog's fur. "It's a good thing Sherlock likes you so much, Cate. Otherwise he'd be pretty upset about old Walter's visits."

Cate leaned over and planted a kiss on the dog's nose, her mouth brushing Adam's fingers. He withdrew them abruptly. Cate looked up at him. "Sherlock's a good sport, Adam. Thank you. Both of you."

His hand curled around his cane, and he stood up, turning away from her. "Take care, Cate." He halted, his back to her, his shoulders rigid under the gray cashmere. "Please."

April 14, 5:12 A.M.

Her hair was still wet from a rushed shower when Cate's blow dryer blew a fuse and gave up the ghost, smoke pouring out of its plastic nozzle. "Damn it!" She glanced at the clock, cursing again. Where was she supposed to get another hair dryer at five fifteen in the morning? Throwing the useless appliance into the garbage, her eyes lit on the answer, and she hauled out the small fan she used on the hottest summer nights. She was bent under it when the phone rang.

"Yeah."

"Cate? Did I wake you?"

"Noah!" Did the man ever sleep? "No, I was already up. Our flight leaves in about ninety minutes."

"Have you looked at the morning paper yet?" His voice carried a hint of something ominous.

"No, I've been busy murdering small appliances. What's up?"

"Small appli—"

She imagined him shaking his head. "Did Hamm say something stupid that we missed, Noah? Remember, we can't follow the guy twenty-four hours a day."

"No, it has nothing to do with Governor Hamm, Cate. Well, not exact-ly."

Cate clutched the portable phone under her chin and held the table fan over her head, shivering as chilly air whipped her wet hair around. "Noah, you'll have to speak up. I can't hear you very well."

"The paper found Carolee Baldwin. The story is on the front page."

She turned the fan off and looked at herself in the mirror. The hard truth looked back. She'd been scooped. Big time. On a story that should have been hers. "Where'd they find her?"

"At the airport in Vegas. She was coming home from Brazil."

"Shit."

Neither of them said anything for a moment, and Cate became aware of the sound of loud chirping on his end. "Do you have parakeets in your house or are you standing outside in your p.j.s while you deliver the bad news?"

There was a smile in his voice when he replied. "Don't let it get you down too much. They beat us. No getting around that. But I have a feeling you're still going to kick some ass on this story. Call me when you get there."

Cate was on her fourth reading of the newspaper story about Carolee Baldwin by the time they'd crossed the Arizona border and were just a short distance from San Diego. Andy had read it twice over her shoulder.

"What do you think Hamm will say about her allegations?"

Cate looked out the window, puffy white clouds drifting by below them. The paper's scoop was a lump in her midriff, like a jelly doughnut that wouldn't digest. She felt slightly nauseated. "He'll deny it, Andy, but the hotel clerk's report is pretty damning." She clipped her seatbelt as the pilot warned them they would be landing in fifteen minutes. "It doesn't look too good for the Barracuda either."

Andy nodded. "Yeah, if the paper's right and Pine told her all of this that night, there's the motive. The question is, how did she do it and still pull up in her driveway at 11:20?"

"The cops think she had help." Cate folded the newspaper and stuck it into the seat pocket. "I don't know what to think." She squirmed in her seat, hearing the engines shift as they began their descent. "Which leaves us with what even Tom Cruise might agree is a *Mission: Impossible*."

Andy grinned. "You said it, McCoy. Solve the kidnapping and find Millicent Pine. In that order."

The border crossing was a scorched, teeming place that gave few visible hints of the drama played out every day in the no-man's land that divided the two countries. Cars stretched in long lines on both sides, and pedestrians made passage on foot. Some trembled before stern U.S. Customs officers, their progress recorded by the unblinking eye of surveillance cameras. Many were turned away, their papers not in order, their explanations not believed.

There were furtive-eyed Americans, who, once on foreign soil, made their connections and devised ways to slip their spoils back across the line. And there were families who spent the day together on one side of the border or the other, saying their goodbyes near the huge turnstiles that stood in the divided zone.

Cate watched as a young mother held her baby's hand, waving it at the retreating back of a thin bent man as he pushed through the metal rungs of a turnstile, as if entering a stadium or a subway. Dust shimmered in the air, and the sun still broiled in the sky at four-thirty in the afternoon. They'd parked the car at a border lot and walked through, Andy's hidden camera rigged up in her hat, so that the lens peeked through a tiny hole punched in the front of it. The batteries that powered it were in a fanny pack around her waist. She would flip it on if they came across anything interesting.

Now, they sat in a pleasant square, sipping from cool bottles of Coca-Cola, trying to decide what to do next. Cate glanced at her watch. "Let's take a cab into downtown Tijuana. Maybe we can catch the coroner who did the autopsy on the girl with the gold fingers."

"You ladies want margarita? Mexican tequila? You like the worm in the bottle?"

Cate squinted up into the face of a grinning man, his teeth white in his dusky face. He held a thick stack of coupons between his fingers. She smiled, waving him off. "No, sorry. No happy hour yet."

He stepped closer. "You want to get happy, ladies? Maybe you need more than margarita."

Cate and Andy exchanged glances. "We don't want anything. Thanks." They stood up, but the man sidestepped in front of them.

"I sell you some X, all the girls like that. Maybe you make some money. Buy some roofies."

"What the hell is he talking about?" Cate glanced around the square, spotting a police officer on the far side. Lowering her voice, she said, "Listen, *amigo,* if you don't get out of our way, I'm going to call that policeman over here."

He looked over his shoulder, and spitting out a curse, slunk away from them. Cate flagged a taxi, and they watched the picturesque square recede in the rear window as they sped toward downtown. The air rushing in through the open windows felt good, and Cate caught the scent of fried food and garbage and something else she couldn't identify.

She glanced over at Andy, the photographer's dark hair flying in the breeze. For a moment, she wondered what they were doing here, in a foreign country, with only a tape and an autopsy report to go on. Anxiety welled up in her, and Cate reminded herself that she experienced this every time she traveled for the station. Money was being spent and expectations were high as the newsroom managers watched the stories come in via satellite and decided whether they were getting enough bang for the buck.

Cate took a calming breath. Just follow the story, she told herself. One step at a time.

15

Tijuana

3:01 P.M.

THE TAXI LET THEM OFF ON A BUSY STREET, the sidewalk jammed with people sweating in the late afternoon heat. Cate looked around, trying to get her bearings in the unfamiliar city. "I don't see anything that looks like a coroner's office around here. Maybe the cabbie didn't understand us."

Andy peered at the signs that hung over the shops and restaurants crowded next to one another, their windows coated with dust, their doorsteps grimy with dirt. "Suddenly that worm in the bottle doesn't sound too bad, McCoy."

Cate dabbed at the sweat on her flushed cheeks. "Must be ninety-five degrees." She scanned the street. "Wait. Maybe that's it over there."

They crossed the street, avoiding small cars that belched noxious exhaust and nimble scooters that weaved through the heavy traffic. Cate gestured to a small sign. "Luis Ochoa-Alvarez, M.D. Isn't that the name on the bottom of the autopsy?" She drew a copy of the report out of her bag and spotted the signature at the bottom. "Same guy. Our driver did know what he was doing."

Cate pushed on the narrow door, and they stepped up into an office, a window air conditioning unit bathing them with cool air. A young woman sat behind a desk. The waiting room was empty. "Is Dr. Ochoa-Alvarez in, *por favore?*"

The girl shook her head and said in only slightly accented English, "He has been called out on a case. May I schedule an appointment for you?"

Cate shook her head. "I'm a journalist, and I wanted to talk to him about an autopsy he did last year. Do you expect him back tonight?"

The girl's eyes took in their obviously American appearance, and Cate saw curiosity in her expression. She hesitated, saying finally, "He wasn't sure how late he would be, but you might find him at his daughter's restaurant when he is finished. He goes there most nights."

"Where is that?"

"It is called El Champinon."

"The Mushroom," Andy said, earning a look of surprise from her colleague. She shrugged. "High school Spanish."

Cate turned back to the receptionist. "Where is the Mushroom?"

The girl drew them a crude map, and they thanked her, leaving a business card with her in case they missed the doctor. Cate glanced at her watch. "How about some liquid refreshment and then dinner at the doctor's favorite place?"

Andy gave her a thumbs up. "Lead on, McCoy."

Cate was finishing her tortilla soup and tucking into her quesadilla plate when Ochoa-Alvarez entered the restaurant. It was ten-thirty, and the dinner crowd had already turned over once, but Cate and Andy had taken their time, eyes going frequently to the open doorway.

The doctor was huge, his belly spilling over a tooled leather belt, his double chins bouncing as he was greeted by a young woman and led to a secluded table in the back. He sat down heavily and reached for a wine glass.

"I'll go over to him as soon as his daughter goes back into the kitchen. Why don't you try to get a shot of him with the hidden camera in case he blows me off?"

Andy adjusted the ball cap she'd worn all day and unzipped the fanny pack, flipping a switch. She turned carefully in her chair, trying to get a face-on shot of Ochoa-Alvarez. "It's kind of dark in here, McCoy. I don't know how this will look when we play it back."

Cate dabbed her lips with a napkin and stood up. "Just get what you can and come over if I give you the signal. Wish me luck."

She approached the physician's table, wondering if Doctor *El Mucho Grande* would speak English or if she would be forced to resort to her fractured Spanish. "Doctor Ochoa-Alvarez? I'm a journalist from the States. Can I interrupt your dinner for a moment?"

He looked up, tortilla grease shining on his lips. His dark eyes slithered over her body and lingered on her breasts for a long moment. "I don't talk to reporters," he said finally in accented English, grinding his food between large square teeth, "but I'll make an exception for a beautiful girl like you."

He slid over in the booth and Cate sat down, getting a whiff of stale body odor from him. She fit her hand into his huge paw, shaking it and saying, "Cate McCoy. I work for a television station in Minnesota."

"Minnesota," he bellowed, drawing the attention of the tables next to them. "Ah, it's very cold up there! You ski all year round, don't you? I love to ski."

Cate imagined him on a pair of skis, his bulk jiggling as he careened off moguls and barreled down the slopes. "It doesn't snow in May, doctor, but you're right. In the winter, most of us flee to your country to thaw out."

He let out a huge laugh that turned into a grunt of appreciation as his daughter set a large plate on the table. She looked at Cate curiously and left without saying anything. Cate glanced over to see Andy watching, the lipstick camera presumably recording them.

"Doctor, I wanted to ask you about an autopsy you did almost a year ago."

He paused in the act of shoveling rice into his mouth and looked at her, dark brows drawn together. "You are not consulting me about an ailment, young woman? Something you would rather not talk to an American doctor about?"

Cate stared at him. Did he think she wanted an abortion or something? Last time she checked it was still legal in the U.S. She tried again. "Doctor Ochoa-Alvarez, I'm looking into a story that may have something to do with a girl you autopsied last year."

He shook his head, spearing half of an oozing burrito and stuffing it into his mouth. Cate's stomach rolled. "I don't know which one you're talking about, *senorita*," he said with a furtive glance at her ringless left hand. "I am only the substitute when Doctor Miguel is on vacation. He spends a lot of time at his *rancho* in the mountains."

Which accounted for Ochoa-Alvarez's medical practice around the corner. She wondered whether to wave Andy over so she could get a better shot of him. Better have some backup, she decided, for the next time the jerk squeezed her thigh under the table. Cate gave Andy the high sign and watched with relief as the photographer approached the table, her baseball cap fixed firmly on her head.

"Doctor, this is my colleague, Andraya Costinopoulos," Cate said, purposely omitting Andy's job title.

Andy shook his hand and sat down in the booth next to Cate, squeezing her closer to Ochoa-Alvarez. Cate took a deep breath, easing as far away from him as she could. "We're looking into the death of the girl with the gold paint on her fingers, Doctor. Do you remember her?"

He wiped any remaining juice from his plate with a tortilla and swallowed it in two bites, burping softly and smiling an apology at them. Cate gritted her teeth. "That does sound familiar, *senorita*. The gold paint was somewhat unusual." He drew a large toothpick from his pocket and foraged between his teeth for lingering morsels. "She was a paint addict, if I recall. What we call a sniffer here."

Cate nodded, drawing a copy of his autopsy report from her bag and the accompanying translation sheet. He seemed mildly surprised to see it. "So your conclusion was that she died from sniffing paint, Doctor? You found nothing else that could account for her death?"

He stuck the toothpick between his front teeth and let it hang there, eyes tilted up to the ceiling to remember. Cate slid the autopsy report toward him, and he looked at it, finally shaking his head. "She had a small bruise on her head, in the back," he said, gesturing to his own head, "but she hit her head, I believe, when she fell down and died. They found her in an alley not far from my office."

His eyes narrowed. "Why are you so interested, Miss McCoy? You don't have enough crime in Minnesota on which to report?" His gaze held a measure of suspicion now.

Cate put the papers back into her bag and shifted away from him, nudging Andy. There wasn't much more to learn here. She rose, smiling. "The police were never able to identify the girl, Doctor?"

He pushed his plate away. His eyes looked shiny and hard, black beetles in the lumpy dough of his face. "Probably just a young whore, *senorita*, sniffing paint to escape from her misery." He shrugged. "Who knows? We have many troubled people in Tijuana. Like your cities."

Cate thanked him and turned away, eager to get out of the restaurant, but Andy's question stopped her.

"Doctor, what happened to her clothes?"

The big man curved his hands over his sated belly, the way a pregnant woman cradles her unborn child. "They're somewhere in the office. My receptionist has a soft heart, and she could not bear to throw away the girl's possessions." He snorted over his employee's sentimentality. "There was also a necklace, I think."

Cate had turned back to him. "What kind of necklace, *senor?*"

"A cross. Silver, I think." He guffawed, and Cate had the urge to mash one of his fat hands with her fist. Make it a little tougher to feel up his patients.

"And your receptionist still has it?"

"Perhaps." He shook his head, his double chins rippling. "Imagine that. A whore with a silver cross and golden fingers."

His laughter followed them out of the restaurant and into the humid Tijuana night.

April 15, 12 NOON

Edward Hamm clamped his teeth tighter around his soggy cigar and let out a bloodcurdling whoop, bringing his jet ski around in a wide circle, a plume of water shooting out behind him. He imagined the faces of the tight-asses on the shoreline and laughed to himself. He hoped that bitch who'd tried to pass a law banning jet skis was up there at her cabin this weekend, listening to his machine. It would serve her right for bringing a chain saw to the Minnesota House and revving it up right there on the floor.

He grinned, remembering her speech about peace and quiet. He'd vetoed her bill so fast it had made her head spin, and now they called her Chain saw Cahill in the halls of the capitol.

Hamm steered his jet ski into another wide turn, straight for the boat carrying his security detail. They shouted at him, waving him away as if he didn't know what he was doing. At the last second, he cut the throttle, sliding up next to the state patrol's speedboat. "Had you fooled, didn't I," he growled, climbing off the watercraft and over the side of the boat, unzipping his wetsuit to his waist. His stomach, pale and hairy, bulged through the opening.

"Governor, your chief of staff called with an urgent message about ten minutes ago. He wants you to call him back immediately."

Hamm accepted a towel from Pete Escobar and sighed hard, rubbing his thick hair and dripping beard. The lake was was icy cold. "I told Bates no work today. I'm entitled to my weekends, aren't I?"

The troopers were careful not to react. One of them handed him a cell phone, and, with a disgusted sigh, he dialed Lamar Bates' home number.

"Bates, haven't you heard that saying about all work and no play?" Hamm winked at Escobar and exchanged his towel for a Pig's Eye. He listened, finishing the beer in three swallows. "Just give them some crap about the wheels of justice turning slowly, I don't care. And for God's sake, don't tell them where I am. You got that, Bates?"

He flipped the phone closed and crumpled his beer can with his right hand, opening his palm to show them the silver disk. "That's my press secretary's career when a jury gets done with her. They just arrested Liz Barracosta for kidnapping."

Noah Hamilton burst through the back door of the newsroom to find total anarchy. His weekend assignments desk editor was standing on her chair, a phone held out of the reach of the weekend anchor, who was leaping up, trying to grab it from her. Phones were ringing on nearly every desk, and the fax machine was emitting a loud alarm, signaling the usual paper jam. Above the assignments desk, a row of television monitors showed the competition already deep into special reports.

"Megan? Jay! What the hell is going on? Why aren't we on the air like everybody else?"

"Noah! Thank God." The assignments editor climbed off her perch and slammed the phone down, giving the weekend anchor a stinging look. "I was just trying to call you."

He spun around, looking for the weekend show producer. "Where's Nicky?"

"In the bathroom, crying. Jay told her he wouldn't read the copy she wrote for the special report."

Noah spun to confront the weekend anchor and resisted the urge to kick something. Michaela's temper tantrums were legendary, and he'd vowed to do things differently if he ever got the chance. One time she'd yanked a phone right out of the wall and heaved the thing at a producer who'd dared to disagree with her about the lead story. The guy had quit the next day.

"Everyone! Please come up here to the assignments desk. We're getting our collective asses kicked on this story and that's going to end right now." He looked around the half circle of faces, including the tear-stained one of his weekend producer, who had just emerged from the bathroom.

"Nicky, please go finish the special report you were writing, and I'll edit it. I want something on the air in five minutes. Jay, get a tie on and get out

103

there to the set. Megan, start making calls to everyone you can think of—the Barracuda's attorney, the jail, Hamm's chief of staff. We're going to want a response from the governor on this."

They dispersed to their various assignments, and Noah took a deep breath. This was a hell of a time for his political reporter to be mucking around somewhere south of the border.

Adam listened to the phone ring in Cate's San Diego hotel room and wondered for the tenth time where she was. Even with the time difference, it was after eleven o'clock at night there. He imagined her and Andy surrounded by street toughs in some Tijuana alley, their cries for help ignored by the corrupt and lazy local police. He pictured himself reading some anonymous medical examiner's report in Spanish on their murders the way he had in the case Cate was pursuing.

He glanced around his darkened store, the spines of shelved books gleaming in the soft light coming in from the street. Business had been brisk tonight, and he'd been able to push Cate to the back of his mind for much of the evening. But an image of her face had returned with a vengeance when he'd locked the door and flipped the television on in his small office.

Channel Three had been in the midst of a live news conference with Chandler Coates, the attorney representing Liz Barracosta. He'd gleaned from the lawyer's comments that his client was in jail, charged with the kidnapping of Millicent Pine. A reporter had asked about police allegations that Barracosta had had an accomplice who had confessed to his role in the kidnapping. Coates replied that he was not going to comment on any alleged confessions. Adam had begun dialing San Diego right then and was still dialing three hours later.

He hung up the phone and sat down on a stool behind the counter, rubbing his leg. He'd pushed the physical therapy too far yesterday, and he'd awakened this morning, stiff and aching. The pain was a deep icy cold lodged near his spine that always brought back random images of that day nearly three years ago. His brother's blood so startlingly crimson against the white powder. The dusk coming on as they'd waited for help. Grant's face pale and still in the gray twilight.

He remembered how the snow had fallen, covering up the evidence of the accident. As he'd lain in the hospital that evening, he'd imagined skiers gliding by, unaware of the dark splotches of blood at the base of the tree, now hidden by the purity of the fresh snowfall. He'd drifted into a drug-induced sleep with the whispering *shush* of skiers in his mind.

He'd opened his eyes the next morning to find his parents bending over him. They'd told him what he already knew. Grant had died instantly of a broken neck after colliding with the tree. Then they told him something he refused to accept. That the injury he'd sustained in the fall he'd taken after watching Grant smash into the tree had done serious, perhaps permanent damage. That he would always drag his right leg behind him and would never ski or hike or even walk gracefully again.

He'd gone home to recover at his parents' house in northern Wisconsin, refusing to see any of the friends he'd grown up with, taking a long leave from his job as a salesman for a pharmaceutical company and retreating into the mystery novels he'd read casually before the accident. As the winter brought storm after storm, piling up drifts of snow, ice bringing down telephone lines and causing blackouts, he devoured his favorite authors, read the classics and delved into the work of new writers that his mother brought home from the library.

Closing the back cover of Daphne DuMaurier's *Rebecca* one night as the rest of the house slept, he knew he wasn't going back to his old job in Milwaukee or his old life, for that matter. The idea for the Sleuthsayer was born a month later when he read a newspaper article about the demise of yet another independent book store two towns away. He'd dragged himself into the place after a grueling morning with his physical therapist, glad when the proprietor had barely looked up from his inventory as he invited Adam to look around. He still hadn't gotten used to the pitying stares when people saw him approaching.

He'd hobbled up and down the stacks, pulling books out, putting some back, frustrated when he couldn't find some of the older Christies and Chandlers he'd been looking for. When he'd asked the owner about them, the man's eyes had lit up, and a friendship was begun.

Every Monday and Wednesday, Adam would limp, teeth gritted against the pain after his therapy session, into Johanneson Books, and the two men would talk until Finn Johanneson's daughter arrived from her classes at the community college to work the counter. The friends would then head for a nearby café that served happy-hour appetizers and micro-brewed beer.

By the time the fierce winter had melted into a slushy spring, he'd agreed to buy Finn's stock of mystery and intrigue novels and begun searching for a place to put them. On a visit to a surgeon in Saint Paul, he'd spotted the 'going out of business' sign in the storefront on Grand Avenue. He'd returned after his consultation with the doctor and signed a lease with the owner of the building that night.

On the trip home, he'd decided against the surgery, vowing instead to put himself back together with a stringent therapy regime and a can-do attitude. When he'd told Johanneson about the store, his friend had insisted on investing a small sum in the new project as a silent partner, his way of coming to terms with losing his own book business to the big chains. Adam's father had also come up with a sizeable investment, and his own savings account was practically zeroed out.

When the Sleuthsayer opened the following September, Adam felt as whole as he'd been since the accident, especially when he unlocked the front door every morning and glanced into the shop's bay window. Mixed in with a clever display of a detective's tools of the trade and the hottest titles of the season, was a small table, its gleaming oak top covered with books.

His mother had taken it out of Grant's apartment, careful to include the books he'd been reading in the days before they'd left for their ski trip. But the item that Adam's gaze always locked on was the pair of eyeglasses, resting on the open pages of a book about modern architecture. He imagined his older brother removing those glasses and casually tossing them onto the book, perhaps rubbing his eyes as he saw how late it was, forgetting them when he left for the airport early the next morning.

Adam thought of them as a symbol of the way his life had finally come into focus after the dark months following the accident. And he liked the idea of his brother's spirit on such public display, the true meaning of the keepsake known only to him and his family.

He shook off his reverie and picked up the phone, punching in the numbers with urgency. He wasn't going home until he reached her.

16

TIJUANA, MEXICO

April 16, 10:34 A.M.

CATE BLINKED IN THE SEARING SUNLIGHT, her tired eyes adjusting slowly from the musty darkness of the church. A dull headache throbbed at her temples, the result of only five hours of sleep. She knew Andy wasn't feeling much better. "We could be wasting our time here."

The photographer nodded, slipping a bottle of lukewarm water out of her backpack and pouring some into her mouth. "I can't believe it's so damn hot and it's only April."

Cate glanced down at the list of churches they'd gotten from the phone book at the doctor's office. Ochoa-Alvarez's receptionist had been surprisingly helpful, startled when she'd found them waiting for her as she arrived for work, but grateful they were pursuing the girl's death. She'd given them a paper bag with the girl's torn and stained clothing inside. Cate had asked about taking evidence, and the woman had pursed her lips, shooting a dark look at her boss's closed door. "He is finished with this one, and the police don't care. But there is one more thing." Opening her desk drawer, the receptionist drew out a tarnished silver cross hanging from a frayed piece of ribbon and handed it to Cate. "Find who did this, *senorita*," she'd whispered, her eyes filling with tears. "The girl deserves to rest in peace."

Cate drew the jewelry from her pocket and studied the cross again in the brassy sunshine. She'd showed it to a priest in one of the churches they'd been into, but he'd just shaken his head, not recognizing it as something one of his parishioners had worn. Cate closed her fingers over it, the silver warm in her palm. "Andy, let's go back to that church near the alley where the girl's body was found. Maybe the priest will be back by now."

Andy tucked her water bottle back into her backpack and grimaced. "This explains the dog bone on your desk, McCoy. I've finally figured it out."

Cate chuckled, looping an arm around her friend's shoulders as they crossed the street. "I've never told you where that came from?" They stepped up onto the crowded sidewalk, Cate's auburn hair and fair skin drawing stares from the Mexican men. "It came in the mail the day after Big Red Arneson was convicted for attempted bribery."

Andy glanced over at her. "The lobbyist?"

Cate nodded. "I broke the story the day before they arrested him, and he called me a bitch when I tried to get a comment from him." They walked up the shallow steps of the church. "He meant the dog bone to be insulting, of course," she said, smiling as she remembered, "but I like to think he's just mad that I sank my teeth in and wouldn't let go."

The interior of the church was dark and cool, and they could see a man in a dusty black robe kneeling in the center aisle. He was praying to a vivid figure of Jesus hanging in the front of the church, the head crowned with a realistic circlet of thorns, the pale flesh marred with bleeding wounds.

Cate and Andy sat down in one of the wooden pews and waited. When the priest was finished, they rose and approached him. "Father? *Hables Ingles?*"

His face was narrow and weathered as if he spent a lot of time away from the serene recesses of his church and out in the hot sun. "Yes, I speak English." He smiled at their reaction, gesturing them into a pew and sitting down in the one in front of them, twisting around to face them. "I attended college in New Mexico." He extended a hand. "I'm Father Cabron."

Cate introduced them and said, "Father, we're journalists from the States looking into the death of a girl whose body was found near your church. Do you remember that?"

He nodded, his mouth twisting, the long grooves in the hollows of his cheeks, deepening. "I cancelled our Wednesday night Bible classes for a while because I didn't want our young people walking home late at night." He looked at them. "Have you discovered who committed such a crime?"

Cate shook her head. "No. We haven't even been able to determine who she was. That's why we're here. We've been visiting some of the churches to see if any of the priests might recognize this." She held the necklace up, her fingers threaded through the ribbon, as he studied the cross. When he extended his hand, she put it into his palm, the jewelry fragile against his calloused skin. He studied it, turning it over.

"Did you see this?"

Cate bent forward and peered at the other side of the cross where someone had engraved two numbers divided by a colon. "I saw it but I wasn't sure what it meant."

The priest's smile was melancholy, his teeth white in the dusk. "Perhaps you should join my Sunday school class, Miss McCoy. It is a verse from the New Testament. John, Chapter nine, verse four. It speaks to laboring for the Lord, if I remember right." He reached into a pocket of his robe and withdrew a small Bible, it's black cover worn and faded. He flipped through the pages. "Here it is. 'I must work the works of Him who sent Me while it is day; the night is coming when no one can work.'"

Cate and Andy exchanged puzzled glances. "So the girl who wore this was some kind of missionary?"

The priest closed his Bible. "Not necessarily, but I wouldn't be surprised if the necklace was given to her by someone who is." He thought for a moment, a shaft of sunlight piercing the gloom and splashing ruby on his left shoulder. Cate followed the column of light up to a large stained glass window. Its opulence was startling in the plain architecture of the church.

Father Cabron noted her interest. "A gift from a rather well-known drug dealer to my predecessor." He looked up at the window, colored light slashing his face. "I think he was seeking absolution."

He shifted on the hard pew. "Do you have anything else of the girl's? Something perhaps one of my parishioners might recognize if she lived or worked near our church."

Cate shrugged, pulling the bag from Andy's backpack. "Just her clothes." She drew out a thin red blouse that was stained with a darker crimson and a pair of dusty black jeans. She handed the clothing to the priest and frowned as he took it, her attention caught by a sound. "I think there might be something in the front pocket."

The priest slipped his fingers into the denim folds, drawing out a creased square of pale blue construction paper, the kind a child might draw on. He unfolded it, his eyes widening as he studied it. "It's German, I believe. We learned a bit in the seminary." He moved his finger across the page, translating haltingly. "O hasten the hour, send down from above the spirit of power, of health and of love." He paused, struggling with the unfamiliar language. "Of . . . filial fear, of knowledge and grace. Of wisdom and prayer, of joy and of praise."

He gave the paper to Cate. "I believe it's a Mennonite or Amish prayer, Miss McCoy." His lips pursed in a slight smile. "Unlike the Catholics, the Mennonites and Amish pray simply, without a lot of fancy talk."

Cate frowned. "Why is it in German?"

"Some Mennonites still pray in German. Their history goes back to the Swiss Anabaptists who disagreed with baptizing babies. They thought baptism should be reserved for adults who understood what kind of a commitment they were making." He tilted his head, his gaze resting on the piece of paper. "The movement really emerged when Menno Simons assumed a leadership role." He half-smiled again. "Ironically, he was a former Catholic priest."

Cate and Andy looked at each other. Andy said. "I thought all Mennonites lived in Pennsylvania."

Cabron shook his head. "There is a large Mennonite community in Cuauhtemoc, near the Copper Canyon. They came here from Canada and Europe in the 1920s. There are about 50,000 of them there now."

"Mexican Mennonites, huh," Cate said, examining the childish scrawl. "I wonder why she was carrying it like that in her pocket. Not what you'd expect to find in the pocket of a prostitute, which is what the police seem to think she was."

Cabron made a dismissive gesture. "The police—You won't get much help there." He rose, curving long fingers around the gold cross that hung against his chest. "I'm afraid I must attend to some parish matters now. I hope I've helped." His dark eyes lingered on the clothing. "I wish you well in your search, Miss McCoy. Sometimes we wait a long time for justice in my country."

Governor Eddie Hamm shifted the over-sized axe from one broad shoulder to the other and conjured up his fiercest expression. The news magazine photographer chortled and crouched in front of him, firing off more than a dozen shots. "Perfect, Governor. This will be one hell of a cover."

"Governor?"

"What is it, Bates," Hamm growled as the photographer loaded more film and two stylists rushed in to powder his face.

"The Spanish ambassador is here. She's with the First Lady out on the terrace."

"Well, give her a Pig's Eye, and tell them I'll be there when I can." Hamm tilted his head back so the makeup artist could rub some gel into his beard.

"Sir," Bates said, glancing at his watch, "the press are here too, and the news conference is scheduled in five minutes."

"You planning on starting without me?" Hamm closed his eyes as the stylist ran a tiny comb through his thick eyebrows. There was a brief silence. "I didn't think so."

Hamm was still wearing his makeup when he stepped outside to the stone terrace in the rear of the house. He was twenty minutes late, and he winked at Pete Escobar, who was standing behind the media. He smirked as he saw several reporters glance pointedly at their watches.

He apologized to Ambassador Roja for his tardiness and guided the silver-haired emissary toward the podium set up at the edge of the patio.

"Good afternoon, everyone." He opened his glasses case and put on the too-small wire-rimmed spectacles. He glanced down at his notes, obviously seeing them for the first time, and read the introduction. "I'd like to welcome Ambassador Roja to Minnesota." He pronounced her name *row-jah*, giving the second syllable a Minnesota flourish. "She is staying with us here at the residence for a couple of days, and we plan to discuss some business opportunities between our state and her country." He looked up from his papers and set them aside, his mouth curved in a taunting smile. "But I know business deals, and international trade bores you reporters, so here's your lead story tonight.

"Ambassador Roja is also here to scope out the place so the king and queen of Sweden can come for a visit next month."

There was a loud cough, and Hamm turned, spearing his chief of staff with an annoyed look. Bates gestured to the governor's speech. The governor glanced down and smiled sheepishly. "I'm sorry. I meant the king and queen of Spain." He nodded to the ambassador. "Forgive me, Ambassador Roja. Maybe I need new glasses."

There was a ripple of laughter as the ambassador stepped up to the podium, a strained smile on her face. "Thank you, Governor. I appreciate your hospitality and warm welcome."

A reporter called out, "Ambassador, what exactly does 'scoping out the place' entail for the royal visit?"

Someone guffawed, and Bates shot the journalist an angry look. The ambassador said, "I am here to visit some of the places the king and queen might want to see while they're in Minnesota. The governor and I plan to discuss some economic issues that are of interest to King Juan Carlos, and we'll be coordinating a state dinner to welcome the royal couple."

A newspaper reporter said, "Why are they coming to Minnesota now?"

"They followed last November's election very closely." She tilted her head back to look up at Hamm, as if trying to see the top of a skyscraper. "The king, especially, is very intrigued by Governor Hamm." She smiled. "I should also tell you that their five-year-old grandson is a big fan of the Paul Bunyan story."

The governor laughed loudly, his face flushed with pleasure. He nudged the ambassador. "He should've been here the day I took on Big Jac Champenau." He snorted, the sound carried by the microphones. "Champion of the lumberjacks my—"

Bates broke in. "The details of the royal visit will be provided in the next couple of days. Thank you all for coming."

Chandler Coates rubbed his eyes and gritted his teeth. The three cups of coffee he'd drunk for lunch were gnawing at the lining of his stomach, and the aspirin he'd taken for his headache might as well have been sugar pills. He'd been up most of the night composing a convincing argument for bail, but the odds were against it. The cops would try to sweat Liz now that they were convinced she knew where Millicent Pine was, and the judge would likely go along with it.

Coates loosened his tie, looking up blearily as a guard led his client into the room. Liz Barracosta waited, head held high, as the guard unlocked her handcuffs and left the room. He would observe them from a small window.

The attorney looked at her. "How are you?"

She ran a hand through her silver hair, grimacing. "I've been better, Chandler, but I can tough it out until we make bail."

He looked down at the file that held the papers for her case. A case that had looked a lot better just twenty-four hours ago. "All right, I'm going to ask you once. No more lies. Who helped you that night?"

Liz looked at him, her dark eyes steady. A ceiling fan whirred. An inmate shouted in the distance. "They found him," she said, only the slightest quiver in her voice.

His heart thumped, and he remembered the murmur his doctor had mentioned last time he'd been in for his annual exam. Keep the stress to a reasonable level, he'd said. Coates stared at her.

She looked down at her clasped hands, her skin yellowish in the harsh fluorescent light.

He waited.

"I knew if I told you this, you'd never believe I had nothing to do with her kidnapping, especially after they found the notebook in my car." She sighed, as if annoyed with his distrust of her. "Then when Cate McCoy came up with the videotape I figured it was better off left unsaid."

Anger so potent it made his eyes water rushed through him, and he yanked his tie right off of his neck. "So you lied." He shook his head.

She blinked. Twice. And then said, "Yes."

He sat back in the metal chair, arms folded over his chest.

She stood up, turning her back to him, her spine rigid in the orange jail jumpsuit. "Millicent Pine left the restaurant with me that night." Her voice was low, and he strained to hear her. "But I'd had too much to drink. She even asked me about it." Liz turned around, her thin arms crossed at her waist. "While she went upstairs to her room to get her coat, I thought twice about driving after a few too many martinis. So I called a young man I pay to do things around my house. Clean the pool, water the lawn, that kind of thing."

Coates suspected she paid him for something else too, but he said nothing.

"He drove my Camaro to the hotel, left it with the valet and had them retrieve my Jaguar, the car I'd driven that night." She sat back down at the table and leaned across it, her fingers splayed on the fake wood. "I'm sure the valet is the one who told the police about Tonio's involvement. He wouldn't forget a Jag." She thought for a moment. "When we left, Tonio was driving, and Millicent and I were in the back seat."

"Go on." His voice was expressionless, his fury diminished to a bleak foreboding.

"We weren't even out of downtown Saint Paul when her cell phone rang."

Interest flickered in his eyes and Liz continued. "She had a brief conversation and hung up. She didn't say who it was, but she told us she had an emergency meeting. She insisted on being dropped off at Mears Park."

"In the middle of the night? In the dark?"

113

Liz shrugged. "It was probably around ten forty-five," she said, folding one hand over the other on the table, "but it was dark. When we drove away, she was sitting on a bench, obviously waiting for someone." She looked at him, her gaze unflinching. "Chandler, that's the last time I saw her."

17

CUAUHTEMOC, MEXICO

April 17, 4:45 A.M.

MARGUERITE PUSHED THE OLD SHUTTERS back from the window and leaned out, pulling clear air into her lungs. She was still weary from her journey into the mountains, but when dawn broke she would pack her small case and embark on another trip, this one with a very uncertain end.

She glanced at the tickets lying atop the battered chest of drawers in the corner. It had been a long time since she'd been on an airplane, perhaps fifteen years. She smiled, remembering the day she'd flown into Mexico City all of those years ago. The noise and size of the airport had been intimidating, and she'd circled the terminal for two hours trying to figure out where to catch the bus into the interior. She'd arrived in Chihuahua with eight American dollars to her name and a shaky command of the Spanish language, but God had provided, eventually leading her to this community that had become her home.

She lay down on her narrow bed, her mind whirling in the dark. She thought of her classroom with its rough wooden desks and uneven floor. If she had been teaching back in the States she would have had computers and the latest textbooks. Here, the children shared the same textbooks year after year and knew nothing of the Internet, but they were eager and dedicated students, and she found great satisfaction in teaching siblings from the same large families. She knew her own sister had never understood that.

Millicent had visited the second year she'd been here, frowning at the strict rules of the community and the suspicion with which the Mennonites regarded all outsiders, including Marguerite. "Why do you want to live here," she'd asked, her hazel eyes puzzled. "It's so . . . far from everything."

But Marguerite, who'd once contemplated entering a convent, had found peace here. She cherished the structure and the simplicity and appreciated the goodness of the people. The missionary work she did during the weeks she wasn't teaching brought her quiet joy. She lived in a small cottage and grew much of what she ate in a flourishing garden. She relished her solitude.

Marguerite closed her eyes, listening to the pre-dawn sounds of the desert, mentally bracing for the clamor of the city. She would fly from Chihuahua to Las Vegas where Della would meet her and take her to Millicent's house. That's where Marguerite would tell Della of last winter's late night phone call, the secretive and difficult journey to Tijuana, the sisters' shared outrage over such cruelty. And that's where she would try to decide what to do next.

She opened her eyes, staring up at the dark outlines of her ceiling beams. Fear trembled through her, and she stifled a sob. She would be strong. She would remember the Lord's words from Psalm 121. *The Lord is your keeper, the Lord is your shade at your right hand.*

6:50 P.M.

"Guess what Chihuahua is famous for?"

Cate rolled her eyes, turning her face toward the taxi's open window, savoring the swish of cool air on her skin. The flight south had been hot and turbulent, the airport small and crowded. But the city was a pleasant surprise. Broad boulevards were lined with palm trees, and Cate saw several wide squares filled with couples and children, enjoying the cool twilight. To the west, the Sierre Madre thrust purple and blue peaks against the darkening horizon.

"C'mon McCoy, guess."

"Those silly little hairless dogs," Cate said, prompting an amused glance from the taxi driver and a guffaw from Andy.

"Wrong. This is where Pancho Villa lived. The guy who led those revolutionaries in the early 1900s." Andy turned a page of her guidebook, reading with rapt attention. "Cool, huh?"

"A cold Dos Equis would be even cooler. I hope we're almost at the hotel."

116

A few moments later the cab turned into a small hotel, and Cate paid and tipped the driver, accepting his help with their suitcases while Andy handled her camera and other equipment. They entered a tiled lobby with a reception desk of dark polished wood at the far end. A smiling young man stood behind it.

"*Buenas tardes, senoritas.* How may I help you?"

Cate gave him their names, mentioning that they'd called from the airport. He found their card in what looked like a small recipe box, and Cate decided their system was much more pleasant than standing there while the reception clerk pounded on a keyboard for ten minutes, finally informing you that you weren't in the computer.

He handed them a key to their double room, and Cate thanked him, pausing as they were headed for the stairs. "Can you tell me the best way to get to the Mennonite community?"

"Ah. *Campos Menonitas.* It is about an hour and a half from here. You can take a tour. We'll be happy to set it up for you."

Cate hesitated, glancing at Andy. How much investigating could they really do if they were stuck with a bunch of tourists more interested in where the bathrooms were than the life and culture of the people. Then again, the cover of a tour group might be a perfect distraction. "We'd like to go tomorrow. How do we arrange that?"

The reception clerk seemed surprised that the Mennonites were at the top of their sightseeing list, but he shrugged and opened a leather-bound book, writing their names on a page. "We have a tour leaving tomorrow morning at nine o'clock. It is a professor and his students from an American college, and they have been invited to dine with a Mennonite family. Would you be interested in doing that?"

"Will they have Corona on tap?" Andy chuckled, winking when Cate shot her an exasperated look. "I'll just take my stuff upstairs, McCoy."

Cate turned back to the eager receptionist. "We'd love to do that. Thank you." Cate gathered her luggage. "Oh. One more thing. Where are the best eats in town?"

"Eats," he said, confused by the colloquialism.

"Dinner," she said. "*La cena.*"

He grinned. "You want steak or black bass?"

"Black bass? What's that?"

He scribbled a name on a piece of paper. "My cousin's place. Tell him Nicolas sent you."

The city was bathed in yellow lamplight, and the temperature had dropped considerably when Cate and Andy emerged from the restaurant. The photographer patted her stomach. "I never dreamed I'd have the best steak of my life in Mexico. Sunny would love this place."

Cate grinned sideways at her. "So not only does the love of your life ride those broncos, but he eats them too?"

Andy laughed. "Every chance he gets."

They strolled along the sidewalk, peering into the windows of small shops and coming to a plaza with a large monument at its center. Cate groaned as Andy drew her guidebook from her bag. "Pipe down, McCoy. What's the use of traveling if you don't know what you're looking at?"

They approached the huge bronze and marble creation as Andy read aloud, "This life-size figure of Padre Hidalgo and his co-conspirators is dedicated to the heroes of the War of Independence. Hidalgo's decapitated body was buried in Chihuahua's oldest church by Franciscan monks and hidden until independence was finally won. The body was then exhumed and sent to Mexico City."

"That's a lovely bedtime story." Cate stepped into the street to hail a taxi. "Which reminds me. I have to call Adam tonight to let him know what we're up to."

"I think Adam would like to tell you a bedtime story of his own, McCoy." Andy's eyes slid sideways and she smiled in the darkness.

Cate flushed, grateful when a cab darted across traffic to glide up to the curb. They got in, giving the driver the name of their hotel. Cate rolled down the window and sat back against the cheap vinyl of the back seat, the pinon-scented desert air tangling her hair. Was Andy right? Did Adam's arm's-length demeanor disguise deeper feelings for her?

She visualized the lean gauntness of his face and the lines that bracketed his mouth, deepening whenever he set his teeth against the pain. Thick lashes would shield the polished granite of his eyes, hiding those moments of agony, warning any sympathy away. She looked out of the windshield, silently urging the driver to hurry. She wanted to hear his voice.

Noah turned on the lamp in his office and collapsed into the one-size-too-small chair behind his desk. His predecessor, a twitchy, neurotic Ivy Leaguer that Michaela had eaten for lunch, had been just five-foot-five. Noah hadn't bothered to replace the furniture. No telling how long *he'd* survive his boss' carnivorous appetites.

He pushed aside a Beta tape lying in the center of his desk and propped his elbows on the blotter, dropping his head into his hands. The budget meeting with the station's general manager had been hellish, and for a moment he'd wished Michaela had been back. She had a way of smiling charmingly while she told them where they could stick their budget cuts, shareholders be damned.

He thought of his last conversation with his boss. She'd called first thing that morning, twelve hours ago, Noah realized wearily, to tell him she wouldn't be back for another week. She'd asked what was new, how several investigative projects were coming along. She'd never mentioned travel, so he hadn't brought up the trip to Mexico, especially since Cate had called to tell him they were heading south to Chihuahua.

He'd listened to her theories and approved the further expenditure, unwilling to call Cate and Andy off now. But he'd urged them to waste no time. If they broke something open down there, he might be able to deflect some of Michaela's fury.

Noah rubbed his pounding head, scanning his desktop for a bottle of aspirin, when his gaze fell on the tape he'd pushed to the side. Small and rectangular, it had a bright orange label and someone had scrawled the date and the words 'Hamm interview' in black pen on it. He frowned. He'd sent Allison Anderson to do an interview with the governor's wife today when the reporter who was supposed to do it called in sick. The story was scheduled to air tomorrow night, so why was the tape on his desk?

He leaned over and flipped on the Sony player that sat on a wooden table to his right. A viewing monitor was next to it, and as the tape locked into place, he saw a shot of Allison come up on the screen. He pressed "rewind," and the tape spun backwards until the shot changed. He stopped the tape, watching Deborah Hamm. The camera was tight on her face, and he was struck by her plain appearance. How had she and Eddie Hamm ever ended up together? She looked as if she was meant for a career in some distant college, bent over stacks of research. Must've had something to do with her money.

Noah sat back in his chair and listened to the interview, his weariness forgotten. The first lady was talking about a favorite charitable foundation when Allison abruptly shifted gears, asking Mrs. Hamm if she'd ever suspected her husband's press secretary capable of kidnapping.

Noah winced at the way the anchor asked the question, but gave Allison points for having the guts to do it. Deborah Hamm's eyes widened, and the camera shot tightened even further. "Certainly not," the first lady said, a slight flush climbing her throat. "She deserves the presumption of innocence until she's proven guilty, Miss Anderson."

The shot widened a bit more as Allison asked her next question off-camera. "Do you believe newspaper reports that Governor Hamm assaulted a prostitute in Florida when he was a young man, Mrs. Hamm?"

Deborah Hamm blanched, and Noah leaned forward, observing her embarrassment with the guilty fascination of a bystander at an accident scene. Her fingers trembled as she reached for the lapel mike clipped to her sweater. "I'm afraid I've answered all of your questions."

Noah thought she would rip the microphone off and leave in a huff, but he frowned when he heard Allison say off-camera, "Can you please wait a moment, Mrs. Hamm? We need to do one of those TV things while you're still here. It'll only take a minute."

The image on the screen jiggled as the camera and tripod were dragged around and re-positioned, this time facing Allison, the curve of Deborah Hamm's shoulder and head now visible from behind. Noah's stomach churned. He knew what Allison was going to do, and while it wasn't exactly unethical, it was the kind of smarmy reporter tactics he'd seen only in the most tabloid newsrooms.

He shook his head, eyes glued to the screen, as Allison waited for her cue from her photographer. When she'd apparently gotten it, she leaned forward, her eyes intent, her mouth curved downward into a hard line. "Did you ever suspect Liz Barracosta, a woman known to some associates as the Barracuda, capable of kidnapping, Mrs. Hamm?"

Noah covered his eyes. He couldn't imagine what the first lady's reaction to this had been, watching the anchor play-act the question again, so the camera could catch it this time. Allison waited a few seconds and then, eyes blazing, rapped out, "News reports say your husband assaulted a hooker back in his soldier days, Mrs. Hamm. What do you think of that?"

Deborah Hamm was rising, gasping with fury, when Noah stopped the tape.

April 18, 9:16 A.M.

The sun had burned off any lingering coolness by the time the bus approached *Campos Menonitas,* and the shade beneath acres of green-leafed apple trees looked inviting as they rumbled into the center of the community. A woman dressed in a plain dark dress, her hair covered with a lace cap, approached the bus and welcomed them with a shy smile as the passengers disembarked, looking curiously around them.

"Everything cool with credit card-cam," Cate murmured as she and Andy trailed after the students and their professor. The kids had chattered loudly during the hour and a half ride from Chihuahua to the settlement, while Cate and Andy strategized in low voices.

Andy nodded, whispering, "I'm trying to save battery power so let me know when you want me to turn it on." They followed the college students into a large hardware store, its dim interior filled with tools and farming implements, many of them obviously hand-crafted. Cate ran her fingers over the satiny finish of a roll-top desk and grinned at Andy. "Think this would fit in Noah's office? We're going to owe him big after Snow gets done with him."

They emerged with the group back into the bright sunshine and listened as their Mennonite guide gave them a brief history of the settlement. Cate's gaze scanned the area as the woman described how Mennonites had traveled from Europe and Canada in the 1920s, settling on more than a hundred thousand acres of some of the most fertile land in Mexico. She told them that the farmers grew most of the country's apples and seedless watermelons and produced delicious cheese.

Cate spotted a large building with long windows and a double door and nudged Andy, who'd been listening raptly to the history lecture. The photographer frowned, following Cate's nod. "The school, I'll bet." They'd planned to try to question discreetly any Mennonite children they came into contact with about the prayer.

But the rest of the day passed in a blur of visits to the dairy, the orchard, and a Mennonite home, where the family shared a simple lunch of bread and cheese and whole milk with the students. By dinnertime, Cate was sunburned and dispirited, and the constant tittering of the college students was getting on her nerves. She'd seen a couple of the co-eds eyeing a young man who was grooming a horse, his white shirt plastered to his skin. Cate had stared hard at them, and they'd turned away, blushing. The only other young people she'd glimpsed had been from a distance as they left the schoolhouse and returned home to their chores.

"We've got to figure out a way to approach some of these kids, Andy," she said as they were invited into a home for the evening meal. This time, the group had been split up, the students divided between two other homes, Cate and Andy and the professor together in the third.

The family gestured for them to be seated, and they gathered around a large table. Cate counted seven children as everyone bowed their heads for grace. As the father began a lengthy prayer, Cate surreptitiously studied the two oldest children. They appeared to be around fifteen and sixteen years old. Cate noticed the callouses on the young man's hands and the girl's simple hair style and cosmetic-free skin. They were quiet and respectful with none of the disdain that the teen-agers she saw at the mall seemed to have for anyone over twenty-five. She wondered how they'd react if she tried to question them.

The meal was enjoyable, the conversation kept lively by the professor, who peppered the family with questions about their customs and beliefs. They answered graciously, passing large plates of meat and corn tortillas and fresh vegetables to the visitors. When they'd finished, Cate and Andy gathered up the dishes, and carried them into the kitchen to a large deep sink. The mother followed, refusing to permit them to help wash up, shooing them outside into the soft evening air.

Andy said she was going to walk off her dinner. Cate stepped out to a small stone patio behind the house, the scent of herbs borne on a light breeze from the family's garden. She stood there, feeling frustrated and out of sorts, unable to believe they'd learned nothing during the entire day. "*Senorita?*"

Cate turned to see the oldest girl behind her, the setting sun warm on her face. She was beautiful, with eyes the blue of her Eastern European ancestors, her hair the deep coarse black of her Mexican mother.

"Yes?"

"Mama wishes to know if you would like apple pie for dessert."

Her diction was accented but precise, and Cate smiled. "Your English is very good. You must make your teacher proud."

The girl blushed. "Senorita Marguerite is—" she struggled for the word, "wonderful. But she is on a trip right now. Brother Juan is teaching us."

Cate's eyebrows rose. She was under the impression that the Mennonites rarely traveled far from home. She looked at the girl, her heart beating fast.

122

What if she told her parents the *senorita* was asking questions. But what if the girl knew something, and Cate didn't ask. She took a deep breath. "Isabel. Do you have an *amiga* who went on a trip and didn't come back?"

The girl's mouth tightened, and her eyes filled with tears. A stream of rapid-fire Spanish burst from her mouth, and then she whirled around and was gone. Cate could only stare after her.

18

Chihuahua, Mexico

11:22 P.M.

"THINK, McCOY! WHAT DID SHE SAY?" Andy tossed the Spanish dictionary on the bed and sighed in frustration. They'd been trying to reconstruct what Isabel had said to Cate for two hours but had had little success. Cate had been so surprised at the girl's outburst that the flood of Spanish had just washed over her.

She rose and padded across the cool tiles of the hotel floor in her bare feet, going to the window to peer out into the darkness. Her brain was tired from the traveling and trying to puzzle out the story, but she felt too restless to sleep. "We're on the right track, Andy. We can't go back until we figure this out."

Andy stretched out on her bed, rubbing her eyes. "That reminds me. The desk clerk called while you were in the shower. Noah wants us to call him at home tonight."

Cate groaned. "What am I going to tell him? That I have a gut feeling we're headed in the right direction but right now I have zero to show for it?"

"He'll understand, Cate."

"He might, but Snow won't." Cate dug in her purse for her calling card and dialed her executive producer's home number. His voice sounded groggy when he answered. "Noah, it's Cate. Did I wake you?"

"It's after midnight, Cate. Where have you been?"

Cate swallowed, reluctant to spill the bad news right away. "We've been working on something and just got a free minute." She heard the rustle of linens and imagined him sitting up in bed.

"Have you come up with anything?"

Cate sighed. "Not really, but we're close, Noah. I can feel it."

He let out a muffled curse. "Cate, let me tell you what I can feel. The dragon queen's hot breath on my ass. Michaela's coming back. She'll be here the day after tomorrow. You've got to have something by then."

"I understand." Cate scooped up the remote control and flipped over to CNN, her mind barely registering what was on the screen. "What's going on with the Barracuda's case?"

"She's in jail, charged with kidnapping. They arrested her a couple of days ago."

Cate's stomach churned. Not only did she have nothing to show for her trip, but she was missing a huge story back home. "Were we on top of it?"

There was a brief silence. "I wouldn't quite say that."

But Cate's attention was no longer on the conversation. She was staring at the television screen where a story about the drowning of a pair of twins was being reported. The locator in the bottom left corner said "Hermosa Beach, California." "Noah? I've got to go."

Marguerite Pine woke in her sister's bed and sat up in confusion, her heart racing as she looked around at the strange furnishings. It was ten seconds before it came back to her, the dawn trip into Chihuahua, the cramped flight to Las Vegas, the shrieking slot machines in the airport. She rolled over and looked at the clock, shocked to see that it was after ten. She usually had half of her morning chores done by now back home.

The thought brought a pang to her heart. How long would she be away from her garden and her books and her students? Running a hand through her tousled hair, she swung her legs over the edge of the bed and took a deep breath. She and Della had talked until well past midnight, sharing what they knew, anguishing over what they didn't. They'd agreed that it would be a waste of time to go to Minnesota, but Della planned to call the investigator up there again today.

Better, they'd decided, to work together here trying to piece together what had happened after the sisters had last seen each other in Tijuana. Marguerite crossed the bedroom and went into the bathroom, remembering anew that she would not have to haul water from the well for her morning bath. Smiling wryly, she turned on the tap and shed her clothes, shivering with pleasure as she stepped under the steaming water.

Her sister lived well; her house a testament to the high fees she was earning as a freelance journalist. Marguerite had been surprised, though, when she'd put down roots after so many years of traveling. Perhaps Della had played a part in that, although Millicent had rarely spoken of her personal life.

Marguerite let the water pour over her head and reached for a bottle of her sister's shampoo, squeezing the gel into her palm as she thought of the name her sister had made for herself. Their parents had been appalled when Millicent had emerged as an influential activist in the women's movement, marching and demonstrating at large rallies, writing scathing articles about the domination of men in corporate America, pushing hard for the ill-fated Equal Rights Amendment.

In the eighties, she'd roamed the world, writing provocative pieces about the fate of women in Africa, the anguish of mothers in China who were urged to abort female fetuses, the grinding poverty on reservations in the southwest.

But Millicent had seemed to mellow a bit over the last five or six years, Marguerite thought, rinsing her long hair. She'd stayed home more, writing long analysis pieces for national magazines, getting more involved in American politics again. When Marguerite had called last December, she'd been surprised to find her sister at home.

She stepped out of the shower and wrapped her hair in one of her sister's towels, looking into the large mirror over the sink. Millicent had stood here, she thought, noting the evidence of her aging, the outward signs that she was no longer the young idealist who'd stirred thousands with her spoken and written words. But she would have missed what Marguerite still saw in the set of her sister's jaw, in the steadiness of her gaze.

Millicent had been born to right wrongs.

April 19, 9:58 a.m.

It was cooler than the day before, the sun veiled by a thin cloud cover, when they paid off the taxi and got out in front of the general store they'd shopped in yesterday. A woman, clad in a long dark dress, gave them a hard look as she entered the store with her two children.

Andy glanced around the quiet square. "Do you think they'll just let us wander around or should we wait until someone shows up to ask us what we're doing?"

Cate murmured, "Hold your horses. Looks like we've already been spotted." She smiled as the man who'd hosted them in his home for last night's meal approached, whispering, "Remember our story."

"*Senoritas*," he said, puzzlement creasing his sunburned forehead. "I didn't know you were returning."

Cate stepped forward, reaching a hand out to shake his. "*Senor* Bertel, please forgive us for coming back unannounced, but we decided to just take a chance." His dark brows drew together in confusion. "You see, we're researchers who are very interested in your excellent school, and we wondered if we might watch your students at work. We weren't able to do that yesterday, and the college kids, well, you saw how they were." She looked at him knowingly, and his eyes thawed a bit. "We would be so grateful if we could visit your school while the children were working. Would that be possible?" She smiled pleadingly, hoping he'd have the authority to grant the request without consulting anyone.

He pushed his flat-brimmed straw hat back and wiped his mouth with the back of one hand. Cate saw that his palms were split with deep cracks blackened by soil. "I would have to ask Brother Juan if it was permissible. Will you please wait here?"

"Yes, we will. Thank you." They watched as he headed for the large building with the double doors they'd seen yesterday.

"Do you really think this will work, Cate?" Andy shielded her eyes as the sun edged out from behind a dark-rimmed cloud.

"Who knows?" Cate shrugged, looking at her. "But I'm sure that's what Isabel said last night. *Se hermano*. 'Her brother,' when I asked her about a friend who'd gone on a trip. She must've said *se hermano* four times and it stuck in my mind."

"What if Isabel told her family about your questions?"

Cate pushed her hair back and took a swallow from the water bottle she'd shoved into her purse. "I don't think she did, Andy. Her father would've been much more suspicious toward us today." She screwed the cap back on the bottle. "Careful. Here he comes."

"*Senoritas*, Brother Juan is honored that you wish to visit his school. He asks that you sit in the back, and he will talk with you when the children break for their noon meal."

"*Gracias, Senor* Bertel. Thank you for your help."

They followed him to the school and slipped inside, sitting down on crude wooden benches behind children of all ages. The teacher, a tall slim man with deep-set eyes and a sprinkling of silver in his hair, was speaking German and gesturing to the chalkboard. The students appeared to be learning about agriculture from the drawings of trees and vegetables on their papers.

Cate's gaze roamed over the bent heads, wondering which might be the brother of the girl who'd disappeared. Was it the same girl who'd turned up in the Tijuana alley, her clothing cheap and modern, so different from the conservative dress Cate had seen around here? Or was she so eager for a break in the story that she was connecting the dots where there were no connections?

The teacher strolled between the rough wooden desks, whispering to individual students in a mixture of Spanish and German, as they worked on their papers. When he finished, he went to the far corner of the room, and Cate saw that three older students were gathered there, apparently studying something different from the rest of the class. Two boys and a girl were reading from a Bible, the girl reading aloud while the boys listened. Cate saw the oldest boy's eyes flicker over her and then quickly go back to the pages in front of him.

Forty-five minutes passed as the students worked quietly. Andy murmured, "They ought to send some of those brats at my nephew's school down here. They could use the discipline."

Cate smiled, catching the eye of the boy who seemed most curious about them.

At twelve-thirty, the teacher opened the doors, and the students streamed out. Cate nodded to Andy, and the photographer quickly made her way to the front of the classroom, introducing herself to Brother Juan and giving him their cover story of being academic researchers. Cate stepped out into the warm sunshine and scanned the yard for Isabel, spotting her with a couple of her friends under a large apple tree.

The girls stopped chattering and Isabel put her head down shyly as Cate approached. "*Buenas dias, muchachas,*" Cate said, exhausting her command of Spanish.

The girls tittered. "*Buenas dias, Senora.*"

Cate glanced around, making sure Andy was still distracting the teacher, when she spotted the older boy standing behind her. His Bible was loosely crooked in one arm, his eyes somber beneath the shade of his straw hat. "*Buenas dias,*" she said, walking toward him.

He nodded, saying nothing.

"May I speak to you for a moment?"

He studied her, muscles almost visibly bunched, ready to flee like a white-tailed deer sensing danger.

Cate halted a few inches from him. "Can you tell me what happened to your sister," she said in a low voice.

His eyes widened, and he tipped his head forward, his expression hidden by the brim of his hat. She wondered if he was thinking about it when his mouth wrenched open and he let out a strange gasp, dropping his Bible onto the dusty ground.

"Esteban no *hable, Senora.*" Cate whirled to find Isabel and her two friends behind her.

"He can't speak English?"

One of the other girls shook her head. "He cannot speak, S*enora.* Not since his sister left." Her English was halting but understandable.

"What happened to his sister?"

The girls looked at one another and then at Esteban who was looking back with wide dark eyes. "She went to the fields and she . . ." The girl's voice trailed off, and she looked to her friends for help. "She not come back."

Cate frowned. "To the fields?"

Isabel nodded. "*El norte.*"

"Norte . . . norte," Cate murmured, wracking her brain for the translation. "North! She went north to the fields?"

"*Si, Senora.* To north."

Esteban was still standing slightly apart from them, listening, and Cate gave him a sympathetic smile, thinking of more questions. She searched the young faces, about to speak, when Brother Juan came out of the school doors, followed closely by Andy, an apologetic expression on her face. The students scattered, skipping off to their midday meals and chores, and Cate swallowed her frustration, turning to greet the teacher with an admiring smile. "Your students are delightful, *Senor,* and so eager to tell me what they've learned."

He smiled proudly. "Unfortunately, I can only have them in the mornings this time of the year. There is too much work to be done in the fields." His English was excellent.

Cate seized the opportunity. "Do some of the families travel north to work in the fields up there?"

He studied her, the sun picking out the chrome flecks in his short hair. He finally nodded. "Many of our families travel to Canada for migrant work in the late spring and return in the fall. There is a large Mennonite community in Canada, as well."

Cate swallowed, calculating how to ask her next question. "Did something happen to one of the girls last year while she was in Canada?"

His eyes hardened, and Cate cursed silently. "We are a very private community, *Senorita*. What happened last year . . . it is not your concern." He opened his arms. "Now if you'll allow me to escort you back to the store, I believe we can call a taxi for you."

Cate emptied the last drops of water into her parched mouth and stared restlessly out at the passing scenery. She'd been on the verge of learning some key information and now she was in trouble. They couldn't go back to *Campos Menonitas* without raising serious suspicion, and what she'd learned today wasn't enough to give her their next lead. She sighed with frustration. "Maybe we should just give up on the whole thing, Andy, and head for the beach. Blend up margaritas at some Cancun bar."

"One for you, two for me," Andy chuckled. "Think we'd ever get tired of tequila?"

"Your hotel, *Senoritas*."

They paid the taxi driver and went into the lobby, waving wearily at the clerk behind the reservation desk.

"Let's get our suits on and hit the pool."

"Miss McCoy?"

Cate paused at the bottom of the wide staircase. "Yes?"

The clerk was carrying a folded piece of hotel stationery. "You received a call from Minnesota today. Here is the message."

Cate thanked him and took the paper, opening it with a strong sense of foreboding. The message read: 'Return immediately. Expenses denied. M. Snow.'

Cate crumpled it in her hand. "Andy, we're screwed."

19

SAINT PAUL, MINNESOTA

April 20, 8:24 A.M.

"THAT PRICK!"

The governor's bodyguards glanced at each other in the front seat of the car and exchanged frowns.

"How about if we just turn it off, Governor?"

"No! Leave it on. I want to hear what that jerk is saying about me."

Lamar Bates kept his eyes on the file in front of him, trying to tune out the morning drive jock who was roasting Hamm alive on his show. The governor was on his way to deliver a speech to a group of venture capitalists, and he'd only skimmed the text once. "Do you want to read through this again, governor, before we get to the convention center?"

"What I really want to do is wring that flabby fatmouth's neck, Bates. Can you arrange that?"

The bodyguards laughed loudly, quieting abruptly as Bates speared the back of their beefy necks with an angry stare. "Don't let it bother you, Governor. Remember your latest job approval ratings."

Hamm sat back against the plush leather, mollified for the moment by the memory of his spectacular poll numbers. Seventy-six percent of Minnesotans surveyed said he was doing a good to excellent job. His numbers were higher than either of his two predecessors at any time during their administrations. He must be doing something right.

Bates glanced at him, judging the timing. "Governor, I have one other item to mention . . ."

Hamm broke in. "Hey, look at that!" He pointed out the window to a large billboard. "The Powerball is up to eighty-eight million dollars."

The older of the two bodyguards chuckled. "Boy, I'd buy me one heck of a fishing boat with that chunk of change."

"Fishing boat," Hamm snorted. "You could buy yourself a hellacious yacht." He closed his eyes, leaning his head against the leather seat. "I'd take that money and sail around the world a few times. The hell with letting them send me annual checks, either. I'd want the lump sum."

Bates cleared his throat. "Governor?"

Hamm's eyes snapped open, annoyance creasing his face. "Yeah?"

"You may be called to testify at Liz Barracosta's preliminary hearing."

"Christ, Bates!" He caught the eye of the driver in the rearview mirror. "Turn that shit off." The radio went dead. He looked at his chief of staff. His face was flushed an annoyed pink. "Why?"

Bates licked his lips. "Well, it's complicated, sir."

Hamm turned toward him, his thick neck constricted by his buttoned collar. "Give me the short version."

"The preliminary hearing decides whether there is enough evidence to try the suspect for the crime. Miss Barracosta," Bates said, his thin nostrils quivered with distaste, "is claiming that she told you the morning after her meeting with Ms. Pine that you should consider doing an interview with the reporter."

Hamm thought for a moment. "She might've mentioned something about that. I told her to forget it. So what?"

The leather crackled softly as Bates shifted. "Governor, her lawyer is asking why she would've warned you about a potential interview if she already knew Millicent Pine was out of the picture."

"Unless she's smarter than we think, Bates. Maybe she's even smarter than you." He drew his reading glasses from his pocket and put them on as the car swung into the convention center entrance. "Here, let me look at that speech." He glanced at the printed page, then up at Bates. "You tell them if they want me in that courtroom, they gotta send over a peon."

Bates pressed his lips together as one of the bodyguards said over his shoulder from the front seat, "I think you mean a subpoena, sir."

Hamm nodded. "That's what I said."

Bates swallowed. "I'll convey that message, Governor."

The Sierra Madre were indigo silhouettes against the evening sky when Cate and Andy strolled down a narrow side street, in search of a small restaurant suggested by the hotel's desk clerk. Cate looked around, her mouth drawn into a grim line, as business owners closed their shops for the night.

Andy nudged her. "C'mon, McCoy. Lighten up. You're giving me indigestion with that face."

Cate shook her head. "It feels like our timing has been off since we started on this story, Andy."

Andy frowned as they sidestepped a man rolling his garbage can to the curb. "What do you mean?"

"I'm not sure. I just . . . I can't explain it, but it's like we're never in the right place at the right time on this one."

They stepped off the sidewalk to make room for an oversized baby carriage and Cate paused, grasping the photographer's arm. "Andy. At the corner."

Andy peered through the blue dusk. "Looks like a family from the Mennonite camp."

Cate drew her behind a rusting station wagon parked at the curb as they watched a man unload small boxes from an old pickup truck and carry them into a grocery store.

"I think the boxes say cheese in Spanish," Andy said, digging through her backpack for her Spanish dictionary.

Cate nodded. "Oh yeah, the dairy. I think I was asleep when we hit that landmark on the tour."

Andy glared at her. "I thought it was interesting."

Cate leaned over the hood of the car, trying to see who was sitting in the cab of the truck. "That looks like the girl I was talking to at the school today. Not Isabel, but one of her friends."

"What should we do?"

Cate lifted her chin. "We've got nothing to lose. Let's go."

They approached the truck. "I'm going to try to talk to her. Will you go inside and ask the father about his cheese?"

Andy grimaced. "Why do I always have to be the decoy while you do the cool stuff?"

"Do you think being felt up by that masher of a doctor in Tijuana was cool?"

"Point taken," Andy said, "although I haven't heard the word masher for a long time." She held her hands up. "Okay, okay. I'm going."

When she'd disappeared into the grocery store, Cate walked up to the truck's open window and smiled at the girl. *"Buenas tardes.* Remember me?"

The girl nodded, peering anxiously over Cate's shoulder for her father.

"I'm Cate." She put her hand into the window, and the girl shook it lightly. "What's your name?"

"Rosa," the girl said shyly, not so brave without her friends.

Cate leaned into the truck, praying Andy was learning the history of Mennonite cheese inside. "Rosa, today at your school you said that something happened to Esteban's sister when she went up north."

The girl nodded, her two dark braids bouncing on her chest.

"Do you know what happened?"

"She got sick," the girl whispered.

"In Canada?"

The girl shook her head. "She ran away."

Cate bit her lip, stifling the urge to rush the girl. "She ran away on the way up to Canada?"

"Si."

"Do you know where she went?"

Rosa's dark gaze searched for her father behind Cate. "They said she went with Gerte."

Cate leaned further into the truck. "Who is Gerte, Rosa?"

"Her cousin, I think."

"And where was Gerte?"

The girl shrugged.

Cate thought for a moment, her mind racing. "How do you know Esteban's sister was sick?"

"Senorita Marguerite brought her home." Rosa crinkled her nose. "But Estella . . . *es morte.* She died." Tears welled up in her eyes, and Cate put a comforting hand on her shoulder.

"I'm sorry, Rosa. I didn't know." She watched tears trickle down the girl's cheeks. "Estella was her name?"

"Si."

Cate glanced over her shoulder as she heard voices approaching. Leaning back in toward the girl, she said, "Is Marguerite Esteban and Estella's mother?"

The girl shook her head. "No. She is our teacher."

Cate held up a wide, shallow glass filled to the brim with tequila and lime juice and touched it to the rim of Andy's glass. "Cheers. To being in the right place at the right time."

"How quickly the tide turns, eh, McCoy?"

Cate took a deep swallow and set her glass down, looking around the restaurant. "Okay, so I can be a bit of a drag when things aren't going my way, Andy. But you have to admit the pressure is on."

"Just because the Snow Queen has cut off our expense account, we still don't know crap about what we're digging up down here, and you've got a case of Montezuma's revenge?" Andy crunched a tortilla chip. "You worry too much."

"Somebody has to." Cate paused as the waiter put their meals in front of them. "Good thing Mexican food is cheap." She cut into her enchilada. "Let's lay out what we know so far."

"Okay." Andy took a large bite of her chimichanga and chewed it happily. "Delish. All right. We know that Millicent Pine was working on something involving the murder of that girl in Tijuana."

Cate nodded. "Right. And we know that she interrupted that story to come to Minnesota to turn a piece about Eddie Hamm."

"That's Governor Hamm to you," Andy said, taking a mouthful of her drink.

Cate smiled. "Remember the time he got so mad during an interview that he threatened to have the Highway Patrol put me under surveillance?"

"Not that you ever speed or anything."

"Anyway," Cate said, sipping her margarita. "Millicent Pine had been investigating the murder of the girl with the gold paint on her fingers."

"Don't forget about the tape."

"The tape." Cate acknowledged, licking salt from her lips. "Somehow that taped interview is linked to the girl in the autopsy report. We know that they're not the same girl. The voice on the tape is much younger than the murder victim." Cate looked at Andy. "You know what I think?"

"What?"

"I think the girl in the alley was this Gerte that Rosa mentioned tonight."

"That's kind of a leap. How did you come up with that?"

"Well, we know that the alley victim had some connection to the Mennonite community from the prayer she was carrying in her clothing."

"How do we know that it wasn't Estella? The boy's sister?"

Cate pushed her plate away and leaned back in her chair, looking around. She liked the ambience of the small restaurant with its lazy ceiling fans and walls full of unusual photographs. "Because Rosa said that Estella was brought back to Cuauhtemoc by her teacher. She apparently died some time after that."

Andy finished her drink and signaled the waiter for coffee. "I wonder where the teacher is? I didn't get the impression that the Mennonites travel much further than Chihuahua."

Cate said, "If we could talk to that teacher, we wouldn't be sitting here playing guessing games." She pushed her hair back behind her ear and cupped her chin in her hand. "Rosa said that Estella got sick, but she didn't seem to know any specifics. I think they kept this very hush-hush out there, even among themselves."

The waiter delivered their coffees, and Andy stirred sugar into hers. "Cate," she said, the spoon frozen in her hand. "What if the autopsy is Gerte and the audio tape is Estella? If the girls were together, wouldn't it make sense that Millicent Pine would have been digging up information on both of them?"

Cate's eyes widened. "Andy, that's it." She scrabbled through her bag, drawing the translation of the taped interview out of it and laying it on the table. She scanned it quickly. "I'll bet Estella wasn't 'sick' when her teacher brought her back here. She was *injured* from the attack in the desert." She put her finger on the translated sentence. "She tells Pine that she was in a car and that the driver raped and beat her." Cate read further. "She says she woke up in the desert and saw *el arbol de Navidad*." Cate glanced up at Andy. "For you English-speakers, that's a Christmas tree."

"Thanks," Andy said dryly.

"God, Andy! Here it is." She turned the paper around so that the photographer could follow along. "At the end she says, 'Gerte is dead . . . She saw them.' I forgot about that!" She grinned at her friend. "You're a genius."

Andy pulled some pesos out of her pocket and laid them on the table. "So where does that leave us?"

Cate stuffed the translation back into her purse and stood up. "Back to Tijuana. We need to know what those girls were doing there and where they lived." She paused. "I also want to know how they were supporting themselves."

Andy followed her out of the restaurant into the cool night air. "How are we going to do that?"

Cate looked at her. "I figured my genius *amigo* would think of something."

Dawn was painting the Sierra Nevada range a warm gold when they checked out of their hotel, Cate grimacing as she put the charges on her credit card. They took a taxi to the train station and just made the first one headed north to Tijuana. Settling back against the cracked upholstery for the long trip, Cate let her mind drift, an image of Adam filling the vacuum. She'd called him late last night to tell him how she'd begun to put the pieces together, but they hadn't talked long. His voice sounded strained, as if it had been one of his bad days with his leg, and she'd told him she'd call again when they got to Tijuana.

She closed her eyes, lulled by the rocking of the train and the memory of his shuttered gaze the morning he'd told her she reminded him of autumn.

20

Tijuana, Mexico

April 22, 4:56 P.M.

THE PRIEST'S EYES WIDENED WHEN HE SPOTTED them silhouetted in the church's old doorway, dusty late afternoon sun at their backs. Knots of worshippers stood in the aisle, gossiping, after the four o'clock mass, and he brushed by them, his eyes wary as he approached. "Miss McCoy, isn't it?"

Cate nodded. "Yes, Father. Do you have a few minutes to talk?"

The priest gestured for them to follow, and they trailed him up the center aisle and into a small office tucked behind the ornate altar. "I gather you've discovered something more about the girl in the alley," he said, waving them into hard wooden chairs.

Cate glanced at Andy. "We think so, but we need your help again."

Cabron's fingers worked a dark-beaded rosary. "I'll do what I can."

Cate leaned forward, elbows on her thighs, her hands clasped. "Father, we think the victim in the alley was a Mennonite girl who slipped away from her family as they were traveling north last summer. We were told that they go up to Canada for migrant work every year." She paused, her throat dry. "Excuse me, but do you have any water? The sun and the dust . . ."

He rose quickly, pouring cold water from a ceramic pitcher into glasses shaped like wine goblets. Cate thanked him and sipped, continuing, "We believe the girl's name was Gerte. We also think she was accompanied by another girl, her cousin, Estella."

138

His eyebrows rose. "You think these girls ran away?"

Cate nodded. "Gerte might've been seventeen or so, but we think Estella was closer to fifteen or sixteen years old."

"*Dios*," he murmured, slipping the rosary into a pocket of his robe. "What happened to Estella, then, after her cousin was killed?"

Andy said, "We're pretty sure that Estella is the girl in an interview taped by a journalist who was investigating Gerte's murder. We think Estella died several weeks after the interview. She'd been raped and beaten pretty severely."

He frowned, clearly puzzled. "So you are helping another journalist . . . ?"

Andy glanced at Cate. "It's kind of complicated."

Cate added, "We're following up on this other reporter's work because she can't, at the moment. That's why we've come to you."

He waited.

"We're trying to figure out where these girls lived and how they were making enough money to eat. We started in this neighborhood since that's where Gerte was found dead."

Andy said, "Chances are she was killed somewhere in the vicinity of where she lived or worked."

Cabron smoothed the front of his robe. "Perhaps another plea to the congregation for help." He tucked the rosary away. "I will discuss it at the close of Sunday mass."

"Thank you, Father." Cate scribbled a number on the back of her business card. "This is where we're staying. Please call if you come up with anything."

By sundown, they'd visited more than a dozen rooming houses, mentioning the names of the girls to uninterested landlords, gladly escaping the dark and seedy interiors for the hot sunshine. "This is needle and a haystack time, McCoy," Andy said, rubbing her eyes as they paused on the sidewalk, the temperature finally cooling as twilight set in. "There must be five hundred boarding houses in this five block area."

Cate nodded, frustration welling up in her chest. They were running out of time. She could fend off the Snow Queen for only so long before her job was in jeopardy. "It would help if we had a picture of one of them. How do we know they didn't use different names?"

"I kind of doubt it," Andy said. "Even though they were trying to hide from their families, I'll bet they weren't very sophisticated about it." She took a sip of tepid water from the half-empty bottle in her backpack. "What's our next plan?"

Cate looked around. "Well, a lot of these businesses are opening again after siesta. Let's drop in on some of the food shops, maybe even the laundries around here. If they lived in this area for four months, someone saw them, maybe . . ." Cate's voice trailed off as she followed Andy's gaze to a nearby bus stop. Dozens of passengers were disembarking from a large, noisy bus, many of them young women apparently arriving home from their jobs.

Cate and Andy trotted toward the bus, catching the driver just as he was closing the door. Cate said, "You talk to him. Your Spanish is better."

Andy leaned into the opening, smiling up into the driver's impatient face. "Senor? *Yo soy* . . . uh . . . looking for *dos mujeres* who rode your bus every day."

The driver spewed a mouthful of annoyed Spanish at her and pulled the lever, closing the door. "So much for that" Andy said, watching the bus as it pulled out into traffic.

"Yeah, but I think you've got something here." Cate said, peering through the gathering dusk at the clusters of young women walking away from the bus stop. "This is the closest stop to the alley where Gerte was killed. What if she was walking home from the bus when she was attacked? Maybe some of the girls who ride the bus every day will remember her and Estella." She glanced at her watch. "I wonder what time the first bus leaves in the morning?"

Andy sighed. "If we're going to be back here at sunrise tomorrow, McCoy, it's time for a plate of enchiladas and some sack time. I'm beat."

They walked back past Father Cabron's church, skirting a plaza where mariachis were playing, and turning down a narrow street in search of a restaurant. Andy paused to read the menu posted outside a small eatery.

She shook her head and set off again, turning to Cate as they strolled. "You think it was the girls' teacher that called Millicent Pine and got her down here?"

Cate nodded. "I think the Mennonite teacher knew Millicent Pine somehow, either personally or from her writings. Think about how many tip calls I get from people who say 'I saw you on television and knew you'd be interested in this story.'" She shrugged. "Most of the time it's crap, but every now and then there's a juicy story in there. I think Millicent knew she was onto something."

140

"Then why did she drop it to come do the story on the Big Hamm?" Andy steered her into a small restaurant that had a large fish hanging by a hook in the front window.

"I thought you wanted enchiladas." Cate said, following Andy inside. As they waited to be seated, she said, "I think Pine believed that stuff from West Palm Beach about old Eddie was too good to pass up. She probably figured she'd be back to this story pretty quickly." At the table, Cate gave her drink order to the waiter and picked up the menu, eyeing Andy over the top of it. "Her ambition may've gotten the better of her."

Large raindrops splattered on the governor's head, curving sideways to drip into his beard, and he glared up at the gray skies. He was standing at the edge of the memorial site, mud caking his shoes, as Pete Escobar described the progress he'd made so far. Not much, thought Hamm. Holes had been dug for the arch footings, but the ground remained raw and barren, and the governor exhaled impatiently. "Pete, I want this done by the time the king and queen come next month. What's holding things up?"

Escobar stared down at the dirt. "Cash. The money isn't coming in like we thought it would."

Hamm thought for a moment and put a hand on his friend's shoulder. "Don't let it get you down, pal. I've got an idea."

Escobar waited, rain sparkling in his brush cut.

"Those movie people are set to start filming any day now. How 'bout if I get them to come to a little memorial fund raiser at the mansion, bring along a few of the actors. Deborah can throw something together."

"Do you really think they'd do that?" Escobar wiped moisture from his face.

"Hell, yes, they'll do it, Pete. Don't forget about that tax break I pushed through the legislature for movie productions here." He curled an arm around the other man's shoulders. "They owe me. Now, let's get out of the damn rain."

April 23, 6:23 A.M.

Clad in jeans and mini-skirts, cigarette smoke curling into their ponytails, the cluster of girls at the bus stop watched Cate and Andy approach with wary suspicion. The smell of diesel fumes and frying cornmeal hung in the air, and shopkeepers were raising their metal security doors with loud clangs. The sun looked like tarnished brass through the morning smog.

"*Buenas dias, senoritas,*" Cate said, her smile met by a dozen bland expressions. "Does anyone speak English?"

No one answered.

Andy said, "We were hoping you could help us. Do any of you remember the girl who was found dead in the alley last December? Near the church?"

A ripple of recognition so subtle it was almost imperceptible swept through the group, but, again, no one replied.

Cate said, "We're trying to figure out what happened to her. Do any of you know where she lived or worked?"

Stony silence.

Cate tried again. "Maybe you saw her riding this bus in the morning. We think she was with her cousin, a younger girl."

One girl, who looked like she might be fifteen, ground out her cigarette beneath a stiletto-heeled shoe and whispered something to her friend. The other girl giggled.

Cate cursed under her breath. Why wouldn't they help? She was certain at least some of them understood what she was saying. A red bus belching oily smoke pulled up, wheezing to a stop. "Look," Cate said, her voice less friendly, "whoever did that to her could do it to you. We're staying at the Padre Kino motel. Please call us there if you have information that would help."

The young women boarded the bus and Cate could see the fifteen-year old take her seat near the front. Their eyes met as the bus pulled away.

"Well, that was productive." Andy glanced at her watch. "Wish I was getting overtime for starting my day at seven a.m., but I guess I'll be lucky to find a paycheck waiting for me." She pointed to a nearby restaurant. "Let's buy ourselves *el grande desayuno*, McCoy, and contemplate how our lives suck right about now."

"Hold on, Andy." Cate spied an old woman standing a few yards away behind a wheelbarrow-shaped fruit cart. The wood was unpainted, and the wheels were rusting, but it was filled to the brim with bright oranges, bananas and tomatoes. She'd felt the tingle of someone watching her during the exchange with the young women.

"*Buenas dias,*" Cate said, looking over the produce and selecting two oranges. She pulled some pesos from her pocket and handed the coins to the woman, watching as the money disappeared into the folds of a voluminous cotton skirt.

"*Gracias, senorita*," the woman replied, her dark eyes steady on Cate's face.

Cate made a quick decision. "Do you know why those girls wouldn't talk to us?"

The old lady smiled, and Cate caught the shadow of missing teeth. Her face was heavily wrinkled. "Too many questions. They think you are the *policia*."

Cate nodded. It made sense. "Do you know anything of the young woman who was killed near here? We think her name was Gerte."

The woman waited, and Andy murmured, "She wants more money."

Cate pulled a wad of pesos from her pocket and passed them to the woman without counting them.

The money was quickly hidden, and the woman said, "The little one like my bananas. Some days I give them to her for free."

"Because she had no money to pay for them?"

"*Si.*"

Cate's heart quickened. "How do you know they're the same girls we're looking for? The one who was murdered in the alley?"

The woman said something in Spanish that Cate didn't understand, and she turned to Andy. "Did you catch that?"

Andy said, "I think she's saying there was a picture in the paper."

The woman shook her head. Andy leaned in to listen again. "No . . . not a picture . . . but a description." She struggled to translate the rapid-fire Spanish. "*Los dedos d'oro*," she murmured, reaching for her backpack and pulling her Spanish dictionary from it. The fruit vendor watched expectantly, repeating the phrase. Andy flipped through the book.

"I've got it! Fingers of gold." Andy grinned.

Cate held up her hands and wiggled her fingers. "Gold on her fingers, Senora? Gold paint on her fingertips?"

"*Si. Los dedos d'oro.*" The woman smiled broadly.

"Do you know where they lived?"

The woman shook her head. "They not take the red bus," she said, enunciating the words carefully in heavily accented English.

Cate thought for a moment. "Did they get on a different bus?" She pointed to the bus stop behind her.

The woman nodded. "*El autobus especiale.*"

"A special bus," Andy said, looking around as if it might materialize before her.

"Do you know where the special bus goes, *senora*," Cate asked.

The woman shook her head, her expression suddenly closed. The conversation with *los Americanos* was clearly over.

"I guess she thinks we got our money's worth," Cate said, thanking her and moving away from the fruit cart. "And we did. We've confirmed that Gerte and Estella boarded a bus here most mornings. That means they probably lived somewhere nearby."

They walked down the sidewalk, heads close. "So what do we do now," Andy asked. "After breakfast, that is."

"Breakfast," Cate exclaimed. "How can you eat when we've finally got our first serious lead?"

"As they say in those hallowed halls of journalism, McCoy, a well-fed photographer is a happy photographer, and you don't want no pissed-off photog on your back. Let's eat."

21

LAS VEGAS, NEVADA

9:31 A.M.

BRIGHT SUNSHINE LIT UP HER SISTER'S BOOK-LINED OFFICE as Marguerite drew the drapes back and looked around, wrinkling her nose at the musty smell. "Millicent started buying books when she was ten years old," she said to Della, "and I don't think she ever sold one of them." She pointed to a high shelf. "See? There's her Nancy Drew collection."

Della smiled. "She is constantly trying to get me to read but—" Her voice trailed off, and the two women looked at each other, the present tense hanging in the air. "Give me *Kiplingers* or *Money Magazine* any day." The phone rang in the kitchen, and Della tensed. "Maybe I'd better get that."

She hurried to answer it, and Marguerite could hear the murmur of conversation as she circled the room, eyeing her sister's collection. Several shelves were devoted to feminist literature and thick research treatises on discrimination and poverty. But Millicent also read for pleasure, and the shelves were lined with authors that ranged from Agatha Christie to P.D. James to James Lee Burke.

Della entered the room carrying two mugs and handed one to Marguerite. "A telemarketer." She sipped her coffee. "Relentless bastards, aren't they?"

"That's one thing you don't have to worry about in the Mexican desert," Marguerite said softly, slipping into the chair behind Millicent's desk. She put her fingers on the dusty computer keyboard. "I used to picture her writing here."

145

"I learned to leave her alone when she was working on a project," Della said. "She'd emerge from this room when it was finished like a little mole coming out of its hole, blinking in the sunlight." Della took a mouthful of hot coffee, blinking back a rush of tears. "What are we looking for, anyway?"

Marguerite shook her head. "I'm not sure. Anything that would tell us what Millicent did after she returned from Tijuana."

Della perched on the arm of a leather chair. "Why didn't you or Millicent call the police after Estella told you what had happened?"

"For all we knew, it was the police who had done it to her." She looked at Della. "The police are very corrupt in Mexico, Della. The people don't trust them, even in the little town I live in."

"What did Millicent tell you she was going to do?"

Marguerite sighed. "We agreed that I would take Estella back to Cuauhtemoc, and Millicent would investigate. She was convinced there was more to this than just the rape and beating of a young girl."

"Why?"

Marguerite smoothed a strand of hair back into the twist at the nape of her neck. She still felt tired from the trip. "I'm surprised she didn't tell you any of this."

"When she was researching something, she didn't talk about it." Della shrugged. "Journalist confidentiality, I guess. But she did give me that envelope. The one I gave to the reporter." She winced. "Maybe that wasn't such a great decision."

Marguerite withheld comment, saying instead, "My sister was convinced there was more to it because Estella's cousin Gerte had disappeared the day before. Millicent believed the two were connected."

Della finished her coffee and placed the mug on the edge of the desk. "But you said that the girl didn't know who her attackers were?"

Marguerite shook her head. "She just remembered being driven out into the desert and the driver forcing her to get out. She was running such a high fever that she was in and out of consciousness on the journey home."

"You were never able to find out what she and Gerte had been doing in Tijuana?"

"Estella had pneumonia by the time we got to Chihuahua," she said, her eyes glistening. "She didn't even recognize her mother."

Della thought for a moment. "Why wouldn't Estella have contacted her parents after the rape? You were her teacher, right?"

"I'm very close to the students, and quite honestly, Estella was afraid," Marguerite replied. "When the girls ran away, it was a very shameful thing for their families. Gerte's father declared that his eldest daughter might as well be dead." She wiped some dust from the dark screen of Millicent's computer. "It's been a huge scandal in our community, but one that no one talks about. Except for the kids, of course. They whisper it between themselves."

"Aren't Gerte's parents beside themselves to know what happened to her?" Della's eyes were puzzled.

Marguerite nodded. "I'm sure they are, but they're keeping it quiet." She shuffled some papers on the desk and looked at the other woman. "I think we should call that reporter. Maybe she can give us some indication of what Millicent had come up with."

Della said, "I remember the night you called. We were watching a movie here and talking about going skiing over Christmas." She rose and walked over to the window, her back to Marguerite, "Up until that night she hadn't mentioned her family hardly at all." Della turned. "I had no idea you were a Mennonite."

"I'm not, in the strictest sense of the word. It's a very closed community. But I do missionary work in the mountains and teach the kids." Marguerite's mouth tightened. "It fulfills me, just like Millicent's work satisfied her." Her gaze met Della's. "But I'll tell you, Della. If I'm responsible for involving my sister in something dangerous, I'll never forgive myself."

Noah saw the "Special Report" slate suddenly appear on one of his competitor's broadcasts, and he fumbled for the remote with a sinking stomach. Aiming it at one of the television sets in his office, he punched the volume up in time to see the scene switch to a reporter standing at the edge of a lake, the water a deepening purple in the oncoming twilight. "Shit."

His phone rang. He cursed again. He knew who it was. "Yes, Michaela?"

Her voice was as silky as a rattlesnake's slither. She thought it was sexy. "Channel 8 is reporting a big search going on at White Bear Lake for that writer. Do we have anybody up there?"

He clutched the receiver tightly. *She probably didn't even remember Millicent Pine's name.* "I'm working on it."

"Send Allison."

He bit his tongue, literally, to stop the rush of words that bubbled up. "Fine," he said finally. "But I think we'd better send a second reporter as backup."

She exhaled just loud enough to let him know he'd ticked her off, her tone hardening. "Noah, I want Allison front and center on this one. Dan can handle things back here on the anchor desk."

"I'll get it done."

Adam turned the key in the lock and flipped off the lights, leaving just the lamp at the cashier's desk on to illuminate the store. Business had been brisk, and he was tired, looking forward to a short walk with Sherlock and a long shower to loosen up his leg. But first he would call Cate and fill her in on the latest developments. Let her know what she was missing.

He dialed the phone number she'd given him and listened to it ring in the motel, glancing at his watch. She and Andy were keeping some pretty weird hours down there. About to hang up, he heard a breathless hello.

"Cate? It's Adam."

"Adam!" The receiver dropped on something hard, and he pulled it away from his ear. "Sorry. We just got back, and I could hear the phone ringing while I was trying to unlock the door." She took a deep breath. "How are you?"

"I thought you might want the latest on the Pine case up here."

"That sounds like there's something new." Her tone was cautious. He knew she felt torn about not being there.

"They're dragging White Bear Lake as we speak, for Millicent Pine's body."

"Damn. Who got it first?"

Adam smiled in the dark. He'd always admired her competitiveness. "The Evil Empire."

"Double damn. Channel 8. Noah must be pretty upset."

"I'm sure," he said. "The reporter said the police had received some information that led them to believe Millicent Pine's body had been dumped in the lake."

Cate sighed. "I take it they haven't found anything yet."

"No. How are things going in Tijuana?"

An undercurrent of excitement returned to her voice. "I think we're making progress, Adam." Cate outlined the day's events. "We went back to the bus stop tonight to see if we could spot this so-called 'special bus' but we never saw it. We plan to be there bright and early tomorrow morning, if I can drag Andy's rear out of bed."

He chuckled. "Speaking of asses, any softening in the Snow Queen's position?"

"Hey, I'll pass that one on to Andy," Cate said, laughing, the sound husky on the crackling phone line. "I wish my bottom line was as funny. Get it? *Bottom* line. Anyway, the Snow Queen is refusing to pay any of our expenses. She's ordered us to come back immediately."

"And you've obviously obeyed," he said dryly. "How about if I wire you some cash? You can keep it for when you've maxed out your credit card."

"Adam, I might have to take you up on it, but I've still got some room on the plastic. Thank you. I'm hoping if we break this story, Michaela will be shamed into changing her mind."

"Well, the money is there if you need it, Cate. I'd better go. Sherlock has his leash in his mouth."

"Break your rules, Adam, and give him a kiss on the nose for me. I'll talk to you soon. And . . ." Static buzzed in the silence. "Thank you."

April 24, 6:05 A.M.

The girls' stares were openly hostile when Cate and Andy showed up at the bus stop on the second morning. The old woman with the fruit cart wasn't there, but the fifteen-year old who'd caught Cate's eye through the bus window was, and she whispered something to her friend. Cate murmured to Andy, "Do you think they'd believe us if we said we weren't cops?"

Andy shrugged. "It's worth a try." Her gaze skimmed over the unfriendly faces. "It can't get much worse."

Cate shoved her hands in her jeans pockets and walked up to the young women. "We are not the police. No *policia*," she said.

The girls looked at her.

"We are *journalistas* trying to find out what happened to those young women. Gerte and Estella." She eyed the fifteen-year old. "Do you understand me?"

The rumble of an approaching bus filled the air, and the girls turned away, getting into a ragged line. Anger flashed through Cate. What the hell was wrong with them?

The young women boarded the bus, holding their short, tight skirts down as they ascended the stairs. Cate watched with frustration, her gaze again on the youngest of them. This time the fifteen-year old went to the back and sat down. Cate could see her profile clearly through the windows, the dark fall of her ponytail.

The girl flicked a glance at her. Cate's breath caught. As the bus pulled out, the fifteen-year old turned and pointed toward the back window of the vehicle. Cate followed the gesture, eyes searching the road. A yellow school bus was lumbering up to a bus stop thirty yards away, and a group of young women were boarding it. They wore short skirts and sneakers. Cate turned to Andy. "What's the Spanish word for school?"

Andy bit her lip. "*Escuela*, I think. Why?"

"Is there any chance the old woman said *escuela* not *especiale* yesterday?"

"Hot damn, McCoy, I think you're right!" They watched as the doors of the school bus closed and the vehicle began to gather speed. Tomorrow they'd figure out where it was going.

22

TIJUANA, MEXICO

April 25, 7:16 A.M.

"WISH WE'D BROUGHT BINOCULARS."

Cate murmured an assent, shielding her eyes from the morning sun and squinting toward a cluster of dun-colored buildings surrounded by a rusting metal fence. Fifteen minutes earlier, the school bus they'd trailed by taxi to the far fringes of the city, had entered the gates and disgorged nearly fifty women into what appeared to be the main building. A security guard had stood in the door and watched them enter.

"Must be some kind of factory," Andy said, shifting into a more comfortable position on the hard ground. They were crouched behind a scraggly clump of desert bushes and scratchy chaparral, visible, Cate suspected, to anyone who really looked hard. She studied the buildings.

"How are we going to get in there?"

Andy looked at her. "We're going in there?"

"How else are we going to know what Gerte and Estella were doing there?" Cate slapped at an insect.

Andy eyed the buildings. The cab driver hadn't recognized the place. "I guess we could try bluffing our way in. Tell them we're working on a story about border-town factories or something."

Cate shook her head. "If there's something squirrelly going on in there, they won't welcome a couple of reporters."

They watched as a guard dressed in an olive drab uniform strolled out of the door and walked casually to the gate, waving to a colleague who stood just inside the fence, smoking. "Security seems pretty lax," Andy observed, "except for those machine guns on their belts."

"Makes you wonder what they're guarding."

"We're not even sure that the Mennonite girls were working there, McCoy." Andy scrabbled in the dirt, finally perching gingerly on her backpack. Catching Cate's look, she grinned. "Don't worry, I'm not crushing credit card-cam. I've got it rigged up in my pocket."

"In that case, why don't we roll off some video of this place? Who knows how long we'll have before we're spotted?"

Andy centered her ball cap with its hidden lens and pressed a button as the tiny camera began to record.

"Can you make sure you get a good shot of the security guards," Cate asked, keeping an eye on them as the two uniformed men stood smoking and talking. "Keep rolling, Andy. I think I hear a vehicle coming."

They watched as a small delivery truck, clouds of dust boiling up from its wheels, swung up to the gate. The driver was waved inside by the guards, but instead of pulling up to the door as the school bus had, the delivery truck continued on, disappearing behind the building.

"That's it," Cate whispered. "Our way in."

"We're going to steal a delivery truck?" Andy's eyes were wide.

"Too brazen," Cate said, her gaze still on the buildings. "This calls for subtlety."

Andy snorted. "This from the woman who threatened to ambush Eddie Hamm at his Sunday school class if he didn't give her an interview."

Cate lifted her chin. "Only because he was dodging me after his lieutenant governor was picked up for indecent exposure." Her lips curved slightly. "Got my interview, didn't I?"

Andy sighed. "So what's the plan?"

"We bribe the driver to deliver us to the loading dock."

Andy digested that. "What if those Checkpoint Charlies spot us? I'm not sure I can outrun a hail of machine gun bullets, McCoy."

"Once we're inside, Andy, we wait until things shut down for the night. Then we look around."

"How do we get out?" She smirked, catching Cate's frown. "Hadn't thought of that, huh?"

"We'll cross that bridge when we come to it." Cate rose to a half-crouch, brushing dirt from the seat of her jeans. "C'mon. I want to be waiting on the road when the driver leaves."

The sun had turned Cate's nose pink and given her a powerful thirst by the time they heard the sound of an approaching truck. Stepping into the deserted road, Cate flagged the driver down. When he'd pulled to a stop, she saw that he was a teen-ager, no more than sixteen years old. He was dressed in loose pants and a ragged shirt and his dark eyes were wide with apprehension.

"*Hable Ingles?*"

"*Pequito,*" the boy murmured, his eyes darting back and forth between Cate and Andy.

Cate reached into her pocket and drew out a wad of pesos. "Would you like to make some *dinero?*"

He stared at her, finally nodding cautiously.

"Let us ride in the back of your truck tomorrow to that company," she said, gesturing over her shoulder. "What do you deliver?"

The boy's gaze lingered on the pesos. "*Las camisetas y pantalones.*" He saw her confusion. "Uniforms," he said slowly in English.

Andy looked at Cate. "Maybe the girls change into them when they get there." She smiled at the boy. "Do you ever have help?" He seemed to understand English better than he could speak it. The advantages of a border town.

He nodded. "*Si. Por grande* . . . large . . . orders."

Cate said, "*Manana?*" She gestured to herself and Andy. "We're your helpers." She held the money out to him. "Can you deliver a large order tomorrow?"

He shrugged. "*Si.*" He gestured to the back of the truck. "We wash tonight."

"I'll give you half of the money now and half tomorrow if you'll pick us up here in the morning. Right here." He took the money from her. "Deal?"

He nodded. "You will stay? I leave?"

"Yes."

He tucked the money into his pocket and started the truck. "*Manana.*"

The truck rumbled away. Andy said, "Think he'll really come back for us tomorrow, McCoy?"

Cate began walking, taking a swig from Andy's water bottle. "Yeah, I do." She swallowed, grimacing at its brassy taste. "The money I gave him is probably as much as he makes in a month."

Andy peered down the road, two strips of asphalt carved through the desert. The shimmering heat made the road appear to be undulating. "We should've asked him for a ride. How are we going to get out of here?"

"I saw a bus stop about a mile down the road."

They walked in silence until Andy said, "What if we get caught in there?"

Cate glanced at her, hearing a rare note of concern in her friend's voice. This *was* different, she knew, than shooting their usual surveillance video or ambushing some scurrilous politician. They would be taking a pretty substantial risk.

"We won't. We're going to buy some loose clothes today and tuck our hair under straw hats and keep our faces down while we unload the truck tomorrow. When the boy leaves, we'll hide somewhere, and when the place shuts down, we look around." She nudged Andy, looking sideways at her, as they walked.

"We can do this."

Andy shrugged and Cate kicked some dust, looking up at the cloudless sky. "We've got to break this story." Her voice was low. "We've got to."

April 26, 9:18 A.M.

The land was so flat, the air so hot and still, that Cate spotted the swirling brown dust cloud when the delivery truck was still a mile and a half away. She pulled back the wide sleeve of the shapeless shirt she wore and glanced at her watch. "Not bad. He's only thirty-five minutes late." She tugged on the kerchief she'd tied over her hair to disguise it's auburn color. "This damn thing itches already."

Andy smirked. She was wearing a straw hat laced under her chin with colorful ribbons and a voluminous skirt designed to conceal the mini-camera apparatus. The lens of the camera peeked out through a minute opening in the straw. "Do you think we can really pass for this kid's older sisters?"

"If no one looks too closely. Once everyone leaves for the night, we can change into the uniforms."

They watched the truck approach, waving to the boy as he slowed down.

"*Hola,*" Cate said, greeting the kid and handing him a wad of money before climbing into the back. She settled precariously on a large bundle of starched shirts. Blue smocks and pants hung on racks on either side of the

154

truck, obscuring her and Andy from view, and the uniforms swayed as the teen-aged driver picked up speed again.

"No turning back now," Andy whispered as they made the turn off the road and jounced over the dirt track that led to the factory gate.

They tensed as the truck slowed and heard the shouted Spanish of one of the guards. "He's asking why the boy has returned today," Andy murmured. "The kid is saying his papa finished a large order and told him to bring it here."

Cate sat, unmoving, the oddly comforting smell of the bleach they'd used on the uniforms in her nose. It reminded her of the campus laundry at college, where she'd worked two nights a week to earn money for books and other necessities. She was a long way from Boston University.

The truck lurched, and Cate clutched the sides of the bundle, bracing herself as they made a wide arc. "We must be headed to the back of the building," she whispered.

The truck pulled slightly forward and then reversed slowly, the brakes squeaking as the vehicle came to a halt. Cate and Andy waited for the driver to come around to the back. When the doors were opened, they saw they were backed up to the building's loading dock. One employee, dressed in a tan uniform, sat at a desk in a corner and barely glanced at them.

Cate and Andy stood up, grabbing handfuls of clothing on hangers and followed the boy. He led them into what appeared to be a locker room with stainless steel toilets and sinks and metal lockers. The boy gestured to them to hang the blue uniforms on a long metal bar that stretched the length of the room. For an hour they unloaded the uniforms and then the thick bundles of shirts, depositing them on a counter inside what was apparently the men's room.

When the truck was empty, Cate exchanged a glance with the driver and, with a brief nod, backed into the locker room. The boy slammed the truck's doors and walked over to the man at the desk. After a brief conversation and a signature, the boy went quickly to the truck, got in and drove away.

Cate looked around the room. Cracked tile climbed the walls, and the floor was filthy. She wondered why they even bothered to issue clean uniforms. "The next shift will probably be here in a few hours. We'd better scope out a hiding place."

They kept an eye on the door while they walked around the room. If they were caught, they planned to say that the boy had accidentally driven off without them while they were using the restroom. Trouble is, they'd have to say it in Spanish.

155

"Think we could fit in here?" Andy gestured to a small opening under the sink.

Cate grinned, pulling off the annoying kerchief and scratching her scalp. "Not a chance, especially after that tamale-and-burrito plate I wolfed down last night." She opened the door of a narrow cupboard full of cleaning supplies. "But one of us could hide in here if we move some of this stuff." Cate pulled out a mop covered with cobwebs and several bottles of disinfectant that looked like they hadn't been used in ages and gestured to Andy. "Be my guest."

"Thanks," Andy said, eyeing the dark cupboard.

"It's better than my hiding place."

"Which is?"

Cate pointed to the toilet stalls. "Saw it on my favorite cop show, *Cagney and Lacey*. The perp crouches on top of the toilet. Lacey's the one who figures it out."

Andy frowned. "Which one was which? Was Lacey the blonde one?"

Cate glared at her. "Obviously Sharon Gless was Cagney and Tyne Daly was Lacey."

"Yeah, I knew that." Andy glanced at her watch. "How long do we have to endure this?"

"Well, its twelve fifteen," Cate said. "It probably won't be safe to come out until seven or eight."

"Then I'd better take a potty break now," Andy said, moving into one of the stalls. "I'm not sure my thirty-eight-year-old bladder is up to this, McCoy."

"Let's also change into the uniforms while we have a chance. We can hide our clothes in a locker."

"I'd hate to think what Sunny would say if he'd caught me in this get-up," Andy said, handing her skirt and blouse over the top of the stall and taking the blue cotton shirt and pants from Cate. "I'm also going to replace this dumb hat and rig up credit card-cam in my ball cap."

"It's never failed us before," Cate said as Andy opened the door. The Minnesota Twins cap had an embroidered "1987 World Series" insignia just above the brim. Andy had drilled a small hole through the embroidery and taped the camera lens to her hair. The hole in the cap was the camera's window on the world and no one was the wiser.

They heard voices outside the locker room door and scrambled to hide, carrying the Mexican clothing they'd worn with them. Cate slid the latch on the toilet stall and stepped up on the seat, peering cautiously over the door to see two young women enter and pause before the grimy mirror. They were speaking in rapid Spanish and taking off their clothes to don the blue uniforms. They couldn't be older than seventeen.

Cate stared at the back of the stall door, thinking. Maybe the afternoon shift started at twelve-thirty. She held her breath as one of the girls approached the toilet stalls, pushing on her door and moving to the next one when it wouldn't open. She heard the girl urinate and flush and then the sound of the water running. Her legs were already cramping from balancing on the toilet seat.

When the employees left, Cate emerged from the stall, stretching her legs as Andy slid out of the cupboard. "I think I felt a spider crawl up my back," Andy complained, wriggling her shoulders.

"Would you rather be hunched over a toilet bowl that hasn't been cleaned in ten years?"

Andy's gaze traveled to the dented and chipped stall doors. "I'll stay in my cupboard," she whispered, as they heard more voices approaching. "Thanks anyway."

The man who'd been sitting at the corner desk was gone when Cate and Andy finally emerged from the locker room into the loading dock area. The lights were off, and the hum of factory equipment had ended an hour earlier. No one had been into the locker room for several hours. Cate glanced at her watch. Seven forty-five. She nudged Andy and pointed to a door. Light coming from the other side framed it in the dark. They moved toward it.

Cate curved two fingers around the handle, and laid her right ear against the metal. It felt warm to her cheek.

"Hear anything," Andy whispered.

Cate shook her head and quietly pulled it open, glancing over her shoulder. "Camera rolling?"

"Ten-four, McCoy."

"Let's go."

They slipped through the door and into a hallway that was lit with bare light bulbs hanging on cords from the ceiling. The walls were grimy and full of dark smudges and the floor was covered with linoleum that had cracked and buckled. They pressed against the wall and paused. Cate gulped in oxygen to slow her racing heart. Andy's face looked pale beneath the brim of her ball cap. "Ready?"

Andy nodded and they slid along the wall toward a set of large double doors with square windows. Dim light filtered through the glass. Cate quick-stepped the last one hundred feet of the hallway and went up on her tiptoes to peer through the windows. A large open room lay beyond, illuminated only by a powerful security light that shone in through a window on the opposite wall. The place was empty, shut down for the night.

Cate pushed one of the doors open and held it as Andy slid through. The photographer stood just inside, moving her head in a slow arc so the camera could pick up details of the room. Large ceiling fans hung from metal rafters, and long tables were set up in the center of the floor. The air smelled acrid with a chemical scent Cate thought she recognized but couldn't name.

They moved away from the doors, splitting up, and Cate spotted what looked like an assembly line mechanism toward the back of the room. As she drew closer, she saw that it snaked in from a different part of the factory and she wondered what it carried when it was up and running.

She turned back to investigate a long table in the center, noticing Andy had moved to the opposite side of the room.

Paintbrushes of all sizes were immersed in cans of liquid and clay figurines were scattered down the length of the table, resembling a small village of half-dressed people. Some wore cloaks of vivid blues and reds, their heads and faces unpainted. Others were nearly complete, delicate eyes and features painted in, the bright colors glowing in the dusky light.

Cate picked one up, surprised to see that it had been modeled in the likeness of the Virgin Mary. In fact, she realized, they were all religious figurines, meant to be part of a crèche. She spotted the baby Jesus and was reaching for it when the room suddenly exploded with light and a high-pitched whistle split the air.

"What the hell?" Cate saw Andy freeze, her hand still on the knob of a narrow door cut into the factory wall.

The double doors burst open and a man rushed in, a machine pistol in his hands. He shouted at her in Spanish, and Cate wedged her fingers under the edge of the table and tipped it, sending figurines crashing to the floor. The guard cursed as Cate ducked behind it, a couple of inches of plywood between her and the deadly looking gun.

She gasped for air, praying Andy had found somewhere to hide, and while she was at it, praying that the hidden camera was getting it all.

The guard marched across the room, and Cate tensed, sure he was about to let loose a stream of bullets against the tabletop. Ready to make a run for it, she froze as the man screamed and something shattered against the concrete floor. Risking a look, Cate saw a second projectile, this time an ornately painted wise man, arrow through the air and strike the guard in the head. It smashed to the ground in a jumble of painted clay.

The guard, blood now dripping from his temple, turned with a roar of pain and fired off a burst of ammunition in Andy's direction. Cate crawled to end of the overturned table and grabbed for fragments of the shattered figurines. She gathered pieces of a good-sized angel and lobbed them at the man, who was now only a few feet from her. On the third try, a large shard struck him in the eye, and he gasped, doubling over, his gun wedged at his waist as both hands clawed at his injury.

Cate shouted, "Run!"

23

TIJUANA, MEXICO

CATE AND ANDY REACHED THE DOUBLE DOORS at the same time and burst through them, running down the dimly lit corridor, Cate tripping on the buckled linoleum. They tore into the loading dock and made for a door next to the large dock portal, which had been locked down for the night. The door gave easily under their push, and Andy nearly tumbled down a metal stair-case. Cate steadied her, and they took off across the packed sand, shouts of alarm in their wake. More guards had joined the fray.

They dashed around the side of the building, running full tilt for the six-foot steel fence that encircled the factory. "Can you do it," Cate panted, look-ing at Andy.

"Damn straight," the photographer answered, not sounding nearly as winded. "I'll give you a boost and then follow you over."

They reached the fence, and Cate leapt onto it like a cat climbing a tree. She clawed her way to the top and, with a push from Andy, sprang over it, falling to the ground on the other side. Andy curled her fingers through the openings and scaled it easily, dropping to the sand next to Cate. They breathed hard for a second, Cate's eyes widening, as the roar of a motor came from the factory.

They took off running into the desert, chaparral bushes grabbing at their ankles. Cate glanced over her shoulder and shouted, "Oh, shit," as an all-ter-rain vehicle erupted from the factory gate and rumbled into the desert behind them. She could see one man driving it and a second seated behind him. The headlight hadn't found them yet but it soon would.

Andy was panting now. "Follow me. I have an idea," she said, and Cate fell into place behind her, warm evening air rushing by her ears as she sprinted. They made a wide arc and Cate gasped when she saw where Andy was headed.

"Are you nuts?"

"Trust me," Andy said, running back toward the factory fence. "Otherwise, we're just sitting ducks."

They ran along the fence line, crouched down to avoid the security lights, as the sound of the ATV grew louder behind them. They reached the back corner of the fence and followed it to the backside of the factory, the shadows deeper behind the building. Cate spotted the tall security spotlight that had beamed light into the darkened factory floor. That seemed like hours ago.

Andy clasped her arm. "Same as last time. Okay?"

Cate eyed the fence and then her friend. "Are you sure about this?"

The photographer nodded. "We can't outrun them, McCoy. We can hide back here until they give up and then scale the fence again. Are you ready?"

The ATV thundered by, headed in the direction Cate and Andy had first run, and Cate nodded. She grabbed for the steel wiring and hauled herself up, moving slower than she had the first time. She felt Andy's palms on the back of her legs, and she reached for the top, hanging there for a minute, following the ATV headlight as it bounced over the sand. She dropped down, biting her lip as her ankle wrenched on impact. Andy was beside her in thirty seconds.

"We'll probably be here for a couple of hours," Andy said, taking her ball cap off and shaking out her long hair. The camera lens was miraculously still in place, and she gently dislodged it, slipping it into the pocket of the cotton uniform. "What do you think is in that room that was alarmed?"

Cate rubbed her ankle, her heartbeat slowing as they sat in the building's shadow. They could still hear the ATV's engine but it was further away. "Is that what happened? All I know is that I was reaching for the baby Jesus and all hell broke loose."

Andy chuckled. "That door I tried to open was set with an alarm." She looked at Cate. "What are they hiding in there?"

Cate shrugged, the lethargy that follows an adrenaline rush settling over her. She yawned. "Whatever it is, they don't want the factory girls to see it."

Andy was silent for a moment. "So what did our excursion get us, McCoy, besides nearly an ass full of lead?"

Cate smiled. "Confirmation, Andy. This *is* where Gerte and Estella were working."

"How do you know that?"

Cate looked at her in the darkness and felt a rush of gratitude for her friend's cool head and steady nerves. "Remember the gold paint on Gerte's fingertips?"

Andy nodded. "It was mentioned in the autopsy."

Cate drew a fragment of a clay figurine from her pocket and held it up. "Gerte was painting halos on Jesus."

April 27, 10:12 A.M.

Chandler Coates emerged into the windy spring day and braced himself for the onslaught. Reporters and photographers clustered around him as he tried to walk, and he finally gave up, holding his hands up in surrender.

"Okay, okay. I'll make a brief statement and then take a couple of questions." He looked into the cameras, his eye caught by the red lights that signaled the tape was rolling. He had better get it right the first time.

"As you know, Miss Barracosta has been denied bail. We disagree with the judge's ruling, but we respect his honor's decision." He glanced down at a paper with some notes on it. "Liz Barracosta is innocent. She did not kidnap Millicent Pine, and we will be pursuing a full acquittal when this case goes to trial."

"Has Liz told the police who she thinks did kidnap Millicent Pine?"

Coates eyed the newspaper reporter. "Miss Barracosta has no idea what happened to Miss Pine or even *if* there has been foul play."

A television reporter shouted, "Are you saying Millicent Pine might've just taken off? What about the blood on the notepad in Liz's trunk?"

"We have no idea how that got there or even if that is Miss Pine's blood."

A radio reporter Coates disliked spoke up. "Is Liz Barracosta denying that she threatened Millicent Pine that night in the bar?"

Coates' lip curled with distaste. "She adamantly denies threatening Millicent Pine. They were having a discussion about a potential interview with the governor. Miss Barracosta felt she'd had too much to drink, so she asked a friend to drive both of them to Mr. Bates' house. You all know the rest."

"Is Liz's friend also going to be charged?" There was a sneer on the word 'friend.'

Coates' eyes hardened, and he picked up his briefcase. "That's all for today. Good day."

The photographers broke away, dashing ahead of Coates so they could get long shots of him walking up the sidewalk. The reporters spotted the prosecutor coming out of the courthouse door and circled him. "Mr. Ziegler, the defense says they're not even sure Millicent Pine has met with foul play. Is it possible she disappeared of her own accord?"

Ziegler's dark eyes narrowed against the bright sunshine. His face was pitted, and a five o'clock shadow was sprouting on his chin even though it was only noon. "Would Miss Pine really vanish without any word at all to her employer, to her friends, to her family? Does that make sense?"

"Why did you ask the judge to deny Barrachosta's bail?" The television photographers had joined the circle, and the reporters pushed microphones closer to the prosecutor's lips.

"We feel that Miss Barracosta is a danger to society." He spread his hands. "Look, she is a woman of some means. We felt if bail was set, she might be able to post it. Fortunately, the judge agreed."

"Have the police come up with anything more besides the blood on the notepad and the testimony of Barracosta's driver?"

Ziegler smiled. "If I told you that, then you'd tell everyone else." There was a titter of laughter. "You'll just have to wait until the trial to find out, Mr. Rossi." He looked around the circle of reporters. "But I'd warn you to reserve those courtroom seats early. You won't want to miss this."

Cate saw the white envelope the next day, lying on the carpeting just inside their hotel room door. She and Andy had stumbled in at two-thirty in the morning, kicking off their shoes and collapsing on their beds in the cotton uniforms. They'd walked the entire way back from the factory, the road deserted at that hour of the morning.

At noon, Cate had awakened to bright sunlight pressing in behind the blackout shades and the sounds of the maids in the hallway. She'd gotten up to go into the bathroom and seen the splotch of white on the carpet. Andy was stirring as Cate ripped it open, drawing the single sheet of paper out. "Okay if I turn on a light?"

Andy groaned.

Cate said, "I'll take that as a yes."

The note was from the priest, Father Cabron. It said that one of his parishioners might be able to help in their search for the two girls. He suggested that they meet at his church after the noon mass. Cate glanced at the clock. They had forty minutes.

The church was cool and dark when Cate and Andy entered it, and the smell of incense lingered in the air. Cate could see two figures waiting in the front pew as the priest walked down the center aisle to greet them. "*Buenas dias.* I'm glad you received my message. Good." He ushered them to the front of the church, and the figures turned and stood as they approached.

"This is Senora Marti and her daughter Luz. They heard my plea on Sunday and have come to talk to you."

Cate shook hands with the older woman and smiled at the girl. She was ten or eleven years old and shy, clutching her mother's hand and peeking up at Cate from beneath long dark lashes. They sat down on the front pew, Andy and Father Cabron in the one behind them.

Cate said, "Do you know something about Estella and Gerte?"

Senora Marti glanced at the priest and then her daughter. "My daughter became friends with the younger girl," she said in accented English. "Estella, I think."

Cate's gaze slid to the little girl's face, and she nodded, ducking her head almost immediately behind her mama's shoulder. She turned back to the mother. "How did they meet?"

"They were renting a room in my home."

Cate nodded, her gaze meeting Andy's. "Do you live near the church, senora?"

"*Si.* Luz and I walk to mass three times a week."

"When did the girls first come to your house?" Cate held her breath.

The woman frowned, the fine skin of her forehead wrinkling. She'd drawn her dark hair into a knot at the nape of her neck. "I believe it was last spring. The oldest girl told me their parents had died, and she was taking care of her younger sister." She glanced at the priest. "Was that not true?"

"We think they were Mennonite girls who ran away from their families when they were headed north for migrant work," Cate said. "The youngest girl, Estella, was probably only fifteen."

"*Dios*," the woman breathed. "I was worried about them when they didn't return, but a man came and said he'd helped them find an apartment. He took their belongings."

Cate leaned toward the Mexican woman, eyes intent. "Did the man say who he was, *Senora* Marti?"

A slim hand fluttered at her throat as the woman tried to remember. "I think he said he was a relative. He paid the rest of the month's rent for them." She curled an arm around her daughter's shoulders, drawing her close. "The girls were always a couple of weeks late with their payments, but I didn't press them. My daughter liked Estella so much."

The priest put a calming hand on the woman's shoulder. "*Senora*, do you remember what this man looked like?"

"He was your height, Father, and *muy gordo*."

"Fat," Cabron translated to Cate and Andy. "Did he give you his name?"

She shook her head. "I think he just said he was their *tio*, their uncle, and that he'd found them a larger place to live that would be more permanent." Her mouth twisted with distress. "I should have asked him who he was." She turned to Cabron. "*Lo siento, Padre Cabron*."

The priest patted her shoulder as the little girl squirmed restlessly, standing up and pulling her mother from the pew. Senora Marti rose, murmuring something to her and turning to the priest. "We are late for lunch at my sister's house. I hope this has helped. If I'd realized—" Her eyes filled with tears. "I had no idea that the poor girl in the alley was Gerte." She pulled a handkerchief from her purse and dabbed at her eyes as the priest escorted her to the church door.

Cate watched them, her mind working. "Gerte's killer must be the same person or people that assaulted Estella and left her for dead in the desert. Why else would someone show up and make an excuse for both girls' disappearance?"

Andy sighed. "And you think the trail leads back to the factory?"

"Definitely."

"Oh, boy."

Father Cabron returned, spreading his hands in apology. "I'm sorry if the *senora* wasn't much help, Miss McCoy."

Cate rose. "No, Father, she helped put another piece of the puzzle together for us. I appreciate your interest in this."

He straightened the large cross that lay against his chest. "I would only ask that you contact me when you know who is responsible for the girl's death."

Cate promised she would let him know, and she and Andy left the church, pausing outside on the sidewalk. "How about lunch?"

Andy looked at her. "Fine, but I'm laying off the margaritas today."

Cate's expression was quizzical. "It's a little late for the straight and narrow, isn't it?"

"I have a feeling I'm going to need a very clear head, McCoy."

"Oh? " Cate followed her across the street to a small cantina. "Why?"

Andy pulled the brim of her ball cap lower on her head. "Because you're already figuring out how we're getting back inside that cursed factory."

24

TIJUANA, MEXICO

"**D**ON'T BE SUCH A NAYSAYER. IT *COULD* WORK."

Andy chewed a forkful of rice and beans and studied her friend. They were finishing their meal, and Cate had just pitched her plan. "Absolutely everything would have to go exactly as planned." She took a long swallow of Mexican beer. "And it never does."

Cate pushed her plate away. "Remember when the investigative team did that story on the racist security guards at Wolff's department store? Everyone said it couldn't be done."

Andy wiped her mouth with a napkin. "They got very lucky. Who would've guessed those guards would've mouthed off like that in front of the I-team's spy?"

Cate signaled the waiter. "*Dos helados, por favore. Chocolat y fresa.*"

Andy grinned. "Very smooth. You've added ice cream to your vocabulary."

"We can't all be Ms. Berlitz, you know." She finished her iced tea. "Anyway, it wasn't luck that clinched that department store piece. Remember how the guards got so comfortable around the woman the I-team sent in there? They gabbed up a storm to her while they were watching the surveillance cameras. That's when she learned all that stuff about how they targeted black women."

The waiter slid two bowls of ice cream in front of them and left. Cate scooped a heaping spoonful of chocolate into her mouth. "Yum."

"So what's that got to do with your crazy scheme?"

"It's all about keeping your eyes open." Cate pushed her bowl toward Andy. "This is great. Try some."

Andy tasted it, nodding. "Better than the strawberry." She thought for a moment. "So you think Chad's just going to hop on a plane, bring some goodies with him and help you play spy?" She sat back in her chair. "McCoy, be real. The Snow Queen has already cut *us* off. No way is she going to agree to send someone else down here."

Cate nodded. "I've thought of that. If Chad will take vacation time, I'll pay his flight down here and his hotel. Adam has offered to loan me some money if I need it."

Andy stared at her. "McCoy, I think you're losing your perspective. Yes, something weird is definitely going on here, but come on. We're out of money, our bosses are pissed off at us and now you want to drag someone else into this?" She leaned toward Cate, putting cool fingers on her arm. "Besides, it's dangerous to go back in there."

"Andy, if we go home without breaking this story, Michaela will probably fire us. Have you thought about that?" Cate pushed her chair back and scanned the room. Most of the lunch time crowd appeared to be businessmen on leisurely midday breaks. It was nearly three o'clock. "We've got to crack this. How else can we explain ignoring her orders to drop it? I think even Noah has knuckled under to her this time."

"Okay," Andy said. "We're under the gun. I'll give you that. But what makes you think Chad will agree to this?"

"Chad's been on the cop beat for seven years, Andy. This is the kind of stuff he loves." She looked at her friend, impatience stamped on her face. "Yeah, yeah," she said, waving for the check. "Don't worry. I'll tell him all about the guns."

April 28, 6:22 P.M.

Chad's plane touched down in San Diego thirty-six hours later, and Cate greeted him with an icy bottle of beer. Andy took his duffel bag as they walked through the airport. "What did you tell the mis-managers about the time off?"

He grinned at his fellow photographer. "I told them I had twelve weeks of vacation built up, and a freelance offer to do some shooting with the Discovery Channel. They bought it."

Cate squeezed his arm. "Chad, we really appreciate this. We couldn't do it without you."

He patted a small carrying case that hung from his shoulder. "You certainly couldn't do it without this. I've brought some toys that you won't believe."

By dinnertime, Chad had checked in to their Tijuana hotel, and they were sitting in his room, the sliding glass doors open to the warm desert air. His "toys" were spread over one of the beds. He held up a long, narrow pole. "Know what this is?"

Cate shook her head.

Chad pointed it at her. "It's a wand."

Andy snorted through a mouthful of beer. "The kind fairy godmothers have?"

Chad pointed at her. "This is serious stuff, girl. Listen and learn." He laid the pole on the bed. "Okay, say we've infiltrated this factory you're talking about and set up a hidden camera somewhere. You two could be a quarter of a mile away and see everything the hidden camera sees."

Andy picked up the wand. "C'mon, Chad." Her voice was disbelieving.

"As long as you're within line of sight, you can point the wand at the building, and it will pick up the signal of the hidden camera and feed it back to your monitor." He grinned at them. "Cool, huh?"

Cate looked at Andy. "I told you he loves this stuff." She pointed at a piece of sturdy lingerie. "What in the hell is that?"

He picked up the bra. "We had this built a while back at a theatre shop. The camera is hidden in this little pocket between the cups. Makes you look kind of busty, but so what?" He held the bra against his chest. "Might get you a date or two, McCoy."

"Ha ha." She looked at the bra. "How does the lens see through your clothes?"

"You poke a small hole in your blouse. Works the same way as the credit card-cam Andy has been using." He put the bra back on the bed amid a dozen small tapes and boxes of batteries. Two compact monitors sat on the floor. He took a long pull from his beer bottle and set it aside. "Okay, Cate, let's go over this plan again. This time, I'll listen for flaws."

Andy said, "And don't forget to mention the guns."

Chad rubbed his hands together in anticipation. "The more the better."

"She's the one," Chad whispered as he and Cate watched more than a dozen young women disembark from the school bus in the dusk the next day. Andy was at the hotel testing the surveillance equipment. "Let's follow her."

They stepped out of a doorway and fell into place behind a slim woman walking briskly up the hill. She was headed for the tarpaper-and-wood shacks that dotted the hillside. Cate knew that two or three generations often crowded into the crude dwellings. It reminded her of the first time she'd seen third-world slums.

She'd been on assignment with the National Guard, documenting a mission that was part training exercise, part humanitarian effort. They'd flown into Tegucigalpa, Honduras, and as they'd circled for a landing in the big military plane, Cate had seen thousands of shacks clinging to the muddy hillsides around the capitol city. She'd wondered how the Honduran government withstood the shame of a citizenry that lived right under their noses in such primitive poverty.

"She's turning into that house on the right," Chad murmured, stepping up his pace.

"Who's going to do the talking," Cate asked, keeping her voice low.

Chad glanced at her in the deepening twilight as they approached the door their target had slipped through. "I think you should. You have the money, right?"

Cate's smile flickered briefly. "I'm getting pretty good at passing out bribes." She took a deep breath. "Here goes."

They stood at the rough wooden door, listening to the movement inside. Cate could hear the sound of a squalling infant and the rapid Spanish of two women conversing over the baby's cries. She swallowed her trepidation and knocked on the wood frame. The conversation ceased.

When the woman they'd followed appeared at the door, Cate saw that she was younger than she'd originally guessed, appearing to be no more than eighteen years old. "*Ingles, Senorita?*"

Her eyes narrowed suspiciously, but she nodded. "*Pequito.*"

The girl's mother called to her, and she glanced over her shoulder impatiently. Cate knew she had but a few seconds to draw her in. "*Como se llama?*"

"Manuela."

"Manuela, would you like to earn $500 American?"

The girl caught her breath, intrigued but afraid. "I'm no whore," she said, her gaze flickering to Chad.

Cate shook her head. "Nothing like that. We just want you to stay home from work for a couple of days."

She tilted her head, studying Cate in the fading light. "You will pay me to stay home?" She snorted with a cynicism beyond her years. "My son needs to be fed, *Senora. Buenas noches.*"

Cate pushed the money against the sagging screen that divided them and the girl froze. Manuela called something over her shoulder and stepped outside. The door creaked as she pushed it closed. "Who are you?"

"We need to get into the factory where you work, but they're watching for us. We want your identification."

The girl shook her head, gesturing at Cate. "They will know you are not me. You have . . . that hair."

Cate pushed an auburn swathe away from her face self-consciously and shrugged. "A wig and makeup."

Manuela's expression was still dubious, and Cate stepped closer to her. "Manuela, I'll give you the money tonight in exchange for your ID card and your promise that you'll stay home until we bring it back to you."

The baby's cries erupted again, and she shifted nervously, clearly torn. "*Si,*" she said abruptly, unclipping the badge from a belt around her waist.

Cate took it, handing her the money. "Don't tell anyone, Manuela. Just say that you're sick if someone asks."

The money disappeared into her skirt pocket, and she turned to go into the house.

"One question," Cate said, stopping her. "Do you know what's behind the door with the alarm on it?"

Something moved so swiftly in the girl's eyes that Cate would've missed it if she hadn't been just a few inches from her. Manuela shook her head. Cate stared at her. They both knew the girl was lying.

The hotel swimming pool glowed a luminous blue and Cate wished she had the energy to slip into a bathing suit and kick out twenty laps. Instead, she took another pull from her beer bottle, savoring the sharp tang as it slid down her throat. She knew she was drinking too much on this trip, but she didn't care. Without the anesthetizing effects of the booze, she probably wouldn't be getting even a few hours of sleep a night. Every time she put her head on the pillow, her mind picked at the complicated skein of the story and the prospects of failing to unravel it.

She spotted Andy coming through the wrought iron gate, carrying two more beers. "Hey."

Andy sat down next to her and dipped her feet in the warm water. The smell of too much chlorine rose from the surface. "Chad's in his room. Asleep, I hope."

Cate nodded. "Nerves of steel," she said, her mouth twisting wryly.

"He just got here, McCoy. He hasn't been living this like we have." She tipped her beer back. "Besides, we'll be outside while you go in there again. Alone."

Cate stared into the rippling blue water. The aftertaste of the beer was bitter. "I wish we knew how much of this Millicent Pine had put together, Andy. That's what keeps pounding away at me." She scratched at the Dos Equis label with her fingernail. "She disappeared in Minnesota. What's that got to do with what she was working on down here? It doesn't make sense."

Andy wriggled her feet underwater, sending bubbles to the pool's surface. "We know that she had linked Gerte's death in the alley with Estella's rape and beating. I think we can assume that she knew of the Mennonite connection."

"I'm sure she did. I think when she recorded that interview with Estella the girl told her, before the tape had been turned on, about where they were living and working. The question is what did she do next?"

They were silent for a moment. Then Andy said, "Chad gave me the name of a DEA agent he and Barry have worked with before. The guy was transferred from the Twin Cities to San Diego a couple of years ago."

Cate said, "And?"

Andy finished her beer. "He wants to call this guy if the shit hits the fan. He says the guy has plenty of connections in Mexico."

Cate pulled her feet out of the water and stood up, glancing at her watch. It was after one a.m. "If we have to call in the cavalry, Andy, *le merde* will most definitely have hit the fan. Let's just hope we're not in the way when it does."

25

TIJUANA, MEXICO

April 30, 8:41 P.M.

HEAT LIGHTNING FLASHED TO THE WEST OF THEM, flickering on and off over the desert like a disco strobe, and Andy glanced around uneasily. She and Chad were hidden behind a snarled clump of cacti and desert brush on a shallow rise behind the factory. The large windows on the backside of the factory floor glowed with light in the dusk. The day before, Cate, her auburn hair hidden under a black wig and her face covered with a convincing layer of dark makeup, had gotten on the school bus with Manuela's identification. She'd been warned to stay away from anyone who got too curious. She'd entered the factory and worked her afternoon shift, a camera rolling in her bra, a second tiny camera placed on the sill of the window when the guard went out for a cigarette break.

Now, on Cate's second day inside, Andy held the wand and pointed it, as Chad instructed, toward the cluster of factory buildings, aiming for the window where the camera was hidden. The monitor, attached by a cord to the wand, showed them the factory floor, with its long tables of employees bent over their work. They could also see a burly Mexican guard with a gun slung over his shoulder, and the alarmed door, it's metal face maddeningly implacable.

"What do you think is in that locked room," Andy murmured, eyes on the small screen.

"We'll find out before this is all over," Chad said.

"I'd guess it's drugs," Andy said, shifting the wand where it was propped on her bent knees. The picture on the screen rolled a bit as she moved. "Cocaine or something."

He nodded slowly. "Could be. Plenty of it in Mexico." He adjusted something on the equipment. "Maybe they're shipping it out of there inside those crèche figures."

Andy arched her back, working out the stiffness from two days of sitting on the ground. "Could be that the customs people don't look at that stuff as close, you know, because they figure it's going to churches."

Chad nodded. "It would be a good cover."

They watched the monitor for a few minutes, the nocturnal sounds of the desert around them. Andy glanced at her watch, restless with the waiting. "I wonder if Cate should hold off one more day before she tries anything on that alarmed door."

Chad shrugged. "The sooner the better. I'm worried that someone will notice the ID doesn't match her face. Those guards are lazy, but they do have eyes in their heads." He put a hand over hers. "She can do this, Andy. We'll see everything that she sees."

"We're almost a quarter of a mile away, Chad. What happens if she's discovered?" She'd swallowed that question every time it had risen to her lips. Cate had not wanted to hear it. Chad didn't answer.

They were quiet, watching the men and women working at their tables, and Andy thought of the drudgery of the job. They were paid a fraction of what American factory workers made, even though they were working long hours and doing painstaking work. No wonder so many of them risked their lives to cross the border.

Andy nudged him. "Look. Must be the end of the shift."

The workers were putting away their brushes and paints and filing out of the room, and Andy thought she caught sight of Cate's back near the middle of the line. She watched as the employees moved slowly through the double doors when a young woman suddenly spun backwards, screaming. The sound was tinny and somewhat distant through the hidden camera. Smoke filled the air as other workers threw up their hands in confusion.

Andy grinned. "The diversion."

Chad nodded, watching the chaos erupt, his dark eyes bright. "Another cop trick. The civilian version of a flashbang."

"But fortunately your homemade cherry bomb isn't as destructive," Andy said, remembering a SWAT operation she'd covered years ago in which the device the cops had used to frighten the hostage-taker inside the house had started a fire.

They watched intently, smoke drifting over the hidden lens, as Cate backed away from the swinging double doors. Frightened workers streamed around her, headed for the corridor, as Cate slipped away from them and out of view of the camera. Andy knew she'd be crawling into the hiding place she'd spotted earlier in the day.

She let out the breath she'd been holding and patted the monitor. "Damn! That girl's got balls."

Chad chuckled. "I believe that's *cojones* in the local parlance, my friend."

They grinned at each other in the dark and settled down to wait.

Cate slapped herself smartly on the cheek and rubbed her eyes, trying to keep the weariness that draped itself over her like a heavy cape, at bay. Her face felt numb, and her head throbbed, and she would've given anything to stretch out on a bed, pull the cool sheets over her shoulders and succumb to sleep.

Stop it, she warned herself. Don't think about sleeping. She looked at her watch. Fifteen minutes after midnight. The late shift workers had been dismissed as guards tried to figure out what had happened when she'd dropped the cherry bomb.

They'd finally turned off the lights two hours ago and Cate had just crawled back behind a stack of shipping boxes after switching tapes in the hidden camera, when she heard the footsteps. Slithering into place and breathing hard, she watched as a guard pushed through the swinging doors, followed by a second smaller man who was dressed in Bermuda shorts and a Hawaiian print shirt nearly open to the waist. The guard had held the flashlight while the second man had punched in a code on the alarmed door.

Cate had strained to catch a glimpse of what lay beyond as Hawaiian shirt had slipped inside but all she could see was a weird blue glow that filled up the doorway. Since then she'd stared, eyes burning, at the smooth surface of the door and fought off the exhaustion that tiptoed up and brushed her with its dark wings.

Andy awoke with a start and peered at her watch, the Indiglo face telling her it was thirty-five minutes past midnight. She sat up, scrubbing the weariness from her face. "What's happening," she croaked, bending close to the monitor.

"Nothing yet."

Andy took a long swig of water, wiped the mouth of the bottle and handed it to Chad. She reached in her backpack and palmed an orange, the dry air filling with the tang of citrus as she peeled it and gave half to him. They ate the fruit, eyes glued once again to the monitor.

"What the . . . ?" A loud pop had come through the monitor speaker.

"Uh, oh. Oh, shit!" Chad said. "I think one of the batteries in the bra just exploded."

Andy stared at him.

"It's happened once before." He was staring at the monitor but the room was empty. "We were doing an investigation on a cop who was taking bribes, following him around, you know." He glanced at her, and Andy nodded, still speechless. "We put the bra on this television producer and sent her in to the restaurant kitchen where the deal was going down. She was posing as a dishwasher. Well, all of a sudden the battery in the bra explodes, and the guy freezes. 'What the hell was that?' he says. We were watching the whole thing on another hidden camera, and we're freaked out!"

Andy said, "So what did she do?"

He smiled grimly, eyes still on the small screen. "She put a dish towel up to her face and said she had a medical condition that forced her to wear some special equipment. Everyone was embarrassed as hell and she ran for the bathroom so she could change the battery."

Andy glanced at the monitor. Still nothing. "Did you catch the guy?"

Chad nodded. "Oh, yeah. He's in Stillwater prison right now."

Andy remembered Chad showing Cate how to change the batteries but what if someone had heard it? She was gathering up the orange skin and stuffing it into her pack, when she heard Chad catch his breath.

"What?" She turned back to the monitor to see the metal door opening, a strange light that appeared bluish gray on their screen, spilling from inside.

"Oh, God," Andy breathed as a man emerged from the room and paused, peering around the factory floor.

"He won't see her," Chad whispered, watching as the man's gaze traveled the circumference of the industrial space, looking straight at the hidden camera lens for a second.

He was short and stocky and not Mexican. He glanced around once more and then drew a thick cylindrical object from his back pocket, running it under his nose with apparent satisfaction.

"He's going to smoke a cigar," Andy said, confusion in her voice.

Chad shook his head. "That's no cigar," he said. "That's a monster joint."

The man glanced at his watch and moved away from the alarmed door, crossing the room and disappearing through the swinging double doors. Chad and Andy waited to see what would happen next.

12:53 A.M.

Cate's fingers shook as she unbuttoned the simple cotton blouse she wore and reached behind her back for the battery pack that powered bra-cam. The sound of the battery exploding had burst through the silent room like a gunshot, and she'd jerked hard, nearly toppling the stacked boxes behind which she was hiding. She'd held her breath as the echo died away, believing she was safe until the metal door had swung open and Hawaiian shirt had come out.

Cate had watched as he'd stood there looking around the room, his gaze settling for a split second on the hidden camera and then circling on to the corner where she hid and then past her. He'd drawn something from his pocket and sniffed it, and she'd smiled to herself when he'd pushed out through the doors.

He'd left the alarmed door open, the strange blue light splashing neon on the factory floor.

12:57 A.M.

"Oh my God! What's she doing?"

Chad gripped Andy's hand, his fingers curling hard around hers, and she bit back another exclamation. On the small monitor screen, Cate was walking toward the spill of light, her head turning every few seconds in the direction the man had gone. As they watched, she disappeared inside.

Cate stood in the doorway, eyes adjusting to the neon light. She spotted two television screens sitting atop large metal boxes. She approached the small screens. On the right were strange colored lines with breaks in them. But it was the left screen that drew Cate closer and made her gasp when she saw what was on it.

Nine small images dotted the monitor, the details of each crisp and clear. The first image showed a girl Cate guessed to be around fourteen years old, half nude, her clothing torn, her face streaked with tears. The next image exposed her whole body, her hands held behind her by a man with a dark hood over his head. The third in the sequence showed the girl lying on a thin mattress, her arms stretched above her head, her legs held wide by more hooded men.

Cate's gaze roamed over the set-up and she shook her head. This was the latest technology in digital editing, far removed from the tape editing that many television stations had used for years. She knew that with this equipment, the editor downloaded his images onto a hard drive and then used a computer to assemble a digital version of the product. Channel 3 had just begun training photographers on this equipment, and Cate remembered Andy saying how easy it was to do fancy effects on it once you got the hang of it.

Her eyes focused again on the images of the girl about to be raped. The terror on her face made Cate turn away, and when she did her eyes met the shocked stare of Hawaiian shirt, poised in the doorway.

26

Tijuana, Mexico

1:07 A.M.

Andy watched Chad's retreating back disappear in the darkness, her breath coming in frightened pants as if she were the one doing the running. Two minutes ago they'd watched the man with the marijuana joint re-appear in the factory and amble leisurely toward the open alarmed door, clearly unaware that Cate was inside.

Andy had grabbed at the monitor with both hands, gasping as the man approached. "Look out, Cate," she'd whispered, her stricken gaze on the small screen.

Chad had been silent, his mouth in a stern line, his eyes narrowed, as the man had paused in the doorway, and then disappeared inside.

That was when they'd decided they needed help. Chad had whisked his cell phone out of her backpack and called his friend with the Drug Enforcement Agency. The agent had told him it would take at least forty-five minutes to gather some people and drive to their location. Chad had arranged to meet him on the road and bring him over the desert the back way.

Now, Andy sat hunched over the monitor, the wand pointed toward the factory window, desperate for any sign of what had happened inside the alarmed room. It seemed like a century since Chad had left, but only three minutes had gone by since the man had come back from his break. Had he killed Cate and was figuring out what to do with the body? Horrible images skittered through her mind, and she took a deep breath of desert air. It tasted metallic from the earlier lightning. She spotted movement and gripped the monitor.

A figure stood in the wash of blue light at the doorway, and Andy's heart thumped when she saw that it was Cate. Maybe she'd somehow knocked the guy out and was making her escape. But as she watched, a second figure appeared in the door, and Andy saw that it was the man. He was holding a gun, and Cate was walking cautiously, as if afraid that it would go off. The hidden camera tracked them until he pushed her through the swinging doors, and then they were gone.

1:09 A.M.

Cate's mind worked furiously as Hawaiian shirt prodded her with his weapon, forcing her into the darkened corridor. Hours earlier, she'd dropped a smoke bomb out here, everything going like clockwork as she'd slipped into her hidey hole. Things weren't going so smoothly now.

She tripped on a piece of torn linoleum, and Hawaiian shirt shoved the gun into her back. "Nice try, but I'm smarter than that." His accent was American South, his voice deep and gravelly as if he smoked too much, and Cate caught the odor of pot. He'd obviously been outside getting high when she'd slipped through the alarmed door. Too bad she hadn't heard him come back.

She thought of Andy and Chad watching the events unfold on the hidden camera. They must've panicked when they saw the guy return. What would they do now?

"In here." Hawaiian shirt shoved her into an office where three men sat around a card table, playing poker. A small pile of coins gleamed in the center. A man dressed in a camouflage uniform stood up, speaking in rapid Spanish.

Hawaiian shirt replied in Spanish and then switched to English. "She saw the operation."

The guard in camouflage looked at her, his eyes hard. "An American," he said in accented English. He gestured to the other two men. "You know what to do with her. *Senor* del Toro will want proof."

Fear surged through Cate like a rush of hot lava. She'd seen their rape video, and now they were going to kill her. A piece of the jigsaw fell into place. Just like they'd killed Gerte and Estella. "I know what happened to Gerte, the girl you threw in the alley. I've told the police."

The men stared at her, but Hawaiian shirt reared back, his eyes wide. He turned to the man in camouflage. "You killed Gerte and dumped her body in an alley? You bastard!" The hand holding the gun shook, and the men eyed it uneasily.

The guard in camouflage smiled mirthlessly. "What did you think, *Senor* Lusk?" He gave the "k" extra emphasis. "That we patted her on the head and sent her on her way after you showed her what you were doing in there?" His glittering eyes narrowed. "Oh, yes, you were screwing that girl, weren't you?"

Hawaiian shirt choked with fury, and Cate thought he might shoot the man right there. She looked around for somewhere to hide if the bullets started flying. The guard reached out and whipped the gun out of his hand. Hawaiian shirt crumpled. "Del Toro told me you'd sent her back to her family."

The guard's lips curved with real humor this time. He shrugged. "He lied." He gestured again to the other two guards who rose reluctantly from their poker game and came to stand on either side of Cate. "Get some shovels and take her out into the desert. In fact, take both of them. I think *Senor* Lusk has served his purpose for our company."

Cate cried out, "The police know what's going on here. I'm a reporter, and I've told them everything."

The man in camouflage froze, staring at her. He spewed something in Spanish at the other two men, and Cate caught the word *journalista*. He walked up to her, his breath hot and smelling of cigars. "Such dedication to your job," he sneered, turning away. "Get rid of her."

1:48 A.M.

Andy heard the faint sound of an engine and leapt to her feet, searching for the approaching truck. When she spotted its outline in the dark, the headlights off, she sprinted over the sand, relief taking the edge off her anxiety. Four men and one woman, all dressed in black, tumbled from its doors and gathered in a semi-circle around the team leader. He held a small penlight in one hand, shining it on the face of a large watch. He nodded to Andy. "Drake Connelly. Is there anything you can tell us about the situation in there?"

Andy looked around the circle of agents, their grim expressions frightening. Her voice quivered. "Just after Chad left I saw a man come out of the room holding a gun on Cate. They went through the double doors, and I haven't seen them since." She looked into Connelly's eyes. They were light brown, startling in his tanned face. "You know that she was wearing a hidden camera?"

He nodded. "One of Chad's specials, I hear." He smiled fleetingly at the photographer, his expression warming. "I'll tell you the sorry tale of our acquaintance some other time." He turned back to Andy. "If they find the hidden camera, she's in serious trouble." He looked around the small circle at his team. "Y'all volunteered for this."

There were a couple of grunts.

"So you know it's off the books. If something happens, we deny what we were up to 'til the cows come home." He gestured toward the factory buildings. "We begin surveillance in ninety seconds. Any questions?" He waited. "Good. Let's go."

1: 49 A.M.

Cate shivered, trying to quell the nausea rising in her chest. Her legs were trembling like they did after a hard workout at the gym, and she forced her brain to examine every possible avenue of escape. But all she could think of was the final image the hidden camera she wore would record. The bullet bursting from the gun's barrel and racing toward her.

"How'd you get in here?" Hawaiian shirt's eyes burned from hollow sockets, and Cate suspected he'd turned his earlier anger at the guard over Gerte's death on her. The guards had left the two of them locked in the office and gone to look for shovels.

"If I tell you that will you tell me where you shoot those videos you were editing?"

He shook his head, running a hand around the back of his neck, rubbing under the collar of the bright shirt. His mouth was bitter. "I was only doin' this for the cash. Gerte and me were goin' to Zihuatanejo as soon as I had enough stashed."

Cate thought of the tape rolling in her bra. "Why did you tell her what you were doing?"

His round face was flushed with either pot or sunburn or both and Cate wondered what a young Mennonite girl had seen in this dissolute older man. Perhaps the first taste of freedom. "She asked me what happened to her friend, Juanita, and she wouldn't shut up about it." He closed his eyes, remembering. "I warned her it wasn't none of her business, but she kept on at me, so I finally told her." He looked at Cate. "Some of them girls in the factory do other stuff for money."

Cate's brows rose. "They agree to be gang-raped?"

His voice was low. "They think they just have to sleep with the guards, but then the guards give them roofies, and they can't say no."

"Rohypnol?" He nodded and Cate recalled stories about the notorious date rape drug that incapacitated its victims and erased their short-term memory. It had shown up on several college campuses in the Twin Cities.

He nodded. "I just set up the cameras and make sure they're rollin'. Then I take the tapes and edit them into a mini-movie." A vulpine pride flashed in his eyes. "You can't believe the demand for 'em."

"How did your bosses find out you had told Gerte about what you were doing," Cate asked, wondering how much time she had to extract the whole story from the man. How long could it take to find the tools to bury a body?

His lips twisted. "I told her just to shut up about it, but someone heard her tellin' Juanita she should go to the police after Juanita got sick in the factory. She collapsed, and it took them two days to stop the bleeding." He shook his head. "Gerte always had to be a do-gooder."

Cate's stomach rolled, fury replacing the anger that had made it queasy. "They killed Gerte near her bus stop and dumped her in an alley so it would look like a random murder. Then they attacked her friend Estella and left her for dead. Did you know that?"

But Hawaiian shirt seemed beyond shock, his earlier fury long gone, his senses dulled by the drug he'd inhaled. He shrugged. "They're gonna shoot us too. Life in the big city."

Cate stood up and paced the small office, careful to keep him in view of the hidden camera lens. "How do they get the rape movies out of here? It's illegal to bring stuff like that into the U.S."

"There's lots of ways to get anything in." A weary resignation settled over his face. "Sometimes they even hollow out those religious things they're makin' out there and stick roofies and X and other stuff inside. The customs pigs seize the drugs and re-sell 'em and look the other way on the tapes." The doorknob rattled. "Everyone gets their cut, *Senorita*."

The guard wearing the camouflage opened the door and gestured to the two guards behind him. "Take them out of the north door and make them dig their own holes." He glanced at his watch. "You've got thirty minutes to get it done."

1:50 A.M.

Andy clutched Chad's hand, her eyes straining in the dark to make out the figures of the DEA agents as they set off for the perimeter of the factory. "Connelly must owe you one heck of a favor, Chad."

The photographer looked at her. "His sister's son was killed by a guy with nine prior drunk-driving arrests. Barry and I had been following the dickhead around undercover, doing a story on how he had just gotten out of jail and was going from bar to bar to celebrate."

He paused for a moment, listening. The moon edged out from behind a cloud, ripe and bright yellow, throwing shadows of cactuses on the desert floor.

"Long story short, the dickhead struck Connelly's nephew head on. The kid died immediately, and the dickhead died two days later. We gave Connelly the tape."

Andy frowned. "And?"

Chad shifted in the sand, his gaze straying from the factory to their monitor. It showed an empty room, the weird blue light still pouring from the open alarmed door. "And, Drake visited the bars that were serving the dickhead that night, even after the bastard was obviously drunk."

"What did he do?"

Chad shook his head. "I don't know, Andy. I do know that not long after the kid died, two of those bar owners decided they were in the wrong business and closed up shop."

Andy thought about it and said quietly, "I'm glad he came."

27

Tijuana, Mexico

1:56 A.M.

COOL NIGHT AIR BRUSHED CATE'S FACE as she was shoved out of the door, falling against Hawaiian shirt. Her hands were tied behind her, and the guards had summoned a third man to accompany them. She wondered if Andy and Chad could see them in the bright moonlight. They were headed toward a gate in the fence opposite from the one through which the guards had waved the school buses and trucks.

Hawaiian shirt muttered something and the guards shouted at him in Spanish. A coyote howled, and Cate breathed deeply, thinking of Adam. He would be furious when he heard how this had gone down, angry at the risks she'd taken. He didn't like risk. It had claimed his brother and his own free-wheeling life, changing him forever.

She thought of him, fingers grazing the dedication page of a favorite book, eyes lighting up at the mention of a cherished author's name. He lived and worked surrounded by the tales of hard-bitten detectives and adventurous sleuths, but Adam knew that was *fiction*. His own world was predictable, a safe haven against the unforeseen. She realized suddenly that she'd disliked that, scorning his caution without understanding it.

"Here." The guards jerked Cate to a stop, and she looked around. They were fifty yards from the factory fence in a shallow depression studded with small scrubby bushes. Cate's heart thumped painfully. This was probably where they'd brought little Estella.

The guards untied her hands and tossed a shovel at her. She caught it, assessing what kind of a weapon it would make. She could use its point to stab one of them or whack the handle over one of their heads, but it wouldn't take her captors long to fire their guns. Her fingers curved around the rough wooden handle, and her mind clicked over her options. What if she and Hawaiian shirt attacked at the same time?

She bent over the shovel and dug it into the sand, trying to catch the editor's eye, but he was weeping, propping himself up by the handle. His shirt glowed in the dim light. Cate scooped out a small pile of sand and dumped it off to the side, her gaze following it. She caught her breath. A figure in black was rising silently from the sand twenty feet away, his face fitted with night goggles. He held a gun in one hand. He caught her eye and made a calming motion.

Cate took a deep breath, her heart pounding as the seconds ticked by, when the air was suddenly split with bilingual commands to drop the guns. Cate spun, arcing her shovel by the handle and throwing it at one of the guards, striking him hard in the chest. He went down, the other two shocked into babbling pleas as the desert came alive with black-clad agents who quickly disarmed the Mexicans.

Delayed shock jolted Cate. She sank into a heap on the sand, her trembling legs unable to hold her. She'd been digging her own grave, she thought with a shudder. She raked shaking fingers through her hair and reached gratefully for the flask of brandy the female agent handed her.

"Didn't I warn you about the guns, McCoy?" Andy's arms were suddenly around her shoulders, and Cate leaned into her, letting her friend help her to her feet. Chad was talking to a tall man who seemed to be in charge as another agent spoke into a cellular phone.

"I take it that's the DEA agent Chad mentioned," Cate said, sipping from the flask again and offering it to Andy.

Andy nodded, taking a deep draught of the liquor. "God, it's been a long night, McCoy. Watching you creep into that room only to have that jerk come up behind you." She shivered, her smile tremulous. "I was starting to wonder which shots you'd want me to use for your obit story."

Cate laughed, releasing some of the pent-up fear coiled in her stomach. "Just don't use that horrible publicity shot the station took of me if it ever comes to that. Deal?"

"Miss McCoy?"

Cate turned to see Chad walking toward her with the tall agent. He was lean and spare, pared down in the way that former military men are sometimes. His face was angular and hollow under pronounced cheekbones and his mouth was a stern, unsmiling line. His one concession to vanity was longish, prematurely gray hair that swept away from his face and curled on his collar. Cate disliked him on sight. She forced a smile. "If you're the cavalry, you got here just in time. Thank you."

The agent looked at her, his dark eyes expressionless. "If you're finished playing spy, we need to interview you and get a copy of your tape."

Cate shook her head. "I don't think so."

Connelly exhaled hard. "We need it quickly, Miss McCoy. We're putting together a search warrant for that place."

Cate glanced at Chad, frowning. "I'll be happy to tell you everything I saw and heard, but I can't give you a copy of our undercover tape. That's proprietary, and we don't turn that kind of stuff over to the police." She tilted her head, looking up at the man. "If we did, that would make us just another arm of law enforcement, wouldn't it?"

The agent glared at her until Chad stepped between them. "Drake, why don't you take Cate's statement now and get your warrant, and we can argue about the tape later."

Connelly shrugged, turning away to confer with his team. Chad looked at her, shaking his head, pride in his eyes. "McCoy, it's been said before but I'll say it again. You are one tough *broad*-caster."

Cate blushed. Drake Connelly was looking at her, the contempt on his lean face hard to miss.

May 2, 7:58 P.M.

The sun had set the next day by the time the raid on the factory was finished. Officers from Customs, the Border Patrol, and the Mexican police had spent hours carrying out boxes of documents and evidence. They'd discovered the room where the gang rapes took place under the eyes of three different cameras, all of which still had the television station logos on them from which they'd been stolen. Theft of the $40,000 cameras was an expensive problem for the stations and many of them were smuggled into Mexico for use in the porn industry. The agents had also dismantled the elaborate computer editing system Cate had seen, carrying it away in pieces to be reconstructed by a police technician.

The DEA agents had explained their presence by saying they'd followed a known American drug dealer across the border and into the desert where they were certain he was meeting a high-level contact. The other agencies were skeptical, especially when they learned of the media's involvement, but by that time Cate and Andy had sped north to a San Diego television affiliate, where they spent the rest of the night and the next day writing and editing their story. Chad had stayed behind to shoot the ongoing raid.

Now, at nine fifty-eight, central time, seven fifty-eight Pacific time, Cate sat on the newsroom set of the San Diego station and waited for her cue from Saint Paul. She'd checked into a hotel room earlier in the day, showered and changed into the new clothes she'd bought. Her eyes were red from lack of sleep, but eye drops and makeup helped solve that. Andy had finished putting the piece together fifteen minutes ago.

She heard the ten o'clock producer in her earpiece. "Ready to go, Cate?"

"Ready, Annie."

"That's a hell of a story, girl. I saw it when it came in on the satellite. The Snow Queen is spitting nails."

Cate smiled, butterflies in her stomach. The station had been promoting her exclusive ever since she'd called Noah to tell him what had happened. He'd congratulated her warmly, killing a story Allison had done about how to find the best au pair, and putting Cate's story in the lead.

"Okay, Cate. We're coming to you in fifteen seconds."

Cate heard the open of the show and waited for her cue. She heard Dan Gilbert say, "Tonight an exclusive look into a Mexican drug and pornography ring and its possible connection to the disappearance of journalist Millicent Pine. Channel 3's Cate McCoy has been investigating this story for several weeks, south of the border in Mexico, and tonight she joins us from San Diego to tell us more. Cate?"

Cate focused on the camera lens in front of her, her expression somber. "Dan, when prize-winning journalist Millicent Pine disappeared from the Twin Cities in March, she was there to do a profile on Governor Edward Hamm. But Channel 3 has learned that she was also in the midst of an investigation into the murders of two young women from southern Mexico, and police believe tonight that her involvement in that story may have led to her disappearance."

Cate heard her taped story begin and sat back to listen. She and Andy had included everything, from the video they'd shot at the Mennonite community to the details of Gerte's death in the Tijuana alley to the discovery of the tiny cassette tape of Estella's interview in a Las Vegas casino. Cate had drawn the viewers in, weaving the complex chronology into a conversational story, building to the undercover video in the Mexican factory.

In her earpiece, she heard her own taped voice saying, "A warning. What we found inside the Tijuana factory was shocking. Behind a locked door, we discovered a sophisticated system for editing and reproducing pornographic tapes." On the screen, viewers were seeing Cate's undercover video as she approached the computers that had been filled with images of the girl being raped. Andy had edited out the most graphic pictures.

Cate's taped voice continued. "Investigators discovered that the sexual assaults were taking place on the premises of the factory after the victims had been given the date rape drug Rohypnal. These rapes were recorded and then turned into pornographic videos."

The story moved to the confrontation, at gunpoint, between Cate and the editor, the editor's confession, and the intervention of the authorities. Cate glossed over the role of the DEA at their request.

She came back on camera. "Investigators have spent the day going through documents and other evidence at the factory. They believe that the owners knew Millicent Pine was working to uncover their operation, and police are trying to determine whether that is why she disappeared while on a trip to the Twin Cities. Dan?"

"Cate, are you saying that the factory owners sent someone up here to kidnap Ms. Pine?"

"Dan, all police will say here is that they are looking into the connection."

"Thank you. Cate McCoy reporting live from San Diego."

Their plane landed at midnight the next night, delayed by bad weather in Dallas, and the three of them stumbled into the baggage claim, exhausted.

"What, no welcoming committee from the Snow Queen," Chad joked, looking around the deserted arrival gate.

Cate grinned wearily. "Think she's figured out that you weren't on a Discovery Channel shoot?"

They gathered their bags and hailed a cab, the taxi driver dropping each of them off at their homes. Cate rode the elevator to her floor, fumbling with her keys as Walter yowled on the other side of the door. She scooped him up as she entered, surveying the latest damage to her ficus tree. Shredded leaves lay on the living room carpet, just a handful of them still hanging from the spindly branches. "Teaching me a lesson, huh, Walter," she murmured, flipping on lights as he curled his paws around her neck.

"Welcome back." Adam stood in the doorway, a University of Minnesota sweatshirt over navy blue pajama bottoms.

"Hi," Cate said, suddenly shy with him. His dark hair was sleep-tousled, and there were bluish circles under his eyes. He looked thinner. "Did you see the story?"

He nodded, stepping into her apartment and closing the door. "Can I make you some coffee while you unpack?"

Cate nodded, hurt. Maybe he hadn't liked it. She dragged her suitcase into her bedroom, the sound of Adam spooning coffee and running water in the background. She opened the case but the idea of unpacking was suddenly too daunting, and she sat down on her bed.

She awoke to a loud rumble, her eyes opening in alarm before she realized that it was Walter stretched out next to her, purring into her ear. The room was dark, and she was reaching for her clock when his arm curled around her waist, and he drew her back against him. "You . . . really pushed it this time, Cate," he whispered into her hair.

Cate closed her eyes, savoring the scent of him all around, the new sensation of his body against hers. She gasped as he slid his tongue over her ear, and she turned her head, their lips meeting in a long kiss. She shifted, moving beneath Adam and arching her hips up to his, smiling as he caught his breath. "I missed you," she murmured, breathing into his mouth and running her hands the length of his back.

"In between the undercover missions and the gunplay?" He caught the skin at the base of her throat between his teeth and bit gently. Air rushed from her mouth in a smothered moan, and Cate slid her fingers beneath the band of his pajamas, her fingertips lightly grazing the rills and knots of his injured hip.

"Especially then," she whispered, looking into his eyes, remembering those frightening moments in the desert. An image of Drake Connelly's unyielding expression slid into her mind and was gone again. "I thought . . . never mind."

He stroked her hair away from her face and put his mouth to the corner of hers, his words barely a sigh against her lips. "I want you."

The Snow Queen's greeting could've frozen Lake Minnetonka in June. Cate had slept late, sharing Adam's famous eggs Benedict and arriving at the station after the lunch hour to an enthusiastic ovation from her newsroom colleagues. The story had made national news, and Liz Barracosta had been released on her own recognizance. Her attorney was certain the charges would be dropped.

Cate stood near the large assignments desk, accepting the praise with a mixture of triumph and embarrassment. Someone had opened a bottle of champagne, and although it was against station policy, people were sipping glasses at their desks. Andy and Chad were enjoying the backslapping kudos of their fellow photographers, and the celebration had brought a halt to any work, when Michaela Snow appeared on the spiral staircase that joined the first floor newsroom with her second floor office.

Her heels clacked loudly on the steps as she descended, and a hush fell over the newsroom. Employees turned quickly back to their computers, typing gibberish so they wouldn't have to meet her eye. Cate took another sip of champagne and watched her approach. Snow's face was flushed, her blue eyes glittering as if she'd been dipping into the bubbly upstairs. Her lips were pursed and curved, the barest of smiles.

She strode through the newsroom, her head held at a haughty angle, and Cate swallowed the urge to laugh as one of the photographers slid into the Snow Queen's wake, mincing cartoonishly behind her back. "Michaela." Cate's voice was husky from the cold champagne.

"Catherine, very good work down there." She held out a hand, and Cate grasped it, struck by how chilly her skin was. They didn't call her Snow Queen for nothing.

"Thank you."

The news director looked around, her gaze gliding over the bent heads and surreptitious stares. "Well, carry on everyone. We've got some newscasts to put on the air."

28

SAINT PAUL

May 5, 10:20 P.M.

Cate ROLLED THE STIFFNESS OUT OF HER NECK and glanced at her watch. Ten-thirty on a Saturday night. She and Adam had planned to have dinner and catch a late movie, but Cate had called to cancel, spending her evening instead in an editing bay. The Snow Queen wanted an updated story to air Sunday night about the Pine case, capping off their weekend coverage of the Spanish royal visit. That meant going through all of the raw tapes she had compiled from the very beginning of Millicent Pine's disappearance.

Cate thought about the message she'd received earlier. Della DeFrancisco had called the newsroom to say she and Millicent's sister were in the Twin Cities and wanted to meet with Cate. She'd put off returning the call, not sure she had the energy for it. The meeting would be an emotional one as Millicent's loved ones came to terms with what investigators now believed was an assassination.

It appeared that the journalist had stumbled across a multi-million dollar drug and porn operation, and the people that ran it had made sure she couldn't expose them. Cate was still puzzled about how Pine had first learned of the story, but once she had, Millicent had obviously begun digging into the background of the people that owned the factory and that had set off alarms.

Cate slid a tape into the editing deck and pushed rewind, feeling sorry for herself. The newsroom was deserted, and even Andy had gone out to unwind with Sunny. Another editor would edit Cate's script on Sunday morning. The tape sped backwards and stopped, and Cate saw that it was the interview with the nervous husband who lived near the White Bear Lake nature center—Ellington . . . Emerson. That was it. Ellis Emerson.

She watched as he stepped out on his porch, Andy rolling from the street until he said he didn't want any cameras. Cate remembered she'd done a written interview because he didn't want his wife seeing him on television. She stopped the tape and slid the glass door of the editing bay open, going quickly to her desk. She remembered sticking the notes from the interview in a drawer, and she dug her hand into it, pulling out several loose sheets of paper. Cate frowned over her hurried scrawls as she walked back into the bay.

Her jottings said that Emerson had a new baby and went to the nature center for some solitude. That night he was jogging, and he'd lost track of the time. Cate rubbed her eyes, remembering his demeanor. He kept glancing over his shoulder and running his hands through his hair, clearly concerned that his wife would appear at the front door and demand to know what he was doing.

She bent her head to her notes again and let out a startled gasp as someone rapped on the glass door. "Cate McCoy?"

Cate rose to slide the door open. "Yes?" A security guard stood on the other side.

"There are two women here and they're saying they have to see you."

Cate stared at him. "Did they give you their names?"

He pulled a paper from his breast pocket. "Marguerite Pine and Della DeFrancisco." He cupped his hand to the side of his mouth and said in a stage whisper, "I think it's that lady's sister. The one that disappeared." He hitched up his pants. "They're at the back gate."

Cate sighed. She shouldn't have tried to dodge them. "Tell them I'll be right there."

Marguerite Pine was a tall woman like her sister, with short gray hair and penetrating hazel eyes. Her skin bore the bronze tint of someone who spent a lot of time in the sun, and Cate noticed that her hands were rough and weathered. She shook Cate's hand. "I'm very happy to meet you, Miss McCoy. If not for your efforts—" She broke off, her eyes filling with tears.

Cate led the two women into the station's cafeteria and brought them coffee from the vending machine. "I'm afraid this is the best I can offer," she said, sitting down at a table across from them.

Della looked at her. "Marguerite and I have been staying at Millicent's house." She glanced at the other woman, and a signal passed between them. "We found something we thought you should see. That's why we've come."

Della drew a sheaf of papers from a briefcase and put them on the table. They were printouts from a computer. "It took us a few days of fooling around on Millicent's computer, but we finally figured out her passwords."

Marguerite dabbed at her eyes. "Millicent had several orange cats when we were kids, all named Blossom, as in orange blossom. I finally plugged that in one night and *voila*."

Cate tried to imagine the formidable reporter as a little girl lavishing love on a kitten, but she couldn't. Her mind's eye was locked on the last time she'd seen Millicent, standing on the capitol steps, tall and imposing, wrapped up against the chilly March winds in a dark overcoat. Her eyes had been bright with amusement as she watched the governor make a fool of himself with the demonstrators.

She bent over the papers, trying to make sense of them as weariness settled over her. She couldn't remember the last time she'd gotten eight hours of sleep. An image of Adam moving against her, his mouth on hers, slipped into her brain, and she pushed it away. "What is it?"

Della nodded to Marguerite, and the woman pointed to some words on the first sheet. "It's her file on this story. See? That's the notation for my initial call to her about Estella."

Cate broke in. "You knew Estella?"

"I'm the one who first told my sister what had happened, Miss McCoy."

"Cate," she said, her mind jarred from its sluggishness.

"Cate," Marguerite Pine acknowledged. "Estella called me last December. She was injured and frightened and begged me to come for her."

"How did you know her?" Then she knew. "You're the teacher the kids were talking about."

Marguerite smiled. "Yes. Estella was one of my prized students. We'd even talked of training her to be a teacher in the community." Her smile dimmed, and her eyes reddened again. "Her parents would not have allowed her to go to college, even if there'd been money for it."

Cate nodded for her to continue.

Marguerite took a deep breath. "She and Gerte, another of my students, ran away from their families last summer when they were on the way north to Canada."

"For migrant work?"

Marguerite nodded and tilted her head, studying Cate's face. "I noticed in your story that you were filming at *Campos*. They didn't know you were recording them, did they?"

"It was tape from an undercover camera. They would've refused to let us talk to any of the children, Marguerite. We had to do it undercover." Cate paused for a moment, thinking. "Where was Estella when she contacted you?"

"She was at a rancher's house," she said softly. "She'd crawled there after they'd beaten her and left her to die in the desert. I called Millicent and told her what had happened, and she agreed to come talk to the girl." She looked past Cate's shoulder, remembering. "At the time, I had no idea what I was getting my sister into."

Cate rose to get more coffee. The clock on the wall said eleven forty-five, but her exhaustion had vanished. She handed a paper cup to Marguerite, and the other woman sipped the hot liquid, continuing. "Estella didn't want to tell my sister what had happened to her in front of me. She admired me . . . and . . . she was ashamed about the rape." Her mouth twisted. "So I stood in the corner of the rancher's bedroom while she whispered what those pigs had done into Millicent's tape recorder. Sometimes she even asked that the recorder be turned off."

"Did Millicent tell you what had happened?"

"Some of it. She said that Estella believed Gerte was dead. Estella had told her before they started taping that they'd been working in a factory outside of Tijuana, but she was so sick and injured, she couldn't give my sister many details about it."

Cate nodded. "So Millicent must've started by getting the coroner's report of Gerte's death. Then she gave you the tape and the report, Della, for safekeeping." Cate looked between the two women. "Why do you think she interrupted her investigation to take the profile assignment from *Vanity Fair*?"

"Money," Della said quickly. "Millicent wanted to take a year off and go back to Afghanistan to research a book about the Taliban. She knew she needed to build up a reserve to do that, so she was taking work when it was offered." Della glanced at Marguerite. "But Millicent got further in her research on this story than Marguerite knew." She flipped several papers over and indicated what appeared to be the transcription of an interview.

Cate read the first paragraph and caught her breath. It was a narrative very similar in detail to the one given by Estella. This time the girl's name was Nita, and her story raised the hair on the back of Cate's neck. Nita had been offered money to stay late after her shift at the factory. She'd refused to take the drugs and had been raped by three men in a locked room. Warned not to tell anyone, she'd stopped eating and became too weak to work. The girl was eventually told not to come back. Millicent had noted at the bottom of the page that she'd found Nita consumed by tuberculosis in a shack with no running water.

Cate ran her fingers through her hair, flipping the page, expecting to see more of Millicent's notes. Instead, there was a diagram with a single name at the top in bold type. Cate studied it. "This looks like some kind of family tree or something. I'm not sure how it fits in, but if it's in her file, then she must have connected it somehow. I think I ought to run this past the agent that's working the case." Drake Connelly would be thrilled to hear from her.

Della frowned. "The police haven't done much for us since this started. We wanted you to see it first." The two women stood. "We'll be in town for a few more days. We want to take Millicent's things from her hotel room home with us, and the police are checking on that."

Cate led them to the back door. "I admired Millicent's work very much." She shook hands with each of the women and watched them walk to their car in the parking lot. Cate went back to the editing bay and plopped down in the chair, staring at the blank video screens and wondering what Millicent's last moments were like. She shivered. She didn't even know if Millicent was dead, but the odds were high. Even the police believed they were looking for a body now.

Cate rubbed her eyes, her second wind fading fast. There was a bitter irony to it all. The veteran journalist who'd traveled to some of the most dangerous and remote parts of the world could've never dreamed her life would end in a Midwestern city on an assignment that must've seemed so innocuous. She pressed play on the machine and stared at the image of Ellis Emerson, frozen on the monitor. She'd swallow her reluctance and call Drake Connelly in the morning.

May 6, 11:23 A.M.

Governor Hamm fixed a gracious smile on his face and thought about how he'd rather be doing anything else but wear his monkey suit and sweat in the sun on the airport runway. The Spanish royals' plane had landed a few moments ago and was slowly taxiing toward them. He heard the clank and scrape of tripods being moved as the TV hyenas shifted to keep the moving plane in focus. Dots of perspiration popped out on the bridge of his nose. He wished he had a beer.

"Governor, when they come down the steps of the plane, you and Mrs. Hamm will move to the bottom of the stairs and then wait for them to descend."

Hamm nodded grouchily at his aide. All of this protocol bullshit was exhausting, like being back in the military without the fun of jumping out of planes.

He thought of Pete, working outside at the memorial site when he'd left. It had been good to have his old paratrooper buddy in town for the past couple of months. He'd taken control of the memorial with the can-do attitude for which he'd been both admired and feared when they were young recruits.

"All right, here they come." The governor and First Lady approached the staircase and took their places as the door of the plane opened. An attractive woman with caramel-colored hair swept back in a chignon appeared, blinking in the bright sun. The king stood behind her, his bearing proud and upright despite his age. They clutched the handrail and descended slowly.

"Welcome to Minnesota." The governor enveloped the queen's hand and bent toward her in a brief bow. "We're honored that you've come for a visit."

The queen moved on to the rest of the reception line, and Hamm held out his hand to the king, shaking it warmly. "King Juan Carlos, it is a pleasure to welcome you to our state."

"Thank you for inviting us, Governor." The older man's eyes twinkled. "I've looked forward to meeting you ever since I heard about your surprise election." His English was only slightly accented. "I understand you were a paratrooper at one time."

Hamm grinned. "Pulled my dossier, did you?"

The king smiled. "I did a bit of military service myself. We'll have to compare notes."

The two men strolled toward the waiting limousine and Hamm bent to the king. "Maybe we could knock back a few brews before the big shindig tonight. I'd like to introduce you to my favorite beer, Pig's Eye. How would you say that in Spanish?"

5:55 P.M.

Cate blinked at her computer screen, the text shimmering before her weary eyes. She was dressed in a simple black dress, sheer black hose, and her most expensive high heels. She and Andy were headed to the governor's mansion to cover the state dinner, but first she wanted to see what the producer had written to introduce her story. Some producers stole all the good parts instead of creating their own intro while others wrote a minimal toss, doing little to keep the audience watching. When her desk phone rang, she welcomed the diversion.

"Channel Three News. Cate McCoy."

"Drake Connelly. I got your message." His voice was terse.

So he was still angry over her refusal to turn over her undercover tapes, a decision that had been seconded by the station's attorney. "Agent Connelly, I came across something I thought I should ask you about."

There was a brief silence before he said, "Go on."

"Millicent Pine's sister found some information in her computer. It was in the same file as the factory stuff."

"What kind of information?"

Cate heard a metallic creak, and she pictured him tipped back in his chair, his long legs propped up on the desk. "Names."

Another silence and then he said, "Am I going to have to say 'pretty please,' Miss McCoy, or are you going to tell me what they are?"

Cate flushed, scrabbling through the debris on her desk for the papers Marguerite had given her the night before. "There's a name in bold at the top and then a list of names below it."

"Whose name is at the top?"

"Ana Gutierrez Escobar."

There was a muffled exclamation, and Cate heard a thud as his boots hit the floor.

"You've heard of her?"

Connelly didn't answer, and Cate could hear him having a curt conversation with someone else in the room. She caught the words, 'Find out' before he was back on the line. "Are you still there?"

"What's going on? Do you know this woman?"

He was quiet, finally saying, "She's the daughter of one of Mexico's most powerful drug traffickers, now deceased, I'm happy to report."

"How did he get that way," Cate asked, wondering if he'd tell her the truth. "Dead, I mean."

"We didn't kill him, Miss McCoy, if that's what you think. Pablo Gutierrez died in a fall from his horse. About eighteen months ago."

"What happened after that?"

"We aren't sure. There was a pretty bloody power struggle over his business, and bodies were turning up about once a month. Then everything went quiet. Some of our agents believe his daughter is running things now." There was a rustling in the background, and he said, "Hold on."

Cate could hear conversation again on his end, and then he was back on the line. "Could you fax me those papers or would that also violate your station's proprietary policy." He started to rattle off his fax number, and Cate interrupted.

"Wait a minute. If I'm going to share this with you I need something back. What's going on?"

He cursed so ferociously that Cate pulled the phone away from her ear, her cheeks burning. Good thing he'd rescued her *before* they'd had this conversation. "You absolutely cannot go on the air with any of this until we put some people on it."

Adrenaline coursed through her, and she fought to keep her voice measured. "Go on the air with what?"

Connelly rasped, "Are we off the record, Miss McCoy?"

Cate swallowed, aware that she was going to regret this. "Only for this part of our conversation."

He thought about it. "Fair enough. Ana Gutierrez Escobar has been under constant surveillance since her father died." He paused, and Cate's heart thudded with anticipation. "Right now she and her husband, Peter Escobar, are guests of your governor."

29

GOVERNOR'S MANSION

7:13 P.M.

CATE STOOD ON THE FLAGSTONE TERRACE next to Andy as the photographer shot the final preparations for the governor's first state dinner. Hamm and his wife were having a pre-dinner *aperitif* with the king and queen privately before welcoming their guests. Eleven oval tables had been placed outdoors, and the china that bore the state's North Star seal shimmered in the yellow glow of lanterns swinging from wrought iron hooks. The entire menu had been planned to show off Minnesota's bounty, beginning with an appetizer of wild rice soup, moving to a salad of greens and pine nuts and culminating with a main course of fresh walleye.

Cate swallowed, the thought of food making her queasy. Her nerves were jangling, and her chest was tight with apprehension as she remembered the deal she'd struck with Drake Connelly. She would hold off on a story tonight about the governor entertaining a drug kingpin's daughter if Connelly would give her more information about Ana Escobar so she could break the story tomorrow night. Connelly wanted time to work the possible connection between the Escobars and the porn and drug operation at the Tijuana factory, but it made Cate nervous to cut a deal with the cops. What if some enterprising newspaper reporter spotted Ana Escobar and remembered who she was?

Cate shifted on her high heels, the toes of her right foot already numb. Damn shoes. She looked around, watching the mansion staff fuss with the table centerpieces, when a movement in her peripheral vision made her turn. A man was standing in the spacious backyard staring at her, his features indistinct in the twilight, but Cate knew him. Peter Escobar. She recognized him from the news conference the governor had held to drum up support for his paratrooper memorial.

He was leaning against a tree, its green-leafed branches arched over him, the freshly turned dirt of the memorial site at his feet. His hands were clasped behind him, and Cate saw that he wore a military dress uniform, the glitter of medals on his chest. Her pulse quickened. She should ask Andy to get a shot of him, but she hesitated. There was something—malevolent about his gaze. She turned away, nodding as the photographer murmured that the guests had begun arriving.

The mansion filled quickly with the state's business leaders and politicos. Cate spotted a former governor and his ex-wife, carefully cutting wide swathes to avoid each other. Several years back when the former governor had been in office, his ex-wife had written a tell-all book, complete with the couple's nickname for the governor's private parts. It had been a bestseller.

Edward Hamm had his arm around the shoulders of a university president, and Cate saw a local singer laughing with King Juan Carlos, her figure-hugging gown a pale flame in the swirl of color. Cate felt suddenly frumpy in her unadorned black dress and shoes that pinched. Get real, she chided herself. You couldn't spend two weeks slurping up tequila and Mexican beer and look like that.

"Everyone? May I interrupt for a moment?" Deborah Hamm moved to the doorway of the solarium, the governor towering beside her in his black tuxedo. The sunroom, beautiful with its ornate tiles, had been cleared of furniture and was occupied now by a quartet of musicians setting up their instruments. The music would drift out to the guests as they dined on the terrace. "You'll find place cards on the tables, and the first course shall be served in ten minutes, so if you'll make your way to the patio, we can begin. Thank you all for joining us in welcoming the king and queen of Spain to our great state. We're honored that they're here."

Applause rippled through the room as the guests drifted toward the terrace and seated themselves. Cate watched Peter Escobar approach the center table and bow to the queen before sitting down. She nudged Andy, and the photographer swung her camera around. "Keep an eye on the main table," she murmured in Andy's ear. "I need plenty of shots of the governor's buddy."

"Looks like they're waiting for someone."

The chair next to the king was still open, and Escobar was craning his neck, his mouth thinned with annoyance. A low murmur broke out among the guests, and Cate turned toward the glass doors just as Ana Escobar stepped through them, pausing in the saffron spill from the lanterns. Her dress was black and severe, gathered at one shoulder, slashing across her breastbone to leave the other bare. She'd brushed powdered glitter over her skin, and it glowed in the dim light. Her midnight hair was swept high and secured with a diamond pin. It glistened as she approached her table, her slim hand slipping into the king's as he bent low, brushing his lips across her fingers, his eyes bright with admiration. She laughed.

Cate pressed a hand to her chest, sure the thudding could be seen by everyone. Perspiration surfaced on her face, and she drew in a shaky breath. She felt as if she'd been looking at one of those illusion drawings, where two designs are hidden in one scene. Once you saw the concealed figure, you wondered how you'd ever missed it.

Ana Escobar was the *woman* Millicent Pine had been seen with at the nature center. It all fit. The witness' words thundered in Cate's head. Ellis Emerson, the nervous husband, had told her on his doorstep, 'I heard them before I saw them. One of them was laughing.' Cate recalled how she'd paused, looking at him. 'Laughing,' she'd asked. He'd nodded.

Cate shivered, remembering what he'd said next. 'I saw the woman pull the other woman into a hug, and they stood there for about ten seconds.' Cate had written it all down and then forgotten it. A woman.

"Cate, are you okay?"

She jerked, startled as Andy whispered to her. "Why?"

"Well, you're standing in my shot."

Cate apologized, moving further away from the camera lens as Andy rolled on a toast being made by Governor Hamm to the king and queen. Ana Escobar was watching with a slight smile on her lips, her dark eyes roaming the room, then meeting her husband's. Cate wondered what Drake Connelly would think if she told him she suspected that it had been Ana Escobar who had been with Millicent Pine the night she disappeared.

Cate remembered the Barracuda's assertion, after it had come out that she *had* left the Saint Paul Hotel with Millicent Pine, that the journalist had received a phone call as they were driving. Liz Barracosta had said Pine insisted on being dropped off at a Saint Paul park. Could it have been Ana Escobar on Pine's cell phone, summoning her to a meeting?

A thought shook Cate. If the Escobars had gotten rid of Millicent Pine because she'd been investigating their drug-and-porn operation in Tijuana, what was to stop them from going after her?

Waiters were delivering the salad plates, and Cate watched as the sommelier moved between the tables, pouring jewel-hued liquid into glasses. Ana Escobar touched her glass against the king's, and Cate wondered what his highness would think if he knew just who he was sitting next to. They were conversing in rapid Spanish, excluding Peter Escobar, who was eating and drinking little.

A movement to her left made her turn, and Cate saw a uniformed officer with a German Shepherd at the end of a leash weaving through the trees at the edge of the property. The dog's mouth was open and his ears were flattened against his head. Cate knew it was one of the dogs from the Saint Paul Bomb Squad. A half dozen of them had been called in for security. There had been rumors of a bomb threat, but the governor's security detail had refused to comment on it.

She turned back to the tables as a diplomat from the Spanish embassy in Washington rose to make a speech. Escobar was staring at her again, his eyes narrowed, and Cate flushed. He'd obviously seen her reports from Mexico. Their eyes locked, and heat prickled over her skin. She made a show of jotting something down in her notebook, and he looked away.

The serving staff swept in with the next course, whisking the salad plates away and replacing them with artfully arranged platters of walleye and vegetables. Cate's stomach grumbled, and she smiled at Andy. "Hope that didn't screw up your nat sound."

The photographer grinned, gesturing to the guests. "I don't think we need natural sound of people stuffing their faces. Wish they'd give us some."

Cate dug into her purse and pulled out a crumpled candy bar. Half was already gone. She broke the other half in two and handed a piece to Andy. "Lucky for you, I never go anywhere without my emergency stash of chocolate."

They munched on the chocolate bar, surveying the scene in front of them. "Wishing you hadn't cut that deal with Connelly, aren't you," Andy said, glancing sideways at Cate.

"I have mixed feelings about it," Cate acknowledged, swallowing the rest of the candy. "It'll be a kick-ass story tomorrow, but what if the competition gets wind of it? They've got to be sniffing around."

Andy tightened a leg of her tripod, nodding. "True, but wouldn't they need Connelly's confirmation on the DEA angle?"

Cate nodded, about to answer when a flash of tawny fur caught her eye. She turned to see a dog pawing furiously at the soft dirt of the memorial site, black sod arcing away from his feet. "Andy! Check it out." As Andy swung the camera around, the officer gave the dog's leash a hard yank, but the shepherd let out a wild yowl, bracing his paws and refusing to yield.

Peter Escobar stood up at his table and shouted, "Get that animal away from the memorial!" He threw his napkin down, and ignoring entreaties from Deborah Hamm to calm down, rushed across the lawn toward the site. Two other German shepherds, summoned by the howls of their compatriot, braced themselves on the edge of the site and snarled. Escobar fell back, watching helplessly as the third shepherd continued to dig. By now, the officers were exchanging ominous glances, not even trying to hold the dogs back.

Cate and Andy moved off the terrace and onto the lawn, jostling for a clear shot with the guests who'd left their dinners to see what was happening. The king and queen were surrounded by security and the governor's bodyguards were urging him into the mansion as he protested loudly. A flash from a newspaper photographer's camera lit up the odd scene, and the image of the photograph froze in Cate's mind. The dog crouched in the dirt, the tendons in his forelegs straining as he dug. The uneasy expression of the officer, the leash swinging from his hand. The freshening breeze that brushed the grass and spun the leaves of the elm tree.

But Cate knew it was the mix of fury and fear on Peter Escobar's face as he watched the dog that would linger longest in her mind.

30

GOVERNOR'S MANSION

8:48 P.M.

"HOLY SHIT!"

Andy's fingers trembled on the camera lens as she tried to tune out Cate's blasphemy and the crowd's gasps. She was focused on what was unfolding in her camera viewfinder, and it demanded all of her concentration.

"Andy, I hope you've got that shot," Cate breathed more to herself than her photographer. The German shepherd was standing over a large plastic bag, barking and whining. The bag was smeared with mud and slightly torn from the dog's frantic digging. The top was knotted.

The dog whined and yipped as his handler clipped the leash to the animal's collar and urged the canine away. Cate caught fragments of what he was saying. ". . . chief called everybody in . . . no bomb-sniffing experience . . . cadaver dog."

Cadaver dog. A chill shivered through her. She'd seen these dogs work when, as a young reporter, she'd covered the cop beat and been sent out to crime scenes. The dogs were trained to sniff for dead bodies or evidence associated with the decay of human flesh, and they were amazingly accurate.

Her gaze fell on the bag. The dark plastic gleamed wetly. Cate's mind whirled. The cadaver dogs had been known to hit on animal remains, but Cate couldn't picture anyone being permitted to bury a family pet in the backyard of the governor's mansion. The Historical Society would've had a fit . . .

205

She froze, the sounds of the chaos receding in a roar of realization. The only person who'd been digging in that area was Peter Escobar. He'd been given reluctant permission from state historians to work on the memorial. Cate blinked, her eyes locked on the bag, her brain flashing to the logical conclusion.

Millicent Pine was last seen with Escobar's wife.

Cate gripped Andy's arm, jostling the camera. "Andy," she gasped, "we've got to go live as soon as we can."

The photographer re-focused the lens, keeping her shot firmly on the bag and looked at Cate. "They wouldn't let us run our cables in here. Remember?"

"Then we have to go out to the front gate. I think there's evidence in that bag of Millicent Pine's murder."

Andy blanched. "Let's get some help. Call the station."

Cate scrawled some half-sentences into her notepad as she dialed the station. The weekend producer answered. "Megan? Cate here. We've got breaking news at the governor's mansion and we're going to need some extra crews down here."

The young woman on the other end said, "Hold on. Let me find the assignments editor and conference her in."

Cate heard her shouting across the newsroom. Then she was back on the line, along with the desk person. "Here's the deal," Cate said brusquely. "We weren't permitted to run our cables into the governor's mansion, so we won't be able to take a live picture of what's going on. But I have my cell phone, and I can do a phoner as soon as you get things set up. Then when we're ready, I'll come outside the gates to do a live shot."

"What's going on?"

"A cadaver dog has dug up a plastic bag in the backyard at the place where the governor was going to put his paratrooper memorial."

The young producer gasped. "Is a cadaver dog what I think it is?"

Cate heard her typing on her computer and thanked the gods of journalism Noah had been working with her. Everyone had heard about the meltdown in the newsroom the weekend the Barracuda had been arrested.

"Yes. It's a dog trained to pick up the scent of human bodies."

"Dead bodies?"

"Yes."

"How do we know it's not just a dead animal?"

"Good question, but the dogs are trained to know the difference. So here's what we should do." Cate paused for a second to organize her thoughts. She wished Noah were there. He'd be the next phone call. "Call the anchors and get them ready for a live cut-in. Have an editor pull that video we sent back of the king and queen arriving and roll that over my phoner. I'll give you an update of what's going on, okay?"

Cate heard the assignments editor paging the weekend anchor over the in-house system. Megan said, "Give me three minutes to pull this together."

Cate controlled the urge to shout for the producer to *hurry*. "We want to be first on this, Megan. I can see the other stations scrambling to do the same thing."

The young woman was tapping furiously on her computer. "All right, Cate. Two minutes. Call back in two minutes, and we'll patch you right through to the control room."

Cate closed her phone, restless and worried that her competition would get on the air before she would. It was her story, damn it, and she wouldn't lose her edge now. She glanced at her watch. Thirty seconds had gone by. Andy was switching tapes and checking her camera batteries. The memorial site had been roped off with yellow crime-scene tape.

Andy nudged Cate and tipped her head. Ana Escobar was standing at the edge of the terrace, her pale shoulders gleaming in the dusk. She held a cigarette loosely between her index and second finger, her dark eyes half-closed as she brought it to her mouth and inhaled. Cate wondered what she was thinking.

Her cell phone rang. "Hello?"

"Cate? We're ready and coming to you in twenty-five seconds."

Cate marshaled her thoughts. How much could she say?

"All right, Cate, here we come."

The weekend anchor said, "Political reporter Cate McCoy is at the governor's mansion where a police dog has unearthed something investigators appear to be examining closely. Cate?"

"Jay, state troopers here at the governor's mansion have called in crime lab personnel to examine a plastic garbage bag that was dug up by a dog trained to find cadavers. The dog was part of a security detail that was patrolling the grounds of the governor's mansion as Governor Hamm hosted the king and queen of Spain here tonight. The dog found the bag as the governor and his guests were dining on the mansion terrace. The troopers immediately declared the area off limits, which means that no one has handled the bag, so we are unclear as to what's inside.

"This is the first state dinner the governor has hosted since being inaugurated eighteen months ago. King Juan Carlos and Queen Sofia are in an upstairs room of the mansion. We are now waiting on the crime scene technicians. Jay?"

"Cate, can you give us some details about the memorial site?"

"It was conceived by the governor and a close friend of his to honor military paratroopers. As you'll recall, Jay, Governor Hamm was a member of the 82nd Airborne Division. The governor unveiled the design for the memorial several months ago and was trying to raise some private funding for it."

"The fact that a cadaver dog is involved sounds pretty ominous. Have police indicated what they think may be in the bag?"

Cate hesitated, her fingers curling around the phone. Should she go with her gut and reveal what she suspected was in the bag? Or play it safe. Her pulse quickened. She could see the reporters from the other television stations on their cell phones, probably waiting to go on the air. She could taste another exclusive. She swallowed.

"Cate? I asked if you have any idea what is inside the plastic bag?"

"Jay, all the police will tell us is that they are waiting for the crime lab. I'll bring you more details as soon as I have them."

At twenty-five minutes after midnight, police officials announced there would be a news conference in ten minutes. The crime scene techs had been working on the bag and its contents for more than two hours. The guests had been allowed to leave after answering questions and providing addresses. Restless reporters had begun to take bets on what the bag contained, with someone laying five bucks that it was the tongue of the governor's first chief of staff, who'd quit abruptly after only six weeks on the job.

Cate had done two live reports from the front gate of the mansion and slipped back inside, growing increasingly edgy as they waited for news. The governor had refused all interviews, and the king and queen had been kept far away from the media. But now the head of the State Patrol, along with the Deputy Chief of the Saint Paul Police, were ready to make a statement.

As the news crews gathered around a small podium that had been set up on the terrace, Cate saw Ana Escobar step through the glass doors, much as she had hours earlier when the dinner was just beginning. She'd changed into black pants, a black silk blouse, and polished riding boots. Her hair flowed over her shoulders, the diamond pins holding it away from her face. Her expression was one of calm curiosity.

"All right, everyone. Listen up." Colonel Gayle Hastings looked out at the assembled media and grimaced, running a hand through her short blonde hair. She'd been appointed head of the State Patrol three years ago in the midst of a scandal over racial profiling after a newspaper story revealed that blacks were four times more likely than whites to be pulled over for alleged traffic infractions. Colonel Hastings had initiated mandatory record-keeping of the race of all motorists being stopped, and the problem had nearly disappeared, but she was not an admirer of the press.

"We have some preliminary information to report, and we stress that it is merely *preliminary*. Until our lab techs can examine it further . . ."

A radio reporter called out, "I'm live in ninety seconds, Colonel Hastings. Can you please tell us what's in the bag?"

The woman glared at the radio reporter but glanced down at her notes, cutting to the chase. "We have found what appears to be items of clothing. We are not disclosing at this time exactly what they are."

Cate's heart beat faster. She called out, "Colonel Hastings, are they women's clothing?"

The colonel glanced at the Saint Paul deputy chief standing beside her. A signal passed between them. "Yes, they are."

Another reporter shouted out, "Are they bloody?"

Colonel Hastings replied, "No comment."

"Have they been ripped or torn?"

"Do they have anyone's name or initials in them?"

"Is that all that was in the bag?"

The deputy chief stepped up to the microphone and held his hands up. "People, that's all we can tell you. Governor Hamm has been informed about tonight's developments, as have the staff of the king and queen. We will have more for you tomorrow. We're asking that everyone be off the property in fifteen minutes."

"Is anyone under arrest, Chief?" Cate felt the hot pinpoint of Ana Escobar's stare.

"No one is under arrest, at this time."

Cate glanced at her dashboard clock, surprised to see that it was two fifteen in the morning. She'd done another live shot, wrapping everything up and then taken Noah's suggestion that she head home. She'd promised to be in again by nine.

The lights of downtown Saint Paul shimmered in her windshield and Cate put her window down, inhaling the torpid air. A storm was gathering.

She breathed deep, realizing that she wasn't tired, but hungry, and she steered her car toward Adam's favorite pizza place on West Seventh. If the restaurant was still open, she'd grab a couple of slices and tap on his door. Better yet, maybe she'd call to see if he wanted a whole pie.

Cate pulled up to the curb, relieved to see a couple of customers inside. She grabbed her purse and palmed her cell phone, locking her car. She went inside, her stomach grumbling at the scent of warm dough. "Is it too late for a pizza?"

The pizza maker shook his head, gesturing to a menu. "We're open all night. Just let me know what you want."

Cate dialed Adam's number, leaving a message when he didn't answer. "Adam, it's Cate. I'm at Giorgios, grabbing a late dinner to go. Thought you might share it with me." She paused, hoping he'd pick up. When he didn't she said, "Okay, I'm going to get a large supreme. If that," her voice dropped to a sultry whisper, "or anything else tempts you out of bed, come over in about twenty minutes. I miss you."

Cate closed her phone and noticed the battery light blinking. No wonder, after tonight. She turned it off, ordered, and sat down at one of the tables to wait. When the pizza was done, she dug into her purse for some money, drawing out a clump of bills along with several sheets of crumpled paper. She handed the money to the chef and, while he boxed the pizza, she smoothed out the papers. They were her notes from her interview with Ellis Emerson. She'd shoved them in her purse after reviewing them yesterday in the edit bay. Or was that two days ago? Work eighteen hour days, and the days began to merge together.

Cate skimmed down over her scrawls, catching certain words and phrases. She smiled as she re-read what Emerson had said about finding solitude from a newborn and a toddler in the nature center woods. She scanned his description of emerging from the woods and hearing the woman's laugh. And then she stopped, her eyes locked on a sentence. *I figured they must have walked over like I did.* She'd written it down in quotation marks.

"Here's your pizza, miss. Large supreme."

Cate clutched her notes in one hand and balanced the pizza box in the other, setting it on the hood of her car when she got outside. She looked down at the piece of notepaper, straining in the dim lamplight. Ellis Emerson had said that because he hadn't seen any cars in the parking lot. If Ana Escobar had killed Millicent Pine that night, what had she done with the body? She certainly couldn't have carried it out of there. Millicent was at least three inches taller and a good twenty-five pounds heavier.

Cate unlocked the car, sliding behind the wheel and setting the pizza box on the passenger side. She thought about what Emerson had said. Two women alone. An argument. Laughter. A long hug. Maybe Peter Escobar had been waiting in the woods and had helped his wife dispose of the body after Ana had killed her. But then, why bury the clothing at the memorial site?

Cate started her car and pulled out into the empty streets. Thunder boomed, and she sped through a yellow light toward the freeway entrance. North. Toward White Bear Lake.

31

WHITE BEAR LAKE

2:56 A.M.

LIGHTNING TURNED THE TALL TREES IN THE NATURE CENTER into jagged sil-houettes, and Cate eyed them from her car, wondering what the hell she was doing there. She'd eaten two slices of pizza on the short trip north, her brain working the puzzle as she drove, practically on auto-pilot. By the time she'd turned into Tamarack she'd come up with a timeline.

That night, Ana Escobar had summoned Millicent Pine to a meeting, reaching her on her cell phone as Millicent and the Barracuda were on their way to see the governor's chief of staff. Cate believed that only the lure of information about the Tijuana factory could have diverted the journalist from her meeting with Bates. Millicent had asked to be dropped off in Saint Paul and had been met there by Ana Escobar, perhaps in a taxi. She would've been careful that the DEA surveillance team, which she undoubtedly knew about, didn't see her leave the mansion.

Cate looked out at the dark parking lot, trying to re-create the scene. It might have been around eleven by the time the two women had gotten to the nature center. Ana Escobar would have told the journalist that they needed an out-of-the-way place to talk, maybe she'd even confided that she knew about the DEA team.

When they'd gotten there, Millicent had confronted her with what she knew of the porn-and-drug operation in Tijuana. Perhaps she'd threatened her with disclosure. That would have been the arguing Emerson had said he'd heard.

Cate glanced down at her dead cell phone and out through the windshield. Her gaze roamed the park, skipping over and snapping back to the dim outline of a wooden building. Emerson had called it the "clubhouse," but that was too grand of a term for the simple building with the triangular windows in the front.

Cate got out of the car and walked the paved path toward the building. Large trees bent in the wind, and thunder rumbled over the open prairie that lay just beyond the circle of oak and elm. She imagined the deer nestled beneath the trees, sheltering from the approaching storm. She circled the building, peering in the windows to the dark interior. A flash of lightning startled her and she spotted a side door, stepped into its shallow arch and leaned back against it.

She was exhausted, her supply of adrenaline practically used up. What had brought her here? The same sensation she'd experienced earlier when she'd seen Ana Escobar. The hidden secret in the painting . . . the truth if you just knew where to look.

She thought of the way Andy peered through the camera viewfinder, studying the shot composition, zooming in and out, searching for the image that divulged the most about the story. That was how she needed to see this place. She closed her eyes, listening to the rustle of long grasses, and willed herself a fresh perspective. When she opened her eyes, she was staring at a large wooden bulletin board on a pole with flyers tacked up behind glass.

Cate stepped out onto the grass, relieved to see that a small light illuminated the board. She approached the bulletin board and wiped the dusty glass with her arm to inspect the posted messages. One announced a bird watching excursion that would take place every Tuesday evening. Another invited families to an Easter egg hunt.

But the largest flyer on the board was titled "Controlled Burn." It explained that large sections of the nature center would be subject to a burn designed to clear non-native trees and plants that were choking out the native flora. The posting listed dates in which the proscribed sections would be set on fire. Cate stared at the list. There had been a widespread burn the week Millicent Pine disappeared.

"They should've shot you in Tijuana."

Cate spun to see Ana Escobar standing a few feet away, her eyes as hard and flat as polished slate. A cape cloaked her head and draped her body. Her hands were hidden.

A jagged spear of lightning arrowed through scudding clouds and was followed by a loud boom. Cate saw something flash out of the corner of her eye. She struggled to steady her voice. "You lured her up here and killed her," she said. "Then you dragged Millicent Pine's body into the back of the burn area and covered it with tinder."

Ana Escobar nodded, her face expressionless. "Odd how they never thought of the burn site, isn't it? They kept searching the woods." Her eyes flickered. "I knew you'd put it together after they found Millicent's clothes."

Cate's gaze darted over the woman's shoulder. Her car was the only one in the parking lot.

Escobar tracked her gaze. "There are a lot of ways in here." Her eyes narrowed. "I've been watching you for some time."

Cate took a step backwards, tension stiffening her jaw.

The other woman's gaze slid over Cate. She tilted her head, the hood brushing her cheek. "We knew each other in college, Millicent and I."

There were undertones to the way she'd said *knew*. She shifted, and Cate caught a glimpse of metal as her cape parted.

"My father believed in a good education, Miss McCoy, so he sent me to Smith. I met Millicent the second week I was there." There was no warmth or nostalgia in her voice. "She was organizing a protest, and I signed up. She seemed . . . interesting." Something moved in her flat gaze. "My father hated her. He said if he'd wanted me to meet people like that he would've let me go to Berkley."

Ana Escobar pushed her hood back, and it puddled on her shoulders, framing her pale throat. The wind lifted her hair, brushing strands of it against her crimson mouth. She slid two fingers past her temple and drew out a diamond pin, holding the sharp spike between her fingers as she would a cigarette. The jewels glinted in the dim light. Cate stared at the pin, shaking, as realization shivered over her in a wintry gust.

The hug.

The scene unfolded in her mind. Millicent's accusations . . . her threats of exposure . . . Escobar's denials . . . the grip on a wrist . . . the thrust of a pin as she shoved it into the journalist's throat, slicing her carotid artery, embracing her as she died. Ellis Emerson had been gone by the time

KERRI LEE MILLER

Millicent had slid out of her assailant's arms to the grass, unable to scream. Or breathe.

"You took her notebook and buried her clothes," Cate said, fear pulsing through her. "You were the one who planted the evidence in Liz Barracosta's car."

Ana Escobar nodded once. "She and Millicent had tangled before, and then that gun turned up." She looked at the pin in her hand, studying its icepick-sharp point. "But best of all, Miss McCoy, Edward Hamm wanted to believe she'd done it." She took a step closer, her cape rippling in a rush of wind. "Unfortunately, you discovered that videotape." Her voice was laced with mild regret. "I should've taken care of you then."

"Before I saw your movie-making operation south of the border." Cate's throat was tight, and her voice came out as a whisper.

The other woman smiled for the first time. "Following in Millicent's footsteps," she said dryly, "and now you're going to die just like she did."

Thunder rumbled over their heads, and Cate caught the pale gray of swirling clouds in the night sky. Her legs trembled, and she edged back against the bulletin board. Escape lay beyond Ana Escobar, and the deadly sharp pin. She had no choice.

With a sudden spin, Cate turned and shover her elbow high and hard against the bulletin glass, pain exploding through her arm as she grabbed for a jagged fragment. Escobar's cape whipped open, and Cate screamed, diving for the ground, deafened by the roar of the gun.

She kicked out at the other woman, slashing at her as Escobar fell, slashing again and connecting with the woman's face. A jagged tear opened below her eye, and Cate saw blood rush down her cheek and into Escobar's mouth, thick and black in the dim light. She froze, panting, as the other woman swore in Spanish, the guttural threats whipped away by the strong wind.

Ana Escobar knelt, her cloak puddled on the spring grass, the diamond pin jutting from her right hand. Her gun lay a few feet away. She was whispering, her lips moving as rapidly as a priest's saying the rosary. Cate's heart thudded. Who would make the first move.

She rose into a crouch, prepared for the next assault, when she caught the sound of sirens. She saw the other woman's eyes flicker, and the whispering died. They stared at one another. A huge flash bulb burst before Cate's eyes, and she covered them, blinded by repeated bursts of lightning. When she opened her eyes, she caught a glimpse of a dark cape. Ana Escobar was running, her cloak billowing behind her. With a groan, Cate pushed herself of the ground and followed.

She stumbled into a wooded area, and then burst out into an open field. Ana Escobar was fifty feet ahead of her and gaining and Cate, again, cursed her decision to wear high heels to the state dinner. Bending down, she whipped them off, wincing as her nylon-covered feet connected with the stubbly field grass. Her black dress was covered with grass and mud.

Cate picked up her pace and closed some of the distance between them. She saw Escobar glance over her shoulder and heard her curse in Spanish. Cate knew there was little chance of the other woman stopping to draw her gun and steadying it enough to shoot. She would miss in the dark.

They ran down a gentle slope and were suddenly in woods again, tall Norway pines and old oaks blocking out the night sky. Cate heard the scream of sirens and knew the police, alerted by the gun shot, had arrived. She was breathing hard and wondering how long she could keep up the pursuit when Ana Escobar suddenly veered onto a footpath. Cate could hear the slap of her boots against the packed dirt as the other woman pulled further ahead.

The path curved through the woods, giving onto a wooden bridge that arced over boggy marshland. Cate's heart clutched with fear. What if the bridge dead-ended up ahead? Ana Escobar could double back and wait for her, shooting her as she ran right into her arms. She slowed a bit, catching the silvery shimmer of light on water. She knew there were several lakes on the nature center acreage spanned by short bridges. Panting hard she approached the lakes and stepped cautiously onto the weathered wood of the bridge, her bare feet making no sound. What the hell was she going to do if she caught up with Ana Escobar, anyway? She ignored the voice that told her to turn around and go back.

Cate held her breath as she neared the end of the bridge. It led to a short dock that jutted into the water. A small sign said "Tamarack Lake." She crouched down to make herself less of a target and scanned the area. Tall marsh grasses rustled in the gusty winds, and Cate could see the silhouette of cattails swaying at the water's edge. It was too quiet.

Ana Escobar was either gone or setting a trap into which she'd just blundered. The thought had just formed when Cate heard a sharp report, the sound unnaturally loud in the placid bog. Simultaneously she fell to her knees, crying out as the molten heat of a bullet exploded into her shoulder.

Escobar fired again. Cate curled onto the dock, gasping with pain and clutching her shoulder. Blood seeped through her fingers. She tasted metal on her tongue. Ana Escobar could be approaching even now to finish her off. She bit her lip against the anguish and lifted her head to the sound of voices. Did Escobar have an accomplice?

She felt herself slipping into shock, the hand pressed against her shoulder covered with blood. Her head spun, and she closed her eyes, stirring as she heard the muted splash of something heavy and then the swish of oars in the water. She thought hazily of the last message she'd left for Adam. She was glad she'd told him she missed him.

She roused enough to know she lay on the dock and wondered how Ana Escobar's cape had come to be draped over her face, blocking out the stars and the sky. Then everything went black.

32

Forty-Two Hours Later

May 7, 8:49 P.M.

Cate shifted in her hospital bed and frowned at her image in a small hand mirror. Her face and arms were covered with mosquito bites, and she had a serious case of bed head. The last thing she wanted was to go on television, but the station was insisting on a live interview for the ten o'clock newscast. It *was* a ratings book after all.

She applied a coat of lipstick and put the mirror away. She still felt weak from the blood loss, and the pain in her shoulder was unbearable without the little pills the nurses gave her. If the police who'd responded to the sound of the first gunshot hadn't found her when they did, she might have bled to death.

"Feeling better?" Adam's clean scent enveloped her as he bent to kiss her lightly. His manner with her had been reserved. Cate knew he was angry about her imprudent pursuit of Ana Escobar.

"Feeling better but looking worse, if that's possible." Cate smoothed her hair self-consciously. "I wish this interview thing could wait another day."

Adam frowned, using his cane to lower himself into a chair by her bed. "Tell them you're not ready, Cate."

"I'll be fine," she said, looking up as the satellite truck operator appeared in the door with a bundle of cables. "Good thing they put you on the third floor, McCoy. I'd a had a heart attack if I had to pull cable any higher."

Cate grinned. "You can have my hospital bed if you need it, Wes."

The truck operator began setting up equipment as Andy came into the room, hauling her gear on a gurney. "Some nice doctor lent it to me when he saw me carrying all of this stuff up here." She bent to squeeze Cate's uninjured shoulder. "You're looking . . . perkier."

Cate rolled her eyes. "Thanks. If it's one thing I've never been it's *perky*."

A nurse came in to take her pulse and blood pressure and then left as Andy wired Cate up with a microphone. Cate had donned a pale yellow bathrobe over her hospital gown, and she smoothed it nervously. "I'm not sure how I'm going to like being on the receiving end of the interview. It's kind of weird."

Andy plugged wires into her camera and looked through her viewfinder. "Calm down. Allison is doing the live interview. How tough can it be?"

Cate groaned.

Andy laughed. "McCoy, all you gotta do is tell your admiring public how neither porno-makers nor drug dealers nor cheap news directors can stop you from getting your gal." She zoomed in on Cate's face. "Speaking of which, the Snow Queen finally signed off on our expenses."

"But I didn't get her, Andy," Cate said, her mouth tightening. "She got away. For all we know she's lounging on some beach in Ixtapa laughing at us."

Andy shrugged. "It's only a matter of time. Her husband will cut a deal with the feds if it looks like he's going to prison."

Cate adjusted the bed sheet. "I don't know. The paper said there's no evidence linking her to Millicent's death. No fingerprints on the clothing they dug up or anything. Just my word that she confirmed it all in our confrontation that night."

Andy set up her lights, and Cate squinted as she turned them on. "Is this what we subject people to?"

219

"Maybe it's time for another pill, McCoy. Should I call the nurse?"

But a nurse was already entering the room carrying a square item wrapped in birthday paper. Cate frowned. At least it was better than the "get well" cards and overpowering bouquets she was receiving. She'd asked the nurse to take the Snow Queen's wilting carnations to the geriatric floor.

She pulled the birthday paper off and caught her breath. It was a copy of the Drug Enforcement Agency's case file on Ana Escobar, rich with details about her history, her associates, and the agency's surveillance. "Wow," Cate breathed, spotting a note attached to the inside cover. It said: *From: The Calvary. To: One tough broadcaster. You kept your end of the bargain. It isn't over. Drake Connelly.*

Cate scratched a mosquito bite and smiled. Energy surged through her veins, and the pain in her shoulder receded for a moment. She looked up at Andy. "I guess I'm ready for my close-up."